AN INSPECTOR CALLED

IAN MEACHEAM

An Inspector Called
Copyright ©2017 APS Publications

All rights reserved.
The moral right of the author has been asserted.

No part of this publication may be reproduced, stored in or introduced into a retrieval system, or transmitted, in any form, or by any means (electronic, mechanical, photocopying, recording or otherwise) without the written permission of the publisher except that brief selections may be quoted or copied without permission, provided that full credit is given.

Cover photo courtesy of Thinkstock
Editorial consultant Christine Ware

APS Publications,
4 Oakleigh Road,
Stourbridge,
West Midlands,
DY8 2JX

www.andrewsparke.com

For Ann and David

PART 1
Ahead Rings Out

CHAPTER 1

"Requires improvement...requires improvement."

Peter Burlington, Head teacher at Whatmore, muttered to himself as he stood staring out of his office window, looking across the staff car park. Three cars had just driven away. Three expensive-looking cars driven by the three Ofsted inspectors who had left the school after two days of hell. He hoped a few Year 11's managed to inflict damage on the cars before they left so that their tyres or paintwork would require improvement.

"F.... Off in Sted!" were his parting sentiments as he turned round to face his Senior Leadership Team. The defeated group looked back at him in silence from the conference table at one side of the room. They had all aged notably over the last two days. Early on Monday morning Peter had led a team of four men and women, good and true – now all of them required improvement, along with the rest of the staff, the pupils, the governors, the buildings - all *"not good enough"* or *"could do better."* Satisfactory simply wasn't good enough these days.

Charlie Briggs was the first person to break the tension. Around the paper-strewn table punctuated with coffee cups and the residue of the bribes for the inspectors, biscuits, muffins and slices of fruit, Charlie had probably been the least concerned before the inspection. The Deputy Head had seen it all before and was hoping to retire before he saw it all again. This result changed all of that. Her Majesty's Inspectors would be back and next time it could be judgement day for his pension.

"It could be worse, boss. We could have been judged Inadequate!"

"Forgive me if I'm not jumping for joy in celebration. Tell me Charlie; would it make much difference to you if one of your wives had graded your bedroom performance as requiring improvement rather than inadequate?"

"The fact is I have to self-evaluate my own performance these days - Number 3 is usually asleep before I get feedback!"

The other SLT members looked carefully at Charlie to see if he was joking or not and then decided en-masse to look down at the scribbled notes they had made at the feedback session without attempting to crack their faces.

Julie Osborne had made the most notes of all. She was meticulous and thorough; although on careful inspection her writing had deteriorated as the lead inspector summed up their findings. She took a sip of tepid water from her glass. Unlike most people she knew, Julie's glass was never half full or half empty. Her glass varied between being full in public and empty in private. She would smile in the staff room and in classrooms around Whatmore but in her office or in her small apartment she bitterly regretted the day she moved to the school, just over a year ago. At least one of the ever-present bottles of white wine in her fridge, that would have been drunk in celebration tonight if Ofsted had gone well, would now be drunk in misery and isolation. Her glass would be continually empty tonight. She would sit on her settee getting pissed and feeling more and more pissed off, particularly with the Head and the Deputy for leading the school in the wrong direction. Of course she wouldn't tell anyone that, apart from her cat, presently the only living creature sharing her flat.

Julie smiled sympathetically at Peter and Charlie as she placed her glass back on the coffee-stained beer mat. A smile to give that vital *we're all in it together* impression. And tonight she would smile at the wine bottle – her best friend since her long-time boyfriend had left her to find someone "who has a life outside the school gates". Towards the end of the evening, she would also cry and argue with the bottle knowing that she was becoming too dependent on her chilled friends. By morning she would hate herself. Single at thirty-two, an Assistant Head teacher with no prospects of progressing and a hangover on a school day – but no-one at school would ever know. At the weekend she would assess her options and go on-line to look at jobs in the Times Educational Supplement and possibly a dating site. She would need to make some serious decisions about her career path very soon but today was about putting on a brave face. Julie tried to look up from her notes, she wanted to say something positive and reassuring to her colleagues, but she was distracted by the final bullet points in her notebook which looked as if they had been written by someone else.

The quietest person round the conference table, Neil Turner, was on his sixth biscuit and his second black coffee since he entered the Head's office thirty seven minutes ago. He had made a few notes on his iPad during the lead inspector's diatribe but now that Ofsted had left the building he was immersed in the reviews of the next Windows package. Neil, at 29 years and 135 days old, was in charge of all things electronic. He was promoted a year ago to move Whatmore into a brave new technical world – a decision the Head and governors quietly regretted due to his lack of empathy with human beings. He was the *"staff room geek"* a tag hardly deserved as he rarely ventured into that hell hole. It contained only a kettle, a toaster and people, all of which he regarded as low-tech. He was most comfortable in his office or talking to Year 11 pupils (preferably on-line) about the latest RPG or RAM on the market.

He vaguely worried about the next few weeks because one of Ofsted's criticisms was for the school not consistently embracing new technologies. This meant he would have to give even more guidance to the IT users, or to his mind, non-users who were failing the school. It wasn't his fault. He regularly up loaded new and interesting things for the staff to look at and use on the network but received virtually no feedback on his efforts.

"Should we not tell the staff?" asked Sobia Didially. "They've been waiting in the staffroom some time now and most of them will want to get home." That majority included Sobia herself, the school business manager and the only member of the senior management team who wasn't a teacher. Mind you, most of the rest of them didn't teach these days. It seemed to Sobia that all they did was tell everyone else how to teach. As the only qualified manager on the staff she often thought that she should be telling the rest of the management team how to manage and lead. The team had endless professional development sessions on the difference between management and leadership but the more she came away from these training days, the more she was convinced that most of the others could do neither. To her, the teaching staff were overpaid, wishy-washy liberals who wouldn't last three months in the real world. The job as business manager suited her as the Head was happy for her to make decisions on finances, even if he didn't realise it and she had two children she could look after in the school holidays without the need for child minders. She wanted to get home now so she could collect them from her sister's house.

"You're right Sobia, the staff need to know and I suppose I have to be honest and open but it would be handy if I could spin a few positives into the report back. Any ideas?" asked Peter.

"How about announcing you're retiring?" Did Julie say that out loud? She hurriedly looked up and realised by glancing at the team that she was safe.

"Well, the behaviour and safety of the pupils was sort of praised," said Charlie, who was in charge of Pupil Welfare and Safeguarding. It was the only one of the four main judgements that was deemed Good.

"I wouldn't go as far as to say it was praised, Charlie, it just came out better than the other three categories," replied Peter.

"I was just trying to be positive boss."

"Any other thoughts or suggestions?"

Julie felt the need to say something. "Why not just read out the main elements of the report and the action points and thank everyone for their hard work over the last two days. Tonight isn't the time to give a long speech on the rights and wrongs of the judgement or Ofsted inspections in general."

Neil and Sobia nodded agreement.

"I do think we need to say that we judged the school to be Good and yet the inspectors didn't see it that way. What does that say about us? What does it say about me?" asked Peter rhetorically.

In the resulting silence everyone paused to fill in their own blanks.

"Okay. I'll keep it brief and give it to them straight," said Peter.

"That would be a first!" was the silent chorus from the rest of the team.

CHAPTER 2

After texting his wife to give her the bad news, Peter washed his face and straightened his tie in the staff toilet next to his office. He stood before the mirror and looked at the fat conductor staring back at him with pity in his eyes. Chubby cheeks and chubby everything else. His hair had gradually been slipping down the sides of his head over the last ten years or so and he relied more and more on his thick glasses to help him see and to cover up the school bags resting under his eyes.

Peter made his way slowly towards the staffroom. He passed a couple of cleaners who were standing at the far side of the reception desk talking about how overworked and underpaid they were. He nodded and smiled at them and they acknowledged him effortlessly without moving a muscle or a broom.

Peter had decided to give the Ofsted feedback in the staffroom as it was less formal. This arrangement had been made two days ago when he assumed the news would be positive. He reflected that in the light of the judgement he should have chosen the Theatre or the Hall. Too late now.

He had to fight his way into the staffroom. It was standing room only. He had to squeeze his way through to get to the usual place he stood in when he talked to the staff. Once in position he looked up to survey his audience. His senior team, including Neil, were scattered around the room and had blended into the general mass, leaving him feeling alone and in the spotlight. Peter remembered his last speech to the staff on the afternoon of the dreaded phone call when he had said that there is no *Us and them and We're all in this together*. Now forty eight hours later it was clearly "*me and them.*" He would have liked to be flanked by his senior team for emotional support and protection but he was the sole messenger and he could feel the red laser dots dancing on his chest, scattering the butterflies.

The staff room chatter slowly quietened down, not necessarily out of respect for their Head but they were anxious to know the Ofsted judgement and then get home.

"Afternoon everyone, thanks for giving up your time at the end of a very busy and stressful two days. The inspectors have fed back to us and I can give you a verbal summary of their findings. Can I just stress that these judgements and action points are to remain confidential until the report is published in a week or so." There was absolutely no chance that what Peter said would remain confidential. In fact, several staff had their mobiles at the ready, fingers hovering over keys to text.

"Firstly, the Lead Inspector wanted to pass on his thanks for your time and professionalism during the inspection." At the word *professionalism*, Peter could feel himself going off script and moving into the realms of fiction but he had to say something positive as a starter. He looked down at his notes briefly and decided to put everyone out of their misery and into an even deeper collective misery.

"Err... despite the senior leadership team making the case that Whatmore provides a sound education for all of its pupils - the overall effectiveness judgement made by the inspectors is that the school ....requires improvement."

If Peter had dared to examine every face looking at him at that moment he would have seen a wide spectrum of expressions. There was fury, horror, astonishment, disappointment, passive acceptance and indifference. Lips were shaping responses as different as "How can this happen?" and "I'm not surprised."

The immediate outcome was most members of staff spontaneously talking to anyone in listening proximity and venting for a minute or so. In that short space of time, three words seemed to be most commonly used. These were *Ofsted, Head teacher* and *fucking* but not always in that order.

The *fucking Head teacher* raised his hands as a sign for the mob to listen to their great leader. Not wishing to look up, he read out key phrases from his notes outlining the strengths but mainly weaknesses in pupil outcomes, the quality of teaching and learning and the leadership and management of the school. Peter left the personal development, behaviour and welfare of the pupils until last and made a point of stressing that this was regarded as Good - but it was too late; the horse had bolted and no amount of reining back could control the animal anger that had been tethered for the last two days.

Some members of staff did not wait to be invited to speak, some shot their hands up, some were texting and those who were not communicating were planning their next career steps in their heads; any Head but this one.

Peter tried to answer as many questions as possible but the more he explained the more it sounded as if he agreed with the findings. He tried to get across to the staff that there was good practice in almost everything that was done at Whatmore but it wasn't consistent enough. The word consistent was Ofsted's favourite. It was consistently used throughout most reports they generated, usually with the prefix *in* before it.

Peter explained that the inspectors had seen some very good teaching, that some subjects had performed well but not in every case and that leadership was not effective across the whole school. With the repetition of the word inconsistent, the mood in the staff room changed slightly and the sights that had been fixed on the Head's chest started to re-focus on other easy targets. In most people's minds it was not just the Head teacher who had let them down and should be blamed. It was others – other teachers and other subjects. Anyone but them. It was the ones oblivious to the stares and glares of their colleagues who continued to survive in their own worlds of unconscious incompetency.

Peter read out the urgent action points to be addressed according to Ofsted. Teaching and learning needed to be consistently Good in all subjects. Maths results at GCSE level needed to improve along with some other subjects. Leaders at all levels had to evaluate the school's performance more effectively and accurately. Finally, an action plan had to be written quickly and put in place to address all these issues.

"I don't want to keep you long tonight but as you may be aware we will now have a re-visit in the next eighteen months to two years."

This was the first piece of good news for the staff – many months grace at least. Thoughts ranged from *We can turn it round in that time* to *Maybe the Head will retire before the next Ofsted* and even to *I can get another job in that time*. But Peter wasn't finished....

"Her Majesty's Inspectorate will be sending someone here in six to eight weeks to see if we are taking effective action on our targets. So from tomorrow morning we will have to start devising our action plan and begin to change…" As he looked around the room he could see the staff physically ageing and tiring in front of him – hearing was failing, eyes were watering and long term illnesses beckoned.

Some twenty minutes later, Peter watched from his office window as members of staff walked to their cars in bedraggled dribs and drabs. He turned back to his desk and sat down wearily. He usually liked this time of day. It was when he was fairly certain he wouldn't hear a knock on his door accompanied by "Have you got two minutes?" or "Can I have a quick word?" The quick word usually lasted longer than "War and Peace" and two minutes could often stretch to hours. Tonight he knew that the staff were all spent and had no energy to moan or complain. That would come tomorrow. Tonight Peter could go home and slump in an armchair and re-charge his batteries in order to face tomorrow's battles. But as he was slowly tidying his desk he realised he hadn't had time to consider his own position since Ofsted left the building. What did all of this mean for him?

Peter Burlington had been a Deputy Head for some time in another part of the country. He was fairly successful in a fairly successful school so he decided to apply for headships. He wasn't confident that he would ever become a Head teacher at fifty years of age. All the recently appointed Heads seemed about twenty years younger. As a fat, bald old fart he felt his profile was not what selection panels were looking for these days. He applied for four or five posts using more or less the same word-processed letter and CV and sent them out. He didn't expect to hear anything. Nor did his wife – she humoured him by supporting his ambition and secretly liked the idea of the extra money a Head's salary would bring in. She was less pleased when two letters came through the post inviting Peter for interview. The two schools were some distance from their house, their friends and, most important of all, from Rachel's one and only grandchild. She said nothing, having great faith in her husband's inability to impress in person.

Indeed, the first school to invite him for a two-day interview rejected him after the first day. Peter's memory of the process was that it was a cross between *The Krypton Factor*, *Mastermind* and *Big Brother*. In a spare moment he quipped to one of the other candidates sitting passively in the staff room that he was surprised that they had not been asked to learn a *pasa doble* in an hour and then perform the dance with a dinner lady in front of the selection panel. The candidate tried to smile but Peter's sense of humour was lost on the younger man searching for current thinking on leadership styles on his smart phone.

A few days later Peter had his second interview. He had decided that he would go along and if unsuccessful this time he would call it quits.

Whatmore School was at that time, according to Ofsted, a good school. The governing body and the local authority were supportive and the current Head was retiring after ten successful years to take up a position as a School Improvement Adviser. Whatmore seemed just the type of school that Peter would like to lead before he retired and thereafter spent his days as far away from school-age children as possible. Peter arrived for the interview at a swish hotel, suited and booted and ready for battle. He sat in a line of five other candidates on one side of a conference table opposite the selection panel on the other. Peter felt like the fat unfit boy in a PE lesson waiting to be picked last and ending up in goal but during the day he was neither snubbed nor ignored. For some reason various selectors warmed to him and liked his answers to their questions. The Student Council spent half an hour with Mr Burlington and decided he was "nice." The Local Education Authority representative liked the thought that Peter was from another county and could bring new ideas with him, judging him to be a safe pair of hands compared to some of the young upstarts who said a lot but knew nothing.

That night he was still in the game. The second day would be the tie breaker – he was up against two others – with a presentation to deliver and then a formal interview as the penalty shoot-out. Fortunately, the subject now given for the presentation was a God-send. He had power point material already sitting on his laptop cribbed when he went on a course recently that he could just tweak and personalise for the next day.

One of the other candidates dropped out overnight and in the morning it was a two horse race. Peter's presentation went well and his ninety minute Q & A session was gruelling but manageable. He followed the rules of engagement on interview – keep to the point (on the rare occasion you have a point to make), demonstrate a sense of humour (remember the handful of appropriate jokes you downloaded from the internet the night before), give examples of successful practice from your own career so far (use someone else's career if necessary) and always tell the truth and be true to yourself (unless you are comfortable and confident with exaggerating, bluffing and bull shitting your way through).

The selection panel sent the two candidates away after their interviews. They were going to have lunch at the hotel and deliberate during the afternoon, then afternoon tea and cakes and deliberate some more until just after the evening meal when they would make their decision and charge all their expenses to the school. The chair of governors, who was also the chair of the selection panel and liked his food, would contact both candidates later that evening.

It was half way through *Eastenders* when Peter received the phone call. On three earlier occasions he had rushed to the phone only to have to fend off *"how did you get on?"* questions from well-wishers. One was from his anxious daughter and there were calls from his existing Head and an Assistant Head who had their own reasons for wishing him well.

Rachel paused an argument between a *Mitchell* and a *Beale* in mid flow so Peter could take the call. She stared at a freeze frame of the screen and tried not to think of the problems ahead if Peter was successful.

"Oh hello." Peter acknowledged the caller as casually as he could. This was followed by a silence of some twenty seconds in the Burlington living room before he broke the tension. "Thank you, I will arrange a time to visit the school again and fill in all of the necessary paperwork." Peter put down the phone. That was it. He was a boss. He turned to his wife and smiled.

Now, three years on he had somehow managed to transform a good school into one requiring improvement. *What did that say about him? Where did he go from here? Home for the night to lick his wounds? What will Rachel say?* Peter knew that at some point during their discussion that she would reiterate how big a mistake it had been to move, to extend the mortgage and to leave their family and friends. In hindsight, he could now agree. It had been the worst three years of his life and he felt crap. At fifty-three years old, he was too old to move to another school and too young to work at B & Q or Tesco.

CHAPTER 3

Peter was back at his desk at 7.00am. The evening at the Burlington house was as expected. Peter had hoped for sympathy with his tea but he was served a plateful of angry regrets with a side of repercussions from Rachel before she went off early to bed. An hour or so later Peter joined her hoping she would be asleep. She was. Peter was awake most of the night, only managing short periods of sleep punctuated by a series of monologues delivered by spirits reminding him of what had been and what was to come.

At 5.30am, pre-empting the alarm, Peter showered, shaved and silently left the house. In one sense this early start to work was easier on the foot brake. There was little traffic on the road, no 4 x 4s dropping off kids, no school buses and no leaping lollypop ladies trying to commit suicide on the bonnet of his car. Today's journey was fast but flat – no high expectations or serious anxieties - just low-level soap operas ahead. The car radio cheerfully forecast a day of gloom with frequent showers and the possibility of hurricane force storms in his office. He parked up in the Head's reserved space, turned off the engine and car radio and walked into the reception area promising himself something to eat and a five minute break sometime this morning to phone his wife.

As he sat at his desk, he started to predict and plan the day. He'd have a greasy school breakfast with some of the pupils who had been dropped off early by parents desperate to get rid of their offspring as quickly as possible. Then he would stand at the main doors as the majority of the pupils arrived, meeting the little treasures with a welcoming smile on his face, telling most of the boys to do up top buttons and re-tie ties and the girls to scrape off their makeup and to remove the large or multiple earrings that they were trying to wear. Most pupils, by now, were used to this reception routine first thing in the morning and were accepting of the rules, just as Peter accepted that by the beginning of first lesson the ties would again be at half-mast and the girls' ears would again resemble window displays for jewellers' shops. He would then stand at the back of an assembly, showing support to a poor teacher whose turn it was to make a tenuous but imaginative link between a part of the bible and modern day adolescence. Early morning duties as a bouncer would then be followed by meetings and phone calls, break time and lunch time bouncing followed by more meetings and phone calls, then the end of school bus duty and conversations at the school gates with well-meaning and well-mean parents interspersed with brief encounters with ex-pupils, now unemployed, waiting for younger friends to impress with their choice of earrings, quick wit and tattoos.

He was really looking forward to the day ahead! He slowly opened his week-to-view diary to see what unexpected pleasures were in stall for him and maybe write the first draft of a resignation or suicide letter when there was knock on his door. Young *Call me Rick* poked his head round the door and asked if Peter had a minute.

"Sure. You're in early Richard. Sit down. What can I do for you?"

"I thought I'd come to you. The inspectors weren't too complimentary about the Maths department and I wanted to get some feedback on my team."

To Richard it might have looked as if the Head teacher had slumped over his chair and had a heart attack at this moment but he was rummaging in his briefcase on the floor next to him for his notes, mainly to give him enough time to think of some inoffensive platitudes to use in describing the damning criticism of the Maths department.

"Are you sure you want to do this now Richard?"

"Rick, please, and yes I would like to touch base with the team later so I need the feedback now."

Peter couldn't help thinking that *Call Me Rick* had some distance to travel before he touched first base. Richard Perry had been Head of Mathematics for a little over a year now and was only in his third year of teaching. He came to Whatmore as an NQT and his meteoric rise was more by default than any innate skill or talent. The Head recognising this, had only reluctantly appointed him to teach in the school and then later as Head of Department. Compared to the other possible candidates, Richard Perry could walk in a straight line and there were signs of life if you held a mirror to his face. He was the best of a bad crop of square roots and as other members of the Maths department left to gain promotion, re-invent themselves in the world of business or re-gain their sanity by gardening, Rick rose to the top of this rather stunted tree. He had little experience of leadership, teaching or frankly anything but he had huge confidence in his own ability, which was fortunate as no-one else did. He would have been one of Thatcher's children if he had been ten years older or taken any notice of politics. He bought into the philosophy of *Me first, Myself second and I third* but felt a little uncomfortable having to share his stage with two other superstar performers. His self-belief made him feel like a priceless commodity that he could trade around the world of education. His career plan was simple – Head teacher in five years, working in the Department of Education in ten and writing about education and his life story in fifteen years, with a desirable wife and an apartment overlooking the Thames. His plan did not take into consideration his own flaws or pitfalls. How could it, given that self-awareness was his biggest stumbling block?

His boss on the other side of the desk also had a plan for Rick - fifteen minutes and no more. So they sat opposite each other, a million miles apart, wanting very different things from this early morning exchange; Rick to make it clear without sounding disloyal that he was doing a great job, much better than the rest of his team and things were getting better every day; Peter, viewing the real world through weary eyes, needing to convey that *Call Me Rick* was not outstanding, nor good, nor even satisfactory but fell squarely into the category of *could do a whole lot better*.

"Richard…Rick …the lesson observations in Maths weren't good. Only Julie's lesson was *Outstanding*, a few lessons were graded *Good* but the majority were *requiring improvement* or worse."

Rick tried to interject but Peter ploughed on. "Not only was the teaching poor but your self-assessment of your team was inaccurate and demonstrated to the inspectors that you had an unrealistic view of standards in your department." Peter paused for breath which let Rick in.

"I fundamentally disagree with these judgements, boss. An inspector who doesn't know the school, staff or children cannot possibly know as much about what goes on inside Maths lessons at Whatmore as I do."

Mr Burlington gripped the well-worn arms of his chair wanting desperately to say things like *Here we go; heard it all before* and *I would trust their judgements over yours any day*. However, Peter knew it was time to listen to the first of several such rants that he would have to listen to today. He couldn't say too much anyway as it would come back to bite him. After all he was ultimately responsible for the school's performance.

"The teachers were really nervous and didn't perform as well as they do normally. Just because they didn't perform in front of an inspector doesn't make them bad teachers. How can Ofsted get an accurate picture of my team when they just see a snapshot like this?" Peter tried to show sympathy in his expression and wanted to say to *Call Me Rick* "Well them are the rules of the game – play or pass" but he couldn't for two reasons. Firstly, Rick was experiencing his first ever Ofsted inspection. He felt for him and admired him briefly for his passion and his defence whilst being blinded in the spotlight of truth. Secondly, Peter privately agreed with Rick – it was a crazy way to judge teachers – to have an automaton with a clipboard sit at the back of a class for twenty minutes and tick boxes. When did this become a sensible way of helping teachers improve? Had he missed a meeting when it was decided that Ofsted knew everything and staff inside schools nothing?

"Richard, sorry, Rick. I know you feel angry about the Ofsted processes but we have to work within their guidelines. We know the rules of engagement - train and develop the teachers over time, get them used to being observed, then get them to plan and perform excellent lessons for two days. The problem is that your team of teachers are not as good as we (Peter stopped himself saying you) thought they were."

"Well I wasn't alone in observing and judging my team. Julie observed some of the team with me and she agreed with me."

So here it was – the slow start of the shift of blame that Peter was waiting for.

"I know Julie is your line manager but you can't hold her solely responsible for the evaluations that were given to me at the end of last term. She is very busy as Assistant Head and has a lot on her plate."

"Okay but one of her roles is Leader in Charge of the Quality of Teaching, Learning and Assessment."

Peter felt his blood pressure rising. He gripped the chair too tightly and wished he had stayed in bed an hour later this morning.

"Richard, Julie is an ex-Head of Maths, she knows her stuff but you are the person in charge of the teaching of Mathematics at this school. It's your job to make Julie and me aware of the failings of members of your team so we can do something about it if you can't."

"Well, I've been saying for ages that Jerry should have been given an opportunity to go on a course about problem solving. There are also two members of staff who are non-specialists and just take a few lessons of Maths here and there but don't come to my department meetings. I have a teacher who joined us recently from another country who can hardly speak any English and the kids just muck about in his lessons. Sheila is on maternity leave and her cover teacher is useless and then there is......"

"I know you have some issues with your team but that doesn't stop you supporting and improving them." He was going to use a glib line from a course he himself attended some years ago about seeing problems as opportunities not threats but it sounded as twee to him now as it did then. "You need to get out there, in lessons and see if you can help your colleagues."

"It's not easy to get out there. I have a full timetable and I can't work miracles."

Peter sensed that this discussion was going nowhere so he tried to play the praise card to trump Rick's hand of clubs.

"Look, the governors and I believe that you have the capability to make a difference and take the department forward." The first part of this statement was sadly true - he had made a difference for the worse - the second part was undeniably false following the disastrous year that Rick had been in charge of Maths during which Peter had fielded numerous complaints from pupils, parents and members of his own department. Despite Peter's own concerns, he had defended Richard Perry publicly and privately. He was in no position to do anything else - he and his governors had appointed him as there was no-one better out there unless the school was willing to pay big bucks. He had assigned Julie as his mentor and line manager to guide him through the first year. Unfortunately, their working relationship had gradually deteriorated. Julie had bent Peter's ear on several occasions about her concerns. In response, once a term Peter made a point of meeting with Rick to *see how he was getting on* and each meeting ended with both parties believing everything was fine. Peter had begun to hope that Julie, as an ex-Head of Department, was being a little harsh on Rick and judging him by her own high standards. He realised, sitting at his desk and looking at Rick eye to eye, that Julie had been right to question Rick's leadership qualities and he now concluded that they spent a whole year playing a game of double delusion.

"Anyway, it's not just the teaching of Maths that's an issue. The GCSE results last summer were not impressive and you didn't meet your targets. The actual grades were way off your predictions and were 20% below English." Peter was now on the offensive and Rick responded in kind.

"With all due respect," (code for no respect), "you can't compare the two subjects. English and Maths are totally different. Maths is much more difficult and...and the pupils enjoy English which makes it much easier..."

"Calm down Richard...Rick....as you know Ofsted expect English and Maths results to be above average and equally good. I know it will be a struggle to compete with English but you have got to narrow the gap." Peter paused and reflected momentarily on the bullshit he had just uttered. He realised that he had joined the dark side by impossibly expecting everything to be *above average*, even using the Ofsted phrase *narrowing the gap*. One thing was certain, he felt the gap between himself and his staff was widening. He was speaking in a foreign language that was not taught in the classroom and not understood by children or teachers, only by Ofsted inspectors.

"Boss, Jo has been Head of English for years. She has a settled team, all good teachers. It's much easier for her to get the results."

"I'm not sure Jo would say that leading the English department was easy, but I take your point..."

Just then there was a knock on the door and Julie came in holding the first print-off of the cover rota for the day. Peter could see from Julie's face that, as predicted, there had been a sudden overnight epidemic among the staff but just at this moment he was relieved to see her, even if she was the bearer of more bad tidings.

Surprisingly for an ageing heterosexual man, he had managed to read Julie's expression pretty accurately. Julie was concerned about the number of staff that were absent today although she was also concerned about the number of glasses of wine she had consumed on her own last night. She had not slept well, she had not woken up well and she was not feeling well this morning. She had risked black coffee and paracetamol at 5.30 am.; risked looking at her bathroom mirror at 5.45 am.; showered and applied several coats of hide and heal to her face and then stared at her wardrobe trying to decide which combination of blouse and skirt she had not worn for some time. What did it matter she had decided; no-one looked at her in that way anymore. Julie was glass completely empty this morning. She was feeling old, undesirable and disillusioned and her living room kept moving every time she tried to walk in a straight line. She collected her thoughts, briefcase, laptop and handbag and aimed for the door. She would drive to work slowly this morning, making sure that she didn't exceed any other limits. She knew that when she entered her office there would already be flashing messages on her answer phone from teachers graphically describing migraine, sickness and diarrhoea. Most messages would be performed in Oscar-winning death-bed monologues by the terminal teacher or by the concerned partner who would over-elaborate by giving a full medical history from the first sneeze. Julie had had the foresight to book three extra cover teachers for today before she left school last night but she was now thinking that wouldn't be enough. She felt sorry for any staff who would have to cover the shortfall and also for herself. She could have done with a day off to recover from her evening with her friend, the white grape, who had now quickly turned into her worst enemy. But she couldn't have any time off; if she took a sick day she might never want to return. She made and drank another black coffee, answered three more apologetic phone calls and then printed off two copies of the first draft of the cover rota. There would be other drafts to come but any staff in early would need to know if and what they were covering. She slowly walked in a straighter line to the staffroom to pin the cover sheet up on the noticeboard.

There were two ways of dealing with the cover list ritual – fight or flight. At first, when she was given the job, Julie would pin the sheets up and then walk briskly back to her office. Over time she had realised that this method did not avoid staff managing to catch her along the corridor or ambush her at her door with reasons why they shouldn't be *taken for cover*. Nowadays she decided to stand there and take the flack and argue the toss, defending her actions and decisions based on fairness and computer algorithms. Today she had pinned the cover sheets up, smiled, said "Sorry" to the few teachers already in the staffroom and headed to the boss's office only to find Richard Perry sitting there.

"Sorry to interrupt Peter. It's not a good day for staff attendance, do you want to have a look?"

"Yes please Julie," Peter replied enthusiastically sensing the opportunity to dismiss Rick from his office. "Rick, I'll catch up with you later on today after I have spoken to Julie about a way forward."

"Do you want me to stay now and discuss it with both of you?"

"No that's fine. Julie and I have other things to discuss. Thanks for popping in…"

This was a clear instruction to leave. Rick slowly but surely got the message and walked towards the door exchanging a smile of sorts with Julie. She closed the door behind him and took his place in the warm and worn seat.

"We seem to have a number of teachers whose health requires improvement," said Peter looking over Julie's print-out. "There was a time when staff just suffered from *Pre-Ofsteditis*, the fear of inspection. Now they get Post-Ofsted shock as well. I do feel sorry for the ones who performed well over the last two days. They're tarred by the same Ofsted brush and now have to cover for their colleagues who can't be bothered to show up for work."

"To be fair Peter, some absences are legitimate but the sudden plague of locusts and bugs must be the result of Ofsted. It would have been interesting to see what the attendance was like if we had been judged *Good* or *Outstanding*. You know morale will be at rock bottom today. Are you going to say much at the briefing this morning?" This was Julie's way of suggesting he say as little as possible.

"I thought I'd keep it short and simple this morning and explain at greater length to the departmental heads tonight. What do you think?"

"You're right. We can't go through the full feedback with all of the staff. We need to get our heads around the critique first ourselves and then cascade our thinking to the middle leaders." Julie was clearly sobering up and slipping into leadership clichés.

"Okay then. Staff Briefing in 10 minutes, Senior Leadership Team at 9.30 and can you find a time when we can speak to the Head of English and Science separately before we meet all the Heads of Department."

"It may be difficult if I need them to cover lessons."

"See what you can do." Peter looked at Julie closely for the first time since she sat down. "Are you alright? Did you have a rough night?"

Julie's cheeks drained of the remaining colour left on her face underneath her make-up. Of course the Head was innocently suggesting that she was unable to sleep because of the inspection and not implying that she looked as if she had been ravaged all night by the over-familiar effects of too much alcohol.

She gathered her thoughts and her dignity. "Yes I'm fine. I was up early. Caffeine will get me through the day."

"What did you make of the feedback? Were you angry or surprised?" asked Peter.

Taken aback by the bluntness of the question, Julie needed an answer that did not give away her true feelings; something positive without suggesting that she was naïve enough to believe that Whatmore was anything other than as Ofsted had found it to be.

"I suppose I was disappointed for the staff and pupils that we couldn't show that we were a good school. We have some great teachers here and yet at the end of the day we didn't make it count." She was now sounding like a Premiership football manager after a 3-0 defeat. Julie tried batting back the question.

"What about you, Peter?"

"I slept badly and frankly spent most of the night questioning my position and my future. I feel like crap this morning." Peter was opening his heart to the one member of the senior team he felt truly comfortable with. He could trust her implicitly. She was loyal. She was a Head teacher in the making, a good one, he was sure.

What could Julie say in response? "You ought to be questioning your position" or "You feel crap because you are crap" but she defaulted to loyal supporter and spoke with a forked tongue. "Peter, you're doing a fine job. It's not your fault. We're are all to blame. The inspectors were gunning for us the moment they set foot in the place. We can survive this." Julie's glass was brimming over, almost convincing herself that the school would survive the repercussions.

"I hope you're right Julie. We've got to put on brave faces and get through this."

"I... we will, I'm sure. I must get back to my phone in case of last minute accidents and emergencies, I'll see you at the briefing." Julie replied as she headed out. Turning momentarily, she nodded and smiled at Peter as she closed the door. For the first time ever, she felt sorry for him.

Peter, left alone in his office, felt sorry for himself and for everyone else in the school. He wanted to apologise to everyone. He wanted to give a hopeful weather forecast of fine days ahead but he also needed to give gale warnings as he knew that the school's dirty washing would have to be rinsed and hung out to dry. This morning he was still torn between negative deep clean and positive spin. He had ten minutes before the briefing and a blank piece of white paper in front of him waiting for his pearls of wisdom. He would make it brief. Hopefully, the walking wounded who made it into school this morning would not be in a combative mood. They would still be shell shocked from the two-day war.

He had managed a doodle or two on the corner of the page when Penny, his personal assistant, knocked and walked in.

"Good morning Peter." She greeted him with a smile; the same smile he had received every morning since he had begun at Whatmore; the same smile she had given to the previous Head every day since she arrived as a temp many years ago. She had seen many changes over the years, in policy and personnel, but in her quieter moments it seemed to her that the school remained the same. Penny had also remained the same; positive, pedantic but always protective. She knew everything about the school and kept it all firmly filed away in her head, in cabinets and on hard drives. She was the heart, soul and engine and all on 23.7% of the Head's salary. She knew this for certain: a year ago she had had to type up a report to the governors from Peter justifying his annual pay rise. She wasn't resentful; she would have hated having the ultimate responsibility for running the school. She was much more comfortable letting others make the final decisions as long as she knew exactly what was going on.

Penny was the perfect PA; pleasant, patient, well organised and low maintenance. She arrived fifteen minutes before the beginning of the school day and left about thirty minutes after the final bell. During those hours she had seen Ofsted come and go, politicians visit, teachers and pupils striking, parents losing their cool and numerous fire engines arrive at the gates only to be turned away. Whatever had been thrown at the school, Penny calmly carried on and kept her own counsel. She was unflappable but could turn into a Rottweiler when guarding the office from anyone without an appointment to see her boss. Once she was at her desk, no-one, not even Peter's senior team members or his wife could pass without her approval. This meant many staff only ever tried to see Peter after Penny had driven out of the school gates.

"Hello Penny. You've heard about the Ofsted report I suppose."

"Yes, I got the news as I walked through Reception." Penny, unlike anyone else on the staff could detach herself completely from the job, driving out of school and not giving it a second's thought until she parked next to the Head's car each week day morning. She didn't go to the feedback - not because she didn't care but because she was only paid until 3.45pm. She worked like a Trojan during the school day but had come to adhere strictly to her contracted hours once it became clear that she would never receive a pay rise or bonus for her dedication. Only teachers got that sort of reward in their pay packets.

"You have messages from the Chair of Governors and the Local Authority. Can you please ring them back later?"

"Sure. I thought it wouldn't be long before the vultures started circling. I'm off to the briefing. Hold the fort will you?"

Peter knew she would. He left the security of his office and was greeted by a heady smelling mixture of adolescent body odour and overcooked bacon from the school kitchen. He realised that he had missed the delights of the school breakfast he had promised himself and he was starving.

CHAPTER 4

The briefing was short if not sweet. As predicted, the staff were shaken, not stirred, to arms. Peter kept it safe and briefly explained that he would be working with key personnel to produce an action plan over the next few weeks. He listed all of the meetings he was planning and the teachers looked at him as if they were taking it all in whilst resenting the fact that they would spend every minute of their day teaching or covering lessons others should have been teaching. Most teachers would have preferred the Head's day of endless meetings rather than five hours of shouting at obdurate children. Peter finished the briefing with his customary but ill judged "Let's be careful out there!" and walked out, heading back to his office. The staff remained in the trenches until the bell rang for the first round.

Peter stopped to speak to Penny. "Can you get me Ann Brown, Evelyn our School Improvement Partner and Clive Howell from the local authority on the phone in the next thirty minutes or so?"

"Any particular order?" replied Penny.

"No I need to speak to them all today and meet with them separately as soon as possible."

"Can you also see if the Cook can rustle me up something to eat? I missed breakfast."

"I'll try - I'll contact Ann first."

By the time Peter was sitting at his desk, his phone was ringing. Penny notified him that the Chair of Governors was already on the line.

"Hi Peter, sorry I had to shoot off at the end of the feedback last night but I was late for another meeting. How have the staff taken it?"

"Not well, Ann. They're very hurt and some are just looking for someone else to blame."

"I guess that will be you then...I don't mean that it should be you but you're the natural target. No offence Peter, but they see you as the big bad wolf."

"No offence taken. I know what you mean. The problem is that the school requires improvement and everyone has to take responsibility...for the judgement and the school's recovery...including the governors."

"I hear what you're saying Peter. The governors didn't come out of the inspection well and they won't be happy with some of the comments in the feedback. I know I wasn't, particularly about not being up to date with school issues and pupil data."

Almost imperceptibly the *WE are all in this together* was being liberally spread across the whole piece of cold toast. The question was, who was holding the knife - the Head or the Chair of Governors?

Peter moved the conversation on. "I think it would be good to meet up as soon as possible to discuss the feedback and our way forward."

"I agree. I'm in a meeting all morning but I can get to you by lunchtime. Is that any good?"

"That's great."

"I'll try to be with you by 12.15"

"Alright. See you then."

Penny popped her head around Peter's door when she saw the light go off on her switchboard to announce that he was too late for breakfast and too early for lunch but he could have some of the cookies normally sold by the canteen to the children at break time. Peter agreed to a dozen; he thought he and his Senior Leadership Team could do with a sugar rush.

Penny had not been able to contact the School Improvement Partner and she had left a message for Clive. No doubt he was in a meeting.

Peter was not sure about the value of the SIP. In fact, he wasn't convinced by much about Evelyn Chadbourne. He had inherited her as a paid adviser to the school when he became Head. Evelyn had apparently been an *Outstanding* Head teacher at an *Outstanding* school before taking early retirement to advise other schools. At first, Peter had welcomed Evelyn's general advice but in time had come to see her as out of touch after being too long out of classrooms. She kept herself up to speed with the weekly changes to national policy in Education and certainly knew the rules of the Ofsted game but she lacked school corridor credibility, especially as her school had been an all girls' school down in the affluent south and he was leading a mixed up school in the north. Peter felt her visits, usually once a term, were a waste of time and money. While Evelyn felt the regular visits were vital and made all of the difference to such poor disadvantaged schools as Whatmore – and they also paid for her foreign holidays that she took for half the year.

Peter was understandably annoyed that Evelyn, as a critical friend, had turned out to be no better than a door to door salesman, failing to predict any of the major issues found by Ofsted. On the contrary, in her last report she had assessed the school as *Good* in all four areas, a view which had informed Peter's self-evaluation report. In due course he would be having a chat with Ann about ending Evelyn's contract. But this was not a conversation for now. The here and now was the action plan and his team meeting.

They started arriving at 9.25, each of them acknowledging Penny in his or her own way as they walked past her desk. Julie smiled, Sobia nodded, Neil arrived at exactly 9.30 and asked Penny if he could go in and Charlie arrived some five minutes late and made a point of giving Penny his full attention.

"Hello Mrs Hinks, I think you left your underwear at my house last night," Charlie beamed and winked as he moved in close to Penny's desk. Anyone else on the staff would have received corporal punishment for such a remark, but not Charlie. He could do no wrong in Penny's eyes - the more he teased her, the more she loved it. Charlie Briggs was Penny's Achilles Heel. She was putty in his hands and many years ago she would have happily been kneaded and squeezed by Charlie's hands. Although now happily married to an insurance adviser, she still harboured regretful thoughts for him having missed his boat some fifteen years ago. They were the same age, give or take a month but Charlie still looked attractive for his age and kept himself trim even though he hadn't taught PE for some time. Penny could still remember those glorious summer terms when he would wear brief running shorts and sit on her desk semi-flirting.

"Mr Briggs, you are late as usual and I will ignore your comment for now but wait until you need a favour from me." She tried to look stern.

"You can always do me a favour Mrs Hinks. I'll see you behind the bike shed at break time."

Penny tried not to smile as she watched him glide into the Head's office.

"Sorry folks, two kids kicking off outside Room 323. What have I missed, have you finished the action plan yet?"

"We were just about to start," said Peter.

Charlie poured coffee from the pot on the sideboard and took his seat. His demeanour differed from the rest of the team. If Charlie had been able to talk about his feelings, he would have described himself as *low* yesterday but having now bounced back. He would metaphorically stick the Ofsted report in his pigeon hole and let it gather dust as it worked its way to the bottom of an ever increasing pile of junk. This morning he would be the one giving reality checks to the others. He would be the one breaking the sullen atmosphere with jokes. He would be the one that would remind the team that this wasn't a matter of life or death. But he was the one that the rest of the team could not do without, even if they didn't realise it. Charlie was a doer. He loved the kids, he loved sports, he loved blokey blokes and most women but hated shades of grey and theoretical discussions. Action rather than action plans. The Year 11 football team didn't need an action plan when losing a match at half time. He would bollock them and praise them and then bollock them again. But today and for several days to come he would have to sit inactively drawing up an action plan and listening to the rest of the team arguing the toss between aims and objectives or predictions or targets. He decided to sit there and watch porn in his mind while the others made their pointless plans.

"Can we review the feedback first?" Peter said. "It's important we all agree on what needs to be done and who is going to do what. I know we haven't had the draft Ofsted report to check but I want to get started on addressing the key points."

"Before we do that," Sobia said, "can I just make a point?"

"Sure. Go ahead."

"Are we going to just accept the findings? You thought we were a *Good* school until forty-eight hours ago. What's changed? What does that say about your judgement?"

"Our judgement," whispered Neil.

"Pardon me?" Sobia shot a glance at Neil.

"It was OUR judgement. You were part of the decision making," replied Neil.

"Yes, but what I'm saying is we ought to appeal against the decision. If we just accept they're right and we're wrong then we don't have much credibility left with the staff."

"The trouble is Sobia, we can't appeal against the Ofsted judgement without real evidence that their data is wrong. We know our results have been disappointing. We can't argue with that."

"Well what about the judgement on Leadership and Management? Can't we make a case for saying that's *Good*?" Sobia persevered.

"Unfortunately, if our pupil outcomes and teaching are not up to standard then our leadership can't be either," Peter said.

"So the four judgements aren't separate then. It's a house of cards. One goes down, they all go down!"

"Pretty much. From what I gather *Outcomes for Pupils* pretty much trumps the other judgements. If the kids don't perform as well as Ofsted expect then a school must improve rapidly or go into special measures."

"So we were never going to be judged as *Good* because our results were…poor. We went into the inspection without a chance of doing well. So what was the point of trying to convince the inspectors we were something we clearly weren't? Why did we try to convince ourselves?"

"We had to, Sobia," said Peter. "To demonstrate that we were on the right track and the grades would go up next year."

"Well that didn't work either - most of the teachers let us down over the last two days."

"Let's not get into blaming the teachers. As the Senior Leadership Team, we've had our knuckles rapped for not evaluating the school's performance accurately and that has given Ofsted an open goal to shoot at."

Charlie pressed the pause button in his mind for a second or two until he realised the others were still talking a different kind of balls. He mentally pressed play to avoid the various footballing metaphors and clichés about to be deployed.

"Surely if we'd said we thought we were below average it would have shown as managers we were on the ball."

"I take your point..."

Sobia was not finished, "So what's the point of it all - we were always going to get a kicking from Ofsted."

"We might have just scraped into *Good* if the teaching and the pupils' books had been okay."

"Who's blaming the teachers now?"

Peter's tight-lipped smile silently expressed frustration, annoyance and defeat. "We are where we are and now we have to look forward and make rapid and effective improvements to get to *Good* in two years. Can I ask you all to focus on the future and not dwell on the last two days." *Some hope*, thought Peter.

Sobia folded her arms and didn't return Peter's smile. She too felt frustrated; frustrated that she was part of a team that couldn't make an accurate analysis to save their lives or speak up to support her.

"How about looking at the key actions from yesterday's feedback as a starting point?" offered Julie.

"Goo...Great idea," Peter corrected himself, relieved someone else had spoken up to change the direction of the meeting.

"According to my notes there were three main areas that need addressing." Julie cleared her throat and reeled them off...

"Firstly, improve the quality of all teaching and learning. Then improve the progress made by pupils in all subjects particularly in Mathematics. Finally improve the leadership at all levels so that staff and governors have a clear and accurate picture of the school."

Peter gave everyone a few seconds to absorb this before breaking the silence.

"Thanks Julie, so we know where the focus has to be. Anyone wish to comment or start us off on planning our actions? Charlie? Neil?"

At the sound of their names both paused from their screens, the IPad and the mental porn were frozen in time. Both men looked up and stared blankly at Peter.

Neil broke first. "I was just checking my notes and I agree with Julie." Neil hoped that his response to whatever he had been asked would sound convincing.

"So what do you suggest we do Neil? You must have some ideas. We've got a blank piece of paper here. Start us off."

"Well.... I suggest our action plan is related to these three main areas and we have a separate section in the action plan for teaching, pupil progress and leadership and then break down each component into sub-sections that we can target and quantify. We assign each section of the action plan to two of us to take responsibility for, monitor and evaluate. We would have to have strict timelines for each action and measurable targets." Neil lowered his head, exhausted that he had used up more oxygen than normal and had doubled the number of words he would normally say out loud during the school day.

Peter was impressed. "I like it. Very constructive. Great contribution Neil." His eyes moved from Neil's forehead onto Sobia for enough time to make a point before alighting on Charlie.

It was clear that Charlie had to contribute at this point but unable to compete with Neil's analysis, he did what came naturally to him, changing the subject and the tone.

"You know, I've been sitting here and thinking about Ofsted and what we're expected to do and it struck me that it's like having an MOT for your car. You either pass or fail. Whether we like it or not we have failed and have to fix our vehicle right away and make it roadworthy again. But the big difference between a garage and Ofsted is that with an MOT the mechanics will tell you exactly what the car failed on; they will tell you what needs to be done and offer help in fixing the problems. What does Ofsted do? The inspectors tell you the school is not good enough, they give you a vague report stating that everything has to improve in a few months but give you no guidance or help in putting things right. So we're left trying to pass the MOT without actually knowing what exactly is wrong! I'd love to be a mechanic failing an Ofsted inspector's car and saying to him 'Sorry mate your car failed but you will have to work out exactly what is wrong with it yourself and fix the faults but don't worry I will inspect it again when I feel like it to see if you have put things right'."

Charlie's re-direction hit home and seemed to have a positive effect on the rest of the team even though it was just meant to illustrate the stupidity of Ofsted inspections. As he'd started, Charlie decided to finish. "Let's fix the vehicle for ourselves. We're the ones who have to drive it into the future, not some out-of-touch, chauffeur-driven bureaucrats who wouldn't know one end of a spark plug from the other. We've had no real guidance or advice from the inspectors, just that nothing's good enough. But my question to you all isn't do we accept Ofsted's opinion now? In one sense we have to, but did we think that we weren't good enough before the inspectors called? We were hoping to put on a good show and cover up all the cracks but we know deep down there are inconsistency issues here. Without saying it out loud we were all thinking, 'Can we get away with this?' Well, we haven't and now we have to be honest and up front about some of our colleagues and sort this mess out. And not by relying on an action plan that goes nowhere but by banging heads together."

The heads around the table did not bang but nodded. All but the most significant head. Peter slid an inch or two down in his seat. He knew that he would have to be the chief head-banger; not something he found easy. He hated conflict, preferring a quiet life with colleagues knowing instinctively how to be perfect so all he need do was praise them every so often. Some of the staff, the better ones, cynically regarded him as wanting to be everybody's friend. Only the poorer performers on the whole thought of Peter as quite a good Head teacher. If truth be told, Peter didn't want to be anyone's friend; he would have cheerfully opted for a life on a desert island with a satellite television, a music system and a giant book of Sudoku puzzles.

Peter attempted to respond positively. He pulled himself upright to remind his group of nodding and drooling dogs that there had to be an action plan first before anything else was attempted.

Sobia couldn't resist a dig back at him. "So we have to write an action plan before we can act?"

"Well....yes, because we have to have the agreement of the governors and Her Majesty's Inspectorate first."

"So what about the idea that we are the professionals and we know what is best for the school?"

"But Ofsted's feedback on our judgement suggests that we don't know what's best for our school." Peter was digging a huge hole for himself on his isolated sandy beach.

"Then let's do something about it. If they want rapid improvement then we have to show them results, not just write about it on thirty sides of A4." Charlie head butting in.

Peter had the sense of his devoted team all kicking sand in his face. "It isn't that easy. We can't just publicly execute half the staff in the middle of the playground. They have rights and we have to go down the capability route before we get anywhere near firing any of them."

"The trouble is Peter," said Julie, "we haven't ever gone down this road before and it will look draconian if we suddenly target half a dozen or so teachers. It'll also look like a knee jerk reaction and the unions will have a field day."

"The real problem," Peter took a deep breath as Charlie spoke, "is that we should have put some of them on capability ages ago. We knew they were crap and no amount of professional development or training would make them into good teachers."

Peter breathed out, relieved that Charlie's bullet was not aimed exclusively at him." I agree with Julie. If we start doing it now it makes us look like..."

"Proper Charlies?" Neil whispered aloud.

For the first time since the meeting started the entire team laughed as one. As if by divine intervention the bell sounded for the end of the first period, prompting a knock on the door and Penny's arrival carrying a plate of cookies and some paper serviettes. She placed them in the middle of the muddled papers on the table and retreated. She smiled as she left because, unless Peter had a hammer and chisel to hand, it would be difficult for them to eat one of the cook's infamous cookies without the result being a trip to the dentist.

Some distance away from the open door, if anyone cared to listen, there could be heard the sound of pupils going to their next lesson or not going to their next lesson depending on age and inclination. There was also the sound of teachers yelling at pupils to stop shouting, swearing, hitting each other and dropping litter. Most pupils were guilty of one or other of these crimes while the most gifted managed to break all four rules at the same time.

In the secure bunker of Peter's office the Senior Leadership Team was oblivious to the extraneous sounds of open warfare. Penny closed the door behind herself, leaving them to pour more coffees and dunk their cookies in an attempt to protect their teeth.

The second half of the game, (The Head versus the Rest of the World), started with Peter attempting to re-establish the ground rules. It was his ball, his pitch, and his reputation so if anybody objected, they could watch from the side lines. Of course Peter did not say anything like this. He merely reminded his team that he wanted to have something constructive to tell the Chair of Governors at lunch time.

"I think we can incorporate Charlie's call to arms in our plan, so if we go back to Neil's idea of the three sections, perhaps we can divvy up our responsibilities to each of these categories."

There was grudging acceptance of this idea and then followed a twenty seven minute discussion which delayed any action. The first problem encountered was a need for five people to divide up equally into three areas. Should they draft an additional person in to even things up? Who? Should Peter, as Head, just have an overall watching brief? Should Sobia, as a non-teacher lead a section on teaching or learning? Should Neil be responsible for anything other than ICT? Should Charlie just continue to be responsible for pupil behaviour and welfare? Could Julie lead all three areas?

Finally, it had to be agreed that Julie would be responsible for teaching and learning, Neil supported by Charlie would be responsible for pupil outcomes, Peter and Sobia would take on the leadership section of the action plan and most significantly of all they agreed to take it in turns to buy biscuits for future team meetings rather than rely on the canteen.

The rest of the staff would be notified of these decisions (without reference to biscuits) later in the day. The rationale for choosing certain team captains might be harder to justify to the rest of the staff. Peter could not admit publicly that he didn't have much faith or trust in certain members of his senior team so he would have to think about the spin he needed to put on the decisions. He certainly could not say that Sobia was an unexploded bomb on a short fuse with no school leadership experience. He could also not openly admit that although Neil was a nice guy, he came over as having the personality of a *Speak Your Weight Machine* and could never command respect from the more forceful personalities among the staff. He could also not criticise Charlie in open court as having more froth than substance and that his flippant approach to school and life, rendered him unsuitable to develop a serious plan of action. He would also never admit that Julie was the only member of his team, other than himself, that he could trust to lead the staff into battle. She was perfectly capable of doing a fine job in completing all three sections of the action plan on her own but that would be neither fair nor democratic. Peter had great plans for Julie and once or twice recently, as he closed his eyes at night, he thought of the plans he could have had for Julie if he was twenty years younger, three or four inches thinner and with the looks of Clark Gable rather than the personality of Clark Kent.

In the end Peter could only live with the decisions made. Charlie and Neil working together was a bizarre concept deserving of a comedy double act nickname. What would it be? Morecombe and Unwise? The Two Rooneys? Or perhaps Cannon and Ballsup? Maybe the pairing would work? Maybe? Only time would tell.

Peter felt obliged to partner Sobia. He felt that he was best equipped with his bullet proof suit and stab in the back vest to work hand in fist with her towards an agreed and agreeable solution. On the successful conclusion of this project he would certainly be nominating himself for the Nobel Peace Prize.

Julie could cope with leading the Quality of Teaching and Learning section on her own. He was aware that her role was much greater than all the others but she could handle it. She never complained. She seemed to be coping, she kept calm and smiled and carried on. If she needed advice, Peter's door was always open to her, day or night!

The team decided to work on for the next part of the meeting in their new pairings, with Julie happy to work on her own. As is commonly the case, working on one's own is more productive than having to sit and listen to another person giving their views with the listener not listening to the speaker while thinking what to say next; an immediate halving of productivity. Arguments resulting from actual listening would waste even more time. Consequently, by the end of the meeting, Julie had made four times more progress and notes than the two pairs.

Julie's main suggestions involved accurate re-observation of all the teachers against the Ofsted criteria linked to a more rigorous and systematic analysis of the pupils' work books. Julie made the case for individual intervention plans for those teachers who needed help and could be saved. However, she could think of a couple of members of staff with permanent contracts who would need a different approach. By this she meant an exit route. She would also use the remaining professional development budget, held by Sobia and Peter, for targeting individual teachers rather than generic training for all staff, which had been the Whatmore way.

There was general approval of these ideas. Charlie still wanted to name and shame the culprits and Sobia was concerned about funding the training to which Peter and Julie replied in unison that the money would have to be found. Sobia scowled and looked to the skies for the rain cloud overhead that would shower the school with notes of all denominations. Neil pointed out that the staff would not take kindly to being continuously observed and raised the spectre of union disapproval. Peter said that he and Julie would talk to the teacher union representatives in the next few days to gain their agreement.

Charlie and Neil's big idea was more left field. Charlie made the case for publishing termly an internal league table for all subjects to create competition within the school. For the first time this morning in espousing it, Charlie sounded engaged and enthusiastic, standing on his soap box - a party political broadcast on behalf of the Competitive Party. His impassioned presentation was met by a range of responses.

Woolly liberals, in the shape of Peter, had concerns over the self-esteem of colleagues on the staff - he had issues with the notion of improvement through comparisons and criticisms, wanting to foster a happy crew who felt good about themselves.

Sobia, on the other hand, was totally in favour of a *hang-'em high* approach. It was not fair on highly performing teachers if others were letting them down. If duds could not be got rid of quickly then at least everyone in the school should be aware of their shortcomings.

The arguments had not just gone full circle, but felt like they were on a third lap. Julie and surprisingly Neil, expressed concern over publicising performance data in the form of internal league tables. As the senior leaders responsible for the bureaucratic task of producing the data, they weren't convinced it would be a useful way of accurately judging termly progress of pupils and might lead instead to inflated pupil assessments by teachers to make themselves look good.

With Julie and Neil on the brink of sinking Charlie's ship, Peter weighed in with his own take on it. He brought out the old cliché that people who diet successfully do not necessarily lose weight every week. This was enough for Charlie to admit that his idea would need more thought. "So what about you two?" he asked, licking his lips in anticipation of getting his own back by blowing Peter and Sobia's ideas out of the water.

"We have some ideas on improving leadership and would welcome your thoughts," said Peter. "Would you like to summarise our thinking, Sobia?"

"If you like. All staff at all levels are responsible for leading pupils and most staff have a responsibility to other adults, so we need to make improvements across the board. Peter feels that it's easier to say who's an effective teacher rather than an effective leader. But in our senior leadership roles, we should be able to say who below us is good at leading."

Peter couldn't remember this train of thought being explored in their conversation but he let Sobia continue. "Surely, we have to demonstrate and model what it means to be a good leader, tell them how to be effective and then give them targets to improve. Then, if some of our leaders are not up to standard…"

"Yes, thanks Sobia. Do you think we need to have whole school training on this or do we just nominate certain people?" Peter looked to all the other members of his team for an answer.

"I think we know already who needs to improve their leadership style but it wouldn't hurt if all of the staff had training," said Julie. "Including us!" She threw this small hand grenade into the middle of the table in amongst the ever-hardening, remaining cookies. "Didn't you have some training on leadership a few years ago?"

"Yes, we paid some plonker to deliver a presentation and we all had to fill in a questionnaire about our preferred leadership style," remembered Charlie. "It was typical training…death by a thousand PowerPoint slides. It changed nothing but cost the school a lot of money."

"It must have been before my time here but it's clearly a while since we had any training, so it's long overdue," said Peter. "What about targeting the training…anyone think we should just focus on our middle leaders?"

"Like Julie, I think there should be leadership training for all staff," Sobia said. "If we train everyone, then we won't have any excuses."

"What about the staff who have this training and are still unable to lead a team?" asked Charlie.

"I suppose we will have to deal with those afterwards," said Peter weakly.

"But Julie just said that she knows who the culprits are and so do I, so why wait? Let's bend their ears now," said Charlie, spoiling for a fight.

"Hold on, let's make sure that we have evidence before we start taking action against specific individuals. We need to give everyone a refresher course on leadership and management first and then if necessary we will speak to certain people." There was a collective rolling of eyes as the rest of the team spotted Peter backing away from the fight. "I'll ask Clive Howell to talk to the staff as soon as possible."

"Why Clive?" asked Neil.

"Well, he knows the school better than anyone else from the local education authority," said Peter.

"That doesn't say much!" said Charlie.

"Also, he won't cost us anything!"

"Fair enough," said Charlie.

The meeting ground to a halt with Peter summing up what had been decided and achieved. There had been useful discussions on who was leading the three key actions and the beginnings of progress on the actions that will need to be taken. It was agreed they would meet again in two days' time to further develop the action plan. The excitement generated by this one unanimously firm decision was tangibly insincere.

CHAPTER 5

The others left Peter's room and scattered to the four corners of the school. Charlie was first to pass Penny working at her desk. He winked at her, she smiled back and he strode off. Julie and Sobia followed exchanging pleasantries as they headed in roughly the same direction. Neil closed the Head's door securely as he brought up the rear. He tried to acknowledge Penny but she was oblivious.

Charlie stopped several times on his journey to ask pupils why they were out of lessons or why they were standing outside classrooms and to deliver semi-sarcastic jokes about their ties, blazers, shoes and jewellery. At one point he managed a corridor-long shout at a couple of girls who were laughing loudly. They screamed back at him, "Sorry Sir" and disappeared out of sight. Charlie had to admit to himself that it felt good to scream and shout after over two hours imprisonment in the Head's office. He needed to vent and it was cathartic to target his pent up frustration on a couple of teenagers whose only crime was being happy and young.

Charlie arrived at the Pastoral Block, a maze of rooms and offices, which had enjoyed many nick names over the years such as The Black Hole, Cell Block H, Room 101, Bedlam, The Relegation Zone, A&E (Arseholes and Ejits), Guantanamo Bay and Briggadoom. Charlie was comfortable using these appellations with his staff because he had originally coined most of them himself. He had loved his time in Physical Education but somewhere along the white line of his career, Charlie had seamlessly switched from the court of sport to the court of law. Being in charge of all pastoral matters was a role he thoroughly enjoyed. In all his years in education, this was the post that gave him most satisfaction and reward even if most other teaching staff saw it as wholly negative. Yes, Charlie missed the sport, the thrills and spills, the winning and the losing but first and foremost he loved working with kids, good or bad and the cups and trophies were, at the end of the day, less important than the players.

Charlie had a loyal team of pastoral heads, one per year, who worked non-stop to get some balance into pupils with unstable lives. In dealing with pupils' problems there were very few hard and fast rules but Charlie had trained his team to understand and confidently follow the few unwritten regulations he had laid down. When mistakes were made or decisions backfired, he would always support his staff in front of others. He would happily field complaints from aggrieved teachers or parents arguing that punishments were too lenient or too severe or in certain cases that he must have the wrong pupil. Over the years Charlie received fewer and fewer knocks on his door as both parents and teachers came to realise that it was almost impossible to argue the toss with such a formidable opponent.

Charlie let his Year Heads deal with all of the positive praising of their year groups and most issues involving their pupils' misbehaviour but would step in for any serious events or safeguarding issues. It meant that his normal day would be spent working with the 5% of the school's pupils who caused 95% of the problems in the classroom. It sounded thankless but he openly loved it. Admittedly, there were a couple of kids over the years that he was relieved to permanently exclude, mainly for the sake of the rest of the pupils and the teachers, but he was sad and disappointed, even then, that he had failed to put them back on the right track.

It was a tiring work and it was beginning to take its toll on Charlie. He could sense that he was developing grumpy old man syndrome. By the end of most weeks he was suffering from compassion overload as well as being knackered. This worried him greatly. It seemed like only a few years ago he could sprint around the football pitch all day long. Now he refereed games from the centre circle and looked forward to the final whistle and the drinks in the pub afterwards. Consequently, he found himself awarding little, if any, injury time these days. He was determined not to overdo it now so he could enjoy a few fit and healthy years at his local tennis and golf clubs in retirement.

Outside the main pastoral office he found three pupils slouching on chairs. They wrenched themselves upright when they saw Mr Briggs coming. Charlie gave each of them a knowing stare and walked inside. Six desks were positioned around the classroom sized office. Two of the Year Heads were sitting at their desks - one on the phone and one talking to a Year 8 boy who stood with his hands behind his back, trying to look as if butter wouldn't melt in his mouth. Charlie knew better than to interrupt or weigh in because he trusted that everything was under control. He made a round of coffees for his team whilst eavesdropping on the Head of Year 8 talking to the boy and admiring how the Year Head had expertly managed to shift the pupil's story from one of being *nowhere near the fight* towards an admission of starting it in the first place.

From habit Charlie decided to look in on the Penalty Box, his nickname for the withdrawal room, a place where naughty pupils were excluded temporarily from lessons. The room had ten work stations partitioned off from each other to avoid pupils talking or distracting each other. They might work in here for a day or longer depending on the severity of the offence. The room was managed by Charlie and run by the Year Heads on a rota. In the Penalty Box he found five youngsters of different ages working in silence.

He told the Head of Year in situ to have a break. She said "Are you sure?" and "Thanks" and left Charlie to it. He sat down to look over the day's register with the names of the prisoners, their offences and their sentences printed across it. The names were all known offenders but Charlie was stoical, knowing that while they were being quiet and sensible in here, they weren't causing mischief or mayhem around school. The padded chair felt warm and comfortable, he felt he was making a difference and even Ofsted had noticed. The meeting with the Head and his management peers seemed a million years and miles away.

He looked at his watch and considered the rest of his mapped out day. He would stay here until lunch time and then go to the school's dining hall, shout at a few kids and earn a free school dinner from the cook, another member of his fan club. She would make a point of serving him personally, giving him extra portions whether he wanted them or not. The afternoon would consist of a meeting between Social Services representatives and a troubled parent of a troubled child from a troubled family. He would try to make the meeting overrun to make him late for the Peter Burlington's after-school, action planning session. Charlie was not sure how much more bullshit he could cope with in one day but he knew he would have to sit there and give the impression of full support. After that, escaping back to the Pastoral Block to catch up with his own team on today's events. At approximately 5.30 they would, one by one, clear their desks and say good night. He was really pleased that they left at this time every night. It showed they believed him on the importance of work-life balance.

Only then would Charlie venture into his own small office to fill in a few reports and lock them safely away in one of his many filing cabinets.

At some point he would expect a knock on the door and the Head of Year 11 would make an entrance. Also a PE teacher and in her early forties, she would sit opposite Charlie on the only other chair in this cramped cupboard space and small talk for a while. At some point in the ritual she would adjust her short gym skirt and slowly cross and uncross her tanned legs. This was part of a regular warming up and loosening exercise they enjoyed before undertaking a very focused and physical work out together. Both satisfied and de-stressed she would leave his office. And some five minutes or so later Charlie would leave the building too, having warmed down. He would phone his third wife when he got into his car and tell her that he would be going to the club for a quick game of squash before coming home.

Neil Turner, Assistant Head teacher, in charge of the School Network and all matters of information technology, made his way back to his office the long way, extending the shortest possible route by 149 metres. This route took him past only three classroom doors and avoided the staff room. Having evaded all human contact, Neil punched in the key pad code for his door to enter what was literally a large stock room. There was just the one chair in the room, a computer chair, adjusted exactly to suit Neil's slightly bent back and rounded shoulders. There were no filing cabinets in his paperless world. At one end of the room were two tables at right angles to each other. He could sit here and work from his two PCs, laptop, IPad and IPhone without having to stand up. He could also reach down into his mini fridge to swig from bottled water during the day or access his fresh lunch of two slices of wholemeal bread with layers of cheese and tomatoes cut meticulously into quarters.

He systematically fired up all of his gizmos and gadgets. The fixed technology in this room ran off one power socket and a series of four, six-gang extension leads. Once the screens lit up Neil would feel safe and secure in his bunker. He would stay here until the Heads of Department meeting when he would leave his cave at 3.25 to get there on time. Any later and he would feel the eyes staring at him as he entered the staff room. If he arrived any earlier, there was a possibility that staff would want to engage with him. He was already exhausted with too much interaction today and wanted to let his fingers do the talking for a few hours.

If Neil could have allowed his mind to wander away from the busy information highways, he would never have paused to ask himself why he was the way he was. His parents had spoiled their only child with computers and video games and he became obsessed with role play adventures and did all of his fighting and kissing in other worlds. Other pupils at his school gave him an unreality check and banished him to an alternative Coventry. His new land was bereft of pretty maidens and friendly giants that could protect him. He managed to survive Sutton Coldfield Sixth Form College and Aston University studying IT with one life remaining but found it difficult to impress anyone at interview for a position in a commercial company. As a last resort he applied for IT posts within schools and six years and 126 days ago was appointed at Whatmore. After 73 weeks, with the Head of IT retiring, he was crowned prince of a virtual realm. He was uncomfortable in the company of strangers and in truth, familiars too, and now found himself working in a school with 1248 pupils and 157 adults. Fortunately for Neil, he was travelling so fast on a broadband motorway he could not look in his rear view mirror or see any signs, so he missed the turn for his field of hopes and dreams. He powered up his search engines, sat back in the captain's chair and took the second star to the right until morning. Or at least until 3.25pm.

Sobia's world was black and white concrete. There were no grey areas to be found. Her office was not far from the Head's room but it felt to her as if they were in different countries. The teachers not only spoke a different language but behaved differently to the rest of adult society. This alien world of unnecessary acronyms and woolly mindedness was a million miles from her comfort zone. Now she crossed back to the real world on real time, into her domain where she reigned supreme. She micro-managed two ladies busily working away at their stations. Sobia had positioned them facing opposite walls while her desk was facing inwards by the window so that she could see each of her workers beavering away. She expected these two women (she knew their names but very little else) to work hard and leave at 4.00 each day. She would brief them every morning and speak to each of them at the end of each day. There were no other seats in this office; she didn't encourage anyone to cross the threshold, particularly teachers, and she certainly didn't want anyone to get comfortable in her office or distract the others.

Sobia kept a tight rein on school finances and would regard it as a poor day in the office if she had to say yes more than three times. She also kept the same tight rein on the other non-teachers that she was responsible for, namely caretakers, cleaners, technicians and the administration team. Sobia was happy to call them *non-teachers* as opposed to *support staff*. She hated the notion that they supported teachers let alone that they could ever be regarded as crutches for weak teachers. However, she liked the idea that they were definitely not teachers and therefore could be treated as grown-ups.

Sobia believed that her staff respected her and enjoyed the disciplined approach to work. If Cathy and Diane were able to speak their minds then their own opinions of Sobia and her leadership style would be at some variance with their much-loved line manager's take on things.

Julie carried on down the corridor to her office. She didn't share an office; didn't have a PA. She argued this was a sign that her boss found her strong, confident and competent. She was able to hold her own against anyone and capable of doing her job without admin support. In time she came to the conclusion that it was the Head's lack of empathy or funds that condemned her to work on her own, sometimes swimming, sometimes drowning, without a colleague with whom to share the slings and arrows of the school day.

Julie's office looked neat, tidy and well-organised. Her walls were covered with reference displays on timetables and the school's curriculum, each sheet decorated by highlighter ink of different colours that meant nothing to anyone else. Her desk was immaculately ordered with a range of stationery close to hand.

The cleaner assigned to Ms Osborne's office had mixed views about the task. She knew there would be very little to clean but was always worried about disturbing the ordered contents of the room. Things were even worse if she had to clean with the Assistant Head watching her every move.

Julie's office was large enough to take a small coffee table with three comfortable chairs. The table was clear apart from three coasters for drinks and a small vase in the centre of the table containing artificial flowers. She had considered buying real flowers for the inspection but in the mad panic and terror of the first morning she had forgotten them. However, all was perfect and if there had been an Ofsted judgement for teachers' offices then Julie would have been judged *Outstanding*.

Only one drawer at the bottom of one of the two tall lockable filing cabinets could have affected this judgement. In this drawer Julie locked away her handbag every morning, her personal smartphone, a selection of chocolate bars, extra make-up, a range of tablets for headaches and three bottles of still water, one of which had contained water at one time but was now filled with another colourless liquid for emergencies. This small hidden space in her office now represented her personal life. Julie's mobile could be left in the drawer during the day as she knew that few messages would come her way. There had been a time when she was happy to tell the world about her job and the man in her life. She would text her friends and assume that they were all interested and pleased for her. Now there was nothing to report and other people were sending her stuff that made her jealous and sad so, over time, she had to *unfriend* those friends for her own sanity. Chocolate and alcohol were the only two true companions who understood her and stayed close.

At her desk Julie started on her emails and messages, adding things to a *To Do List* that had started long at the beginning of the day and was now even longer without anything having been achieved or crossed out.

A knock on the door broke the silence and her dark spirit. It was *Call Me Rick*. The Gods hearing her prayers for male company had misunderstood entirely.

"Are you busy? Can I just have a few minutes of your time?"

Julie wanted to answer "Yes and No" in that order but opted for a nod.

Rick Perry took his usual chair and dumped several wodges of paper on Julie's coffee table, forming a trench for him to shelter behind. Julie moved to sit opposite him, lightly armed with note pad and pen.

"What can I do for you Rick?"

"I was wondering if you'd had a chance to discuss the Maths Department at this morning's senior leadership meeting? I'm anxious to feedback to my team what was said by Ofsted and what's going to happen now."

"We spent this morning considering only the main key actions based on the general feedback from last night and we don't know what the fine detail in the report will say yet. Having said that, we know Maths has been put under the microscope and significant improvements will have to be made."

"What do you mean? That SLT will make improvements or I have to?"

"Well, as I said, we haven't got to the details of who or what at present but I think you can be certain that we will have to be fairly radical with your department if we want to get to *Good*."

Sirens sounded in Rick's ears. His heart started to beat, drumming out a call to arms. He was ready to go over the top.

Turning the volume control up slightly Rick opened fire with "So what does that mean; radical changes? Hope I'm not getting the blame for the performance of the Maths department. I've only been in charge for a few months and some of my team aren't up to the job." Rick the Maths teacher employed the strategy of rounding down to minimise his fourteen months in post and gain Julie's pity.

There was little pity to be had in this war and Julie calmly retaliated, asking innocently "Aren't you in your second year, leading the department?"

"Yes but I've had little support from...SLT. Some of the staff need a lot of help and I just haven't got the time to help them all." This was now getting personal. In this instance SLT was code for Julie, his line manager and he was also making out that his timetable was too heavy to give help to the rest of his team. Julie was, of course, the person who created his timetable.

"We're all busy Rick and we'll all have to work smarter in the future if we are going to improve the Maths results. You are one of the better teachers in the team, so I can't reduce your timetable too much. I'm afraid you have to teach as many classes as the Head of English. That's fair and equitable. If you need more support from me as your line manager, then you have to ask. You know where I am and it's not as if you're shy at knocking on my door. I admit, we've got some problems within the teaching team but we are where we are and we need to focus our efforts in developing them quickly and effectively. We can't play the blame game Rick; we have to all take some responsibility."

Rick had now tried to get his early retaliation in twice, with the Head and now with his line manager and on both occasions they had kept calm and deflected his righteous indignation, making it almost impossible to build the case that he was not to blame, it was everybody else's fault and he remained a worthy candidate for a senior leadership role in the next year or two. What Rick didn't understand was how easily Peter and Julie could see through him and that both possessed the attribute of returning fire only when necessary. Rick was losing ground and credibility for a second time today. He tried a different tack.

"I can't turn it all around immediately. It will take time to improve some of the teachers. They need support and guidance with behaviour management and help to improve their own Maths knowledge. The pupils find the subject difficult and hate coming to lessons. I can't sort all that out in six weeks before the HMI comes."

"No-one is expecting you to. For a start, we have to write an action plan. Then the HMI will evaluate our plan and judge if it's starting to have a positive effect. He or she won't expect us to magically solve all of the Maths problems overnight. Secondly, SLT are all there to help you so you can lead the team effectively and we will take some decisions with you on ways we can improve the teaching. It's not going to be easy and we have to work quickly to start the improvement process. We can't just sit here moaning and groaning about the Ofsted judgement. We have to be positive and believe that we can make improvements."

"But where do I start? What do I say to the teachers in my department?" replied Rick with a hint of desperation.

"The Ofsted feedback revolves around three areas and they all apply to Maths, but not exclusively. We will have to look at teacher effectiveness, the outcomes of our pupils and the performance of the.....leadership of the Maths department." Julie had tried not to hesitate in delivering this blow but had paused to choose her words carefully. What Julie really wanted to say was that the HMI should be closely examining your misleading title of Head of Maths and questioning what you actually do for the money you earn and consider if a chimpanzee could do a better job paid purely in peanuts.

"So I'm under the microscope then. Great! My department let me down and I'm tarred with the same brush."

'Welcome to my world' thought Julie, bracing herself for Rick's next volley.

Rick, caught in no man's land, could have wept but instead exploded, "It's not fair. I'm doing my best in difficult circumstances, with a bunch of losers in my department, with no offers of help from senior staff other than the occasional *How's it all going?* and *My door's always open*. I was appointed to lead a very challenging Maths Department and I defy and challenge any one to do any better."

With that *Call Me Rick* stood up and attempted to make a dramatic exit by slamming the door on the way out. Unfortunately the door was on a gradual closer. The door catch finally clicked in the frame, reopening to re-admit Rick, red-faced and angry, only to sheepishly scoop up the documents he had forgotten in his fit of pique.

At the second attempt, the door remained shut.

Julie considered the empty page in her note pad. She had finally decided to abbreviate the minutes of the meeting to a one word summary when her phone rang.

CHAPTER 6

Peter had been on the phone non-stop to all and sundry, including concerned parents who had picked up that the school had failed Ofsted, wanting to check the school was still standing and a fictitious *parent* Peter suspected was a local reporter hoping to scoop a story on falling standards in state education.

At one stage when Peter was feeling like he was working in an Indian call centre, Penny put Clive Howell from the local authority through to him. Clive was in between meetings in two schools and was on his hands free.

"Hi Clive, I suppose you heard about Ofsted."

"Hi Peter, yeah, sorry to hear the news and sorry I couldn't be there but we had three inspections in the authority yesterday and I was already booked for the Lightwood feedback. You'll be pleased to know they were judged *Outstanding*"

"Yes, I'm thrilled," replied Peter sarcastically. "Anyway I want you to give us some of your time."

"No probs Peter, what do you want me to do?"

"One of our targets is to improve leadership at all levels and I could do with you giving some training to the middle leaders at a twilight event or for a half day."

"Sorry Peter, the traffic is chocka; did you say leadership training for middle leaders?

"If you can manage it."

"Yeah, but why just middle leaders?"

"I want the other staff to concentrate on training on delivery of lessons."

"I see, but I meant why not the senior staff as well. Didn't the inspectors criticise leadership at all levels?"

Peter could see how this conversation was going. He and his senior team would have to attend the training and appear to be enthusiastic and engaged by Clive.

"No, I mean yes. I see what you mean. I took it for granted that we would all be there."

"Great. Super. We'll need to touch base soon to get the ball rolling. I'll text you some dates and time slots when I'm free in the next couple of weeks and we can spend some quality time together. I think it would be wise to wait until the report has been published so that we can drill down on detail. We need a meeting when we can...outside...box. Perhaps a pre-meeting off line so that we can get our...in a row."

"Clive, you're breaking up. Text me and I'll organise a meeting."

"Sorry Peter, I can't hear you. I'll send you a text and we'll go forward from there. Speak to you soon."

Peter put down the phone and said out loud "Give me...strength!" He was losing the will to live and he could do without a meeting with the chair of governors in another thirty minutes. So he did what any man would do in this position. He would ask a capable woman for support. He phoned a friend.

"Julie, I'm meeting the chair of governors in half an hour and I thought it would be good if you were in the meeting. The conversation will be about many of your key areas and I thought it would be good for your own professional development."

"Well, I suppose I can find the time to come over. By the way I've just had Richard Perry in my office pointing the finger at all of us. I think he's feeling fragile. We need to keep a close eye on him."

"I agree. Perhaps we can catch up on where we are with Maths later this afternoon."

"Okay but I'd like to get away a little earlier tonight. I feel as if I have been living in this place for the last few days. I need to escape and watch some mindless TV."

"I know. I need to spend some time with Rachel. We've been like strangers living in a hotel recently." As he spoke, he realised that he still hadn't spoken to his wife since last night. He would ring her once he'd grabbed a sandwich from the canteen.

Julie put down the phone and quietly berated herself. She had been manipulated by Peter again. This time to help him do his dirty work with the chair of governors and if that wasn't enough she would have to stay at school for a third late night to discuss the Maths Department just because Peter didn't want to go home to his wife.

She opened the top drawer of her desk and her right hand blindly groped behind her pens, pencils and highlighters for a small set of keys that would open the filing cabinets. She was ready to have her lunch. Chocolate and water beckoned.

Peter told Penny that he was going to the dining hall and would be back before Ann Brown arrived. She didn't need to know that he was leaving his office to escape the phone calls and to re-acquaint himself with the rest of the school.

The bell was just about to ring for the end of lesson three and the start of the mad hour when a thousand adolescents would unleash their pent up emotions in a tsunami of food, fighting, fighting for food and fighting with food. This was lunch time. A time when most teachers took cover in the staff room. This was the time when all the good work they had done during the morning, helping to create sensible and thoughtful citizens of the future, was undone in less than ten seconds. From now on the lunatics would be running the asylum. If it was up to Peter he would have started the school day at 7.00am, finished at 1.00pm and let the kids leave to have their lunch at home or at the local chip shop.

Peter grabbed a cheese salad sandwich and made his way quickly to the staff room. He thought it would be a good idea for staff to see him out and about. Along the main corridor that linked the pastoral offices, the staffroom and the dining room Charlie was striding purposely, talking, shouting and teasing pupils as he went. He was off to do his duty.

"Hello Mr Burlington, have you recovered from the SLT meeting yet?"

"Just about," replied Peter, unable to think of anything spontaneously witty to compete with Charlie. "I'm meeting Ann Brown in twenty minutes or so...if you want to join me."

"Sorry boss, I have a meeting with social services and a parent this afternoon. I'll see you at the Departmental Heads." With that Charlie was gone, followed by a small posse of idolising pupils hoping that they could share a table with him for lunch.

Peter despatched the few pupils standing at the staff room door to explain themselves. One had been told to see a teacher during the lunch break and the others just wanted to ask a teacher something. He told them all to come back at the end of lunch time because teachers needed a break too. They would all probably forget to return. Peter walked in feeling as uncomfortable today as he had on his first day as Head. He wasn't sure why. It was his school after all!

The staff room was unlike any other room in school. No-one owned it and everyone abused it but it was still a safe haven for adults. It was a place of comfort, of occasional tears and of much hysterical laughter. Not for Peter any more. As a young teacher he used to love the escape into a happy hour with colleagues. But as he climbed the greasy pole the bonding and bantering time slipped away. He was expected to be out and about on duty or in his own office crunching data or pupils. A senior leadership position became a lonely job. Staff ceased to see you as a normal human being. The Head was usually the enemy, the one to blame, the *highly paid one* and the stranger in the staffroom. So when Peter did venture in nowadays it was for a purpose. To give briefings, lead presentations or to specifically catch hold of a member of staff. He would not out-stay his cold welcome and wouldn't dream of joining in the various staff activities or in-activities. He glanced around the room to see a foursome setting up a game of bridge, one or two of the Food Technology teachers untangling their knitting, a crossword corner, teachers tapping away on their smart phones, staff marking books hurriedly for the next lesson and self-selecting groups who just enjoyed each other's company. These were often arranged in specific cliques of teacher or teaching assistant and subdivided by age, subject or interests. There was the PE staff who sat together and took the mickey out of each other for the whole lunch time. Then there were the young teachers who had survived their first or second years together and were protective of each other, and the English Department who all sat together and talked and talked. Each member of staff once seated were masters of multi-tasking for the remainder of the lunch time. They could eat their sandwiches, drink hot or cold drinks, talk and listen in on various conversations at the same time, share anecdotes, discuss pupils' behaviour, criticise the SLT, Ofsted and the Secretary Of State for Education as well as plan their next two lessons in their heads. The room was supposedly a place of calm and tranquillity and yet ten minutes into the lunch break the space was a noisy, vibrant mad house full of very clever, hardworking, eccentric people who he admired greatly.

Jo Slater, Head of English, walked into the staff room talking with one of her department. She was a stunningly attractive, mesmerising woman. Having had two maternity breaks, one after another, she had regained her figure and position as subject leader at Whatmore in her late thirties. This wasn't surprising because in most people's eyes she was the model definition of an outstanding teacher and leader. Her classes adored her, her team would die for her and she loved her subject. If Peter could have cloned her, he would have used all of the school capitation on the experiment, regardless of what Sobia would say. He caught her eye and smiled as she came over to him.

"Hello Peter, we don't see you in here very often." If anyone else had said this Peter would have assumed they were being sarcastic. Not Jo.

"I wanted to speak to a couple of people and you were top of my list," Peter said. As he delivered the line he worried that he sounded as if he was flirting.

"What can I do for you?"

"I need to talk to you about the inspection and some of the finer details of the feedback from last night. Have you any free time between the end of lunch and the Departmental Heads' meeting. I could do with half an hour of your time." Peter could feel his cheeks blushing. Everything he was saying to Jo seemed somehow suggestive.

"I'm free period 5 this afternoon if I'm not taken for last minute cover," said Jo, accommodating as ever.

"I'll make sure Julie doesn't use you. See you in my office as soon as you can after two o'clock.

"See you then, Peter."

Peter took one more look around the staff room to see if he could spot the Head of Science but Abid was nowhere to be seen. He was probably in his Prep Room having lunch there with the technicians. He would have to speak to him later.

Peter hurried back to his office carrying his uneaten sandwich and asked Penny if Ann had arrived yet.

"She's on her way. She phoned and said she was just leaving another meeting."

"When did she ring?"

"About ten minutes ago!"

Peter slumped back in his chair after pouring a coffee. He took a sip and looked at his mobile and his hermetically sealed sandwich. What should he do next? Phone Rachel or speed-lunch. Just then Ann opened the door and the decision was taken out of his hands.

"Hello Peter, sorry I'm a bit late. My last meeting overran."

"Not a problem. Can I make you a drink?"

"I'll just have some water, I've been drinking Women's Institute tea all morning and I don't think I could face another at the moment."

Peter supplied Ann with a glass of water, told her that Julie should be joining them and that work on the action plan had started.

While Peter was talking, his chair of governors was sorting through her bags to find the Whatmore folders, her pen, mobile phone and reading glasses. Ann lived in organised chaos since the death of her husband six years ago. She busied herself with local societies, clubs and committees and her life was now one long meeting. In a former life she had been the Headmistress of a small primary school before taking early retirement to look after her ailing spouse.

"So what have you decided to do so far? I'm assuming we have to wait until the report is published before you can put a detailed plan into action."

"Yes, you are quite right, we could wait a week but I wanted to make a start while it's fresh in our minds. I think it would be wise to bring forward the next full governing board meeting to coincide with the publication of the report and then we can discuss how we spin the findings to our parents and the local community."

"What's the timeline for publication?"

"The lead inspector said that he would be sending me a copy to check for factual inaccuracies within a week."

"I see why you need to get cracking now Peter but please don't think you have to change everything in the next week or so. Surely you need a period of reflection?"

"I know what you're saying Ann, but I'm not great on that. Looking back just makes me feel sad and useless. I have to be doing something to affect the future," said Peter. "What's done is done."

"Peter, I didn't mean that you should reflect on your own position. Merely that you need to take stock of the judgements and the report before trying to solve the problems."

"But that's just it Ann. I came to the school three years ago after it was judged to be a *Good* school and now look where I have taken it...in the wrong direction. What does that say about me?"

"Ofsted were not just inspecting you Peter, they were inspecting the whole school..."

"I know but I'm the Head and I have to take full responsibility. Perhaps the best action the school could take is to find a new Head teacher."

"Peter, stop feeling sorry for yourself. It's perfectly natural to feel negative on the day after this setback but you have to look at this inspection as a way of moving the school forward. I can't have you feeling down. You need to stay positive. It's not as if someone has died!"

"Yeah, you're right Ann," he said. "My mind has been racing since last night and I haven't been able to tell anyone how this is all affecting me. See...I told you I'm not good with reflection...even that requires improvement!" The mood lightened and they both started laughing just as Julie entered the office.

If she hadn't have been so tired, Julie would have thought *What have the bag lady and Mr Blobby got to be so happy about?*' But she smiled sweetly, asked if it was okay to join them and sat in her third favourite chair.

"Hello Julie, how are you coping?" Ann asked in all innocence and with sincerity.

Julie was floored by the question. Was this a test? How was she supposed to respond? She couldn't tell the chair of governors how she really felt about life and that she wasn't coping at all.

"Fine thanks, a little tired and disappointed." Good answer she thought. Vague but fairly honest.

"Well, keep your strength up and look after yourself. We need you of all people to stay fit and healthy. You know Peter and I really appreciate what you do here at Whatmore."

It was Julie's turn to blush slightly and for the first time today she started feeling a little more positive about herself and her future. It didn't take much for Julie to feel good but the pats on the back when she was first appointed were all feeling like stabs these days.

"Why don't you two tell me what you decided this morning?"

Peter and Julie spent the next quarter of an hour summarising the main issues and their first thoughts on how to drive improvements. Ann listened without commenting and made bullet points in her note pad as they talked. As they ran out of breath, Ann looked up and took her reading glasses off.

"So we have a few big decisions and changes to make in the next few weeks. Clearly you've got to demonstrate how you are going to improve some of the teaching, particularly Maths, and develop the leadership skills of some people. Also, Ofsted are not happy with our understanding of the school's performance. So basically the school hasn't got it right when our own assessment said we had. Forgive me for complicating things but don't you think we need to understand how Ofsted's *Good* differs from ours. They clearly have higher standards than us!"

"I would argue theirs are different, not higher standards," said Peter.

"Quite possibly Peter but in a game of cards whose standards are trumps?" Ann replied. It was her Bridge Night tonight. "I'm not trying to finesse your ideas, I'm just commenting that when the HMI comes in a few weeks we can't claim the Ofsted inspectors had a different set of criteria to judge the school than we do. We have to look at ourselves first and admit we got it wrong and analyse why. Only then can we improve."

Peter sat there as if he were a pupil who had been caught doing something wrong by a deeply disappointed matriarch. How could this dear old lady switch from talking about scones and crochet and half an hour later, make two experienced and effective teachers feel *worst in show*? Ann Brown, Peter had to admit, was a force of nature. She should not be underestimated and although she appeared to be a critical friend, he detected that her barometer had recently swung towards critic and away from friend.

"I agree with you Mrs Brown." Julie came to Peter's rescue, "We will all have to show that we can improve. We over-marked ourselves because we hoped that on a good day, excuse the pun, we could convince Ofsted that we were good enough."

"Please call me Ann. If you remember I attended several of your management meetings last year where you discussed your self-evaluation. I know that it was the Senior Leadership Team's decision to evaluate Whatmore as *Good*. Unfortunately, it now looks like we've changed from admitting that the school was and still is underperforming to accepting that our own judgements are not accurate enough."

Without looking at each other the Head and Assistant Head knew instinctively what to do. Nothing. Sit there and take it. Nod and agree if necessary. Take the blame. Fall on swords. Pour petrol over each other but don't argue or disagree. Partly because she was right and they knew it, and because neither of them had the energy for a fight and because they were both scared to death of Ann Brown.

The next twenty minutes consisted of three performers dancing around the truth. Peter wanted to blame successive governments, secretaries of state for education, Ofsted, and local authorities. He also wanted to lock into Room 101 all academies and free schools, The Daily Mail, the cast of Waterloo Road and anyone who voted for Margaret Thatcher. Ann blamed Peter but could not openly say it at present and Julie blamed herself for agreeing to help Peter out by attending this meeting. They talked around a change of emphasis in the action plan, a focus on Maths, lesson observations, book trawls and when the three of them should meet again. They each silently prophesised that the next meeting would not be a pleasant experience and the hurly-burly would probably involve thunder, lightning and pain.

As Ann closed the door behind her both Peter and Julie started to take in large quantities of oxygen and self-pity.

"That went well," Peter observed. "Can the day get any better?"

Julie, regaining the colour in her cheeks, said what both of them were thinking. "I'm not sure I trust that woman to be on our side."

"I suppose it's natural that Ann wants to save face and blame SLT and particularly me."

"She wasn't just having a swipe at you Peter," Julie tried to give Peter a crumb of comfort but the only crumbs he could see were still sealed inside the sandwich wrapping.

"Before you arrived the conversation was heading in that direction and I didn't help matters by sounding sorry for myself."

"We're all feeling sorry for ourselves today but we haven't become a bad school overnight. We may not have been good enough but we are not the worst school in the world."

"That could be our new school motto." Peter said, trying to lighten the mood. "It's just a bad day. How do you manage to stay so cheerful and positive? I'm the one that should be rallying the troops and looking as if I'm taking all of this in my stride but you're the one keeping me going."

Julie blushed again, this time out of guilt-ridden hypocrisy. 'If only he knew,' she thought. "I suppose I don't have the pressures on me that you do. The buck doesn't stop with me. I go home and try to have a life outside school and keep some sort of work-life balance," She felt so relieved that she was not presently hooked up to a lie detector.

Peter was just about to ask Julie something personal when there was a knock and Penny walked in to announce Jo Slater was waiting to see him.

Julie stood and adjusted her hair and skirt in the vain attempt to compete with Jo as their paths crossed. They smiled at each other as they passed. Jo, inches taller in her heels, looking down slightly at Julie and Julie trying not to look up.

The two women were always polite to each other but that was as far as it went. These were the two most important members of Peter's crew. Both extremely capable, both talented teachers and administrators, neither bringing unnecessary baggage into school. These were the type of staff that any Head would dream of having and Peter did a fair amount of dreaming about both Jo and Julie.

If the pleasant passing smiles could have been frozen in time and analysed by highly-paid psychologists they would have had a field day. They would have noted that Julie looked at Jo, just below the eyes, with personal jealousy and professional resentment.

Julie envied what she had seen of the Slater family at school events. The attractive, and well-groomed husband and the two gorgeous children who never seemed to cry, moan, swear or spit. They were a fairy tale family and Jo herself was not just charming but princess-like with her long blonde hair without a single thread of grey. Julie had fewer years on the clock and a higher paid role and yet would have swapped places with Jo in a heartbeat.

Jo, captain of her own small ship, the HMS English, ruled the waves. Jo, who led a highly performing team of teachers. Jo, the inspirational teacher of English whether she was teaching subordinate clauses or Macbeth. Jo, who everyone loved and respected and would follow into battle each and every school day.

Whereas Julie? Where was the Julie who in the first few years of her meteoric career could make pupils fall in love with Maths and sometimes with her? Gone at the whim of people in high places who recognised her capacity to take on other enemies such as the timetable, professional development and analysing pupil data until the old Julie's enthusiasm for education was expunged and no-one seemed pleased with her anymore. Where was the pleasure in the job? Where was the pleasure outside the job?

Julie headed for the door with an exit strategy in mind. Get through the day by saying very little in the meetings still to come, get home, get on her internet dating sites and get drunk.

Jo's life could not offer greater contrast. Her polite and pleasant acknowledgement of Julie was no different to her approach to every other member of the senior leadership team. She was happy to speak to them, discuss matters relevant to her discipline and make a fuss if potential decisions by others could have a negative effect on the teaching of English. Her professional and personal lives rarely crossed with Julie's. Jo seldom bothered her, taking her rare issues straight to the Head to try to get her own way, which she mainly did. She knew she was in a strong and privileged position, respected by all; even, it appeared, by Ofsted.

Jo didn't mind that her responsibilities meant taking work home but she had a system for that: arrive home about five; dedicate the next two hours or so to the children (her younger sister having picked them up from school) until daddy got back to bath them and get them ready for bed, while she made supper; both sit in the lounge with the TV on, working on their laptops or in Jo's case marking books and put the finishing touches to the next day's lesson plans; log off and shut down by eleven, go to bed. Friday and Saturday nights were different and special for the two of them; no laptops or marking, sometimes glad rags on and a late night and sometimes casual rags off and an early night.

Jo sat down and smiled at Peter. He returned the smile, stood and walked around the desk to sit closer to her. This was Peter's way of putting staff at ease in a non-threatening way by removing all physical barriers. What he didn't realise was that some found this uncomfortable and would have preferred him caged in between the desk and the wall.

Peter employed the strategy with Jo because he needed to manipulate her into helping him out and he assumed that sitting close together as equals would seal the deal. If the highly paid psychologist was still in the room then it would have been noted that they would never be equals. Peter might be the Head of the school but Jo was his superior in every other way – intelligence, popularity, respect and looks.

"Thanks for coming Jo. I wanted to tell you first-hand about the feedback from last night. I know one of the inspectors talked to you at the end of the first day and gave you some very positive comments but I thought you would like to hear what they concluded."

"Nothing bad I trust...I mean about the English team. I know that the school as a whole hasn't come out of this inspection well."

"Yes that's true but just for now I would like to spend a few moments on praise. What came through in the feedback and I'm sure will be reflected in the final report is the outstanding work the English department does on a daily basis. A special mention was made of you and your approach and the way the pupils really enthuse about studying English. It was really heartening to know that what you are doing is recognised by Ofsted."

"Not just me Peter, the team work really well together." Jo was quick to point this out, not for the first time.

"You are quite right to share the glory with your team but let me just for once single you out. You are doing a brilliant job at Whatmore...and perhaps I haven't said that enough to you since I came here. So thank you."

Jo did what politeness demanded at this stage in the conversation. She thanked Peter for the thank you and waited for the inevitable follow up. It was delivered by Peter in his usual roundabout sort of way. On this occasion the delivery resembled the main traffic island at Milton Keynes.

"As you are aware, I'm sure, not every department did as well as yours and the inspectors were particularly critical of Maths. Ofsted will always compare the performance of Maths with English and I'm afraid they had very few kind words to say about Richard Perry and his team."

"I'm sure Richard will turn things around in time. He hasn't been Head of Department for long has he?"

"No he hasn't and in the real world of *slow and steady wins the race*, Richard is doing well but that's not good enough for Ofsted. They want to see an immediate improvement. So he will need to be helped along the way."

There was a deafening silence for a few seconds. Peter was waiting for the cue from Jo along the lines of "Can I help him?" or "Is there anything I can do?" Nothing like that arrived so he was forced to carry on. "When I spoke to the lead inspector last night, he suggested that Richard could do with some help on improving his leadership skills from an outstanding practitioner. He felt you were the best person on the staff to do this and I have to say I agree with him."

"Peter, it's very flattering for the inspector to think of me but I don't know the first thing about Maths, I'm just a dumb blonde who likes reading children's' books. What could I do to help Richard and his team deliver Maths?"

"I'm not saying that you have to help with teaching Maths. Julie's going to help with that. All I want you to do is get him to improve his style of leadership."

"Forgive me Peter, but isn't that a senior leader's job?" Jo was batting back every new delivery.

"Normally we would be the ones to take a special interest in Richard but unfortunately the action plan means our time will be committed elsewhere."

"And what about my time? I have a full teaching commitment, all the marking and two relatively new teachers in the department to look after."

"I don't expect this to take up much of your time...just an hour a week maybe...just to set Richard on the right track...I know you can do it...it would really help out the school and..." Peter was getting dizzy with the number of times he had driven round in circles and he still wasn't getting anywhere. Jo was not saying yes.

Peter wondered why nothing was easy in managing a school. The house of cards was built on good will and the impossible trick was to get your own way without upsetting anyone and for no decision to appear forced. Impossible, of course, but always to be strived for. Machiavellian perhaps but if staff thought something was a good idea, better still that it was their own good idea, then the prospects for success were much better. He had been in schools long enough to realise that bullying might work in the short term but winning the odd battle by force never wins the war.

He could instruct Jo to do his bidding but he still hoped that if he kept talking and justifying this plan of action then her defences could be breached. But Jo continued to dig her high heels in, serving up an unreturned ace in her concern that the high standards in English might drop if her eye was off the ball looking after Richard. She also threw in to the equation that the mock exams were fast approaching and that the papers would have to be re-written due to a government change of mind on the way the subject should be tested. She followed up with what she hoped was a winning volley describing the unique position the English Department found itself in. She was responsible for two vital subjects, English and English Literature, while also carrying responsibility for Literacy standards across the whole school - all the other Heads of Department were only responsible for a single subject. Another back-handed reply was that she felt that she and her team were being picked on because they were performing well.

"Jo, you are not being picked on. You were chosen by Ofsted because you are the best person in the school to do this. Surely you can see that. I know you passionately care about the pupils here and would like them to succeed in all subjects."

There was a pause in the game followed by Jo's final, reluctant concession: "Of course I want the pupils to do well overall...but don't call me Surely!"

Peter beamed, laughed at the film reference and thanked her, offering her support and time to do this task. Jo wasn't fooled in the slightest, knowing that in reality the job she had worked so hard at to make manageable, had taken a turn for the worse and that there would be no extra support or time.

Jo left Peter's office having lost all the delight in leading her team to a glorious Ofsted victory. Somehow the mission that she had accepted under pressure seemed impossible. She was out of her comfort zone for the first time in years.

Peter sat back in his chair, stretching and yawning, and feeling a slight sense of pride and pleasure in his handling of this encounter. He had the outcome he wanted, there was no blood on the carpet and he knew Jo would do a fine job in trying to support *Call Me Rick*. Whether it would work was a different matter but for now he could count it as an action ticked off on the Ofsted plan.

He had ten minutes and two more tasks to complete before meeting all the Heads of Department; to ring his wife and eat his lunch. He used his mobile to phone Rachel but she didn't pick up so he left her a short and semi-sweet message and told her he wouldn't be home too late. He eventually managed to navigate his way into the packaging to eat his sandwich with six bites inside two minutes. What a lunch time!

The HODs meeting was in the school library. The school was by now almost bereft of children. There were just the few hanging about waiting for friends trapped by teachers in tellings-off or detentions. Unlike the days of Ofsted's on-site presence, lorry loads of strewn litter lay waiting for the cleaners to pick up. This was clear evidence that the pupils had existed in school today, even if Peter had had no time to see or speak to any of them. He made a mental note to get around the school tomorrow. Be seen and heard. Walk the talk.

The library was ironically the one area of the school that was now neither tranquil nor calm. The large echoing room was filling up. Some heads of department had got there early to grab a free biscuit and drink before setting up camp in a favoured place around the square arrangement of tables.

The librarian had spent the last forty minutes re-arranging her furniture ready for the meeting, setting up the hot water urn and spreading out digestives and ginger nuts on a large plate. She would be leaving school early tonight, finding it uncomfortable to work in there while others talked at each other. She would have to spend until break time the next day cleaning up the mess and returning the library to its exact specifications. It was a shame that the room had to be used for meetings or indeed used at all but now that Neil Turner had introduced PCs and laptops into the library, the place was over-used at break and lunch times and her stress levels had dramatically increased.

Peter reserved his usual position by placing his suit jacket on the back of a chair half way along one of the sides of the square, the empty side. Usually late arrivals would fill up the seats immediately to Peter's left and right. He made himself a coffee and sat down. Others arrived and sat down in friendship pairs. Neil Turner however was staring at his tablet unaware that he also had empty chairs on either side.

Sobia arrived looking like thunder and Julie walked in laden with diaries, a note pad, a wallet of coloured pens and a bottle of water. She did the decent thing and sat next to Peter. Richard Perry sat by Neil. Jo Slater walked in last, not quite her normal radiant self, Peter thought.

"Thanks everybody...I think we'll make a start. I purposely didn't produce an agenda for tonight's meeting because I intend to focus purely on the Ofsted inspection. I want to keep it short but give you further details from the feedback, a brief description of what the Senior Leadership Team has discussed today and I want to give you some time to ask any questions you have about where we are and what we do next as a school." Peter looked down at the notes he had made at the Ofsted feedback. He had not had time today to prepare anything for this meeting, let alone map out an agenda, so he did what he was trained to do; like a fighter-pilot, he strapped himself in and winged it.

At some point during Peter's rehash of his notes, Neil decided to count how many times the word *improve* would be said aloud and to keep a tally on his IPad. He wondered how many times the word had been used today in school and how many times teachers and inspectors used it in a day or a week or an academic year. Did the word become meaningless the more it was used? Spoken words all seemed fairly meaningless to Neil.

The Head explained who was going to lead on which area for improvement and the timescale for drafting and dissemination of an action plan. He told them that teachers would all be observed again and if necessary be the subject of an individual action plan to drive improvement.

Neil tapped his screen.

"Julie Osborne will work with middle leaders to firm up the judgements on classroom observations and will be peer-assessing lessons and pupils' books so we can be confident in our own judgements. Charlie Briggs and Neil

Turner will be developing new ways to gauge pupil progress in departments and Sobia Didially and I will be looking at improving accountability in middle leadership..."

Peter's monologue was interrupted by a late entry into the library. Charlie raised his hand in apology and squeezed into a corner of the square.

"Has anyone any questions based on what's been said so far?" asked Peter in the vain hope that no-one would move a muscle or a lip. Unfortunately, hands went up from at least 50% of the gathering and Peter knew he was in for a rough flight.

Brian Green, acting Head of Humanities, occasional teacher of History and fully occupied union rep for the National Union of Teachers, seemingly had his hand up from the start of this and any other meeting he ever attended. He was passionate about the rights of teachers, their pay, conditions and workload. To feed his frenzy he would attend conferences and courses and write lengthy emails to Peter explaining the position of his members. Peter would have loved to have responded by sending him a rude graphic illustration of his member's position but so far had always thought better of it. Peter reluctantly invited him to speak.

"Thank you Mr Burlington. I think I can speak for all the members of the NUT and those who belong to other professional associations in saying that we are all disappointed in the Ofsted inspection and that this does not reflect accurately on the hard work and effort of the teachers and support staff here at Whatmore. Ofsted is a crude instrument to bludgeon schools with and my union has real concerns about the way successive governments have used inspections to introduce academies through the back door and de-professionalise teachers. But my concerns today are about what we do here at Whatmore now that Ofsted has been and gone."

Peter was about to correct the speaker and say "Ofsted has been and gone for now" but he checked himself. Brian Green had the floor and wasn't about to give way.

"As a result of the inspection it now appears that we will have to work even harder to be successful. May I suggest to you that the majority of staff here cannot work any harder and that we will not give up any of our hard fought for planning and marking time to create an action plan for Ofsted and if the plan suggests that we have to do more than we currently do then that will become an industrial issue. Also, we have agreed to a lesson observation programme with you which meant that each teacher could be observed three times a year and now, it seems, you are introducing further observations on teachers because the senior management were not accurate in their judgements. My role is to protect my members from the unnecessary stress of an intolerable workload that means that they can't do their jobs effectively."

"Would you like me to reply to your observations now, Brian, or do you want me to speak to you in private?" said Peter, the implied criticism clear for all to hear.

"I believe we all need to hear what you and the SLT will do to safeguard our workload."

"Alright then. But if you have any follow-up issues, please make an appointment to see me. My door is always open to the union as you know...I will try to take the points in the order that you presented them. Firstly, implementing the action plan will be led by the senior leaders but there may be new strategies that we as a school think need to be done in order for us to improve. If that puts too much pressure on an individual then I would want them to see me and find a way around it. I don't want any member of my staff to be over-burdened by what lies ahead, but we will have to work differently." Peter felt like saying "we must work smarter not harder" but managed to avoid the overworked cliché.

He moved on to a more difficult issue to peacefully resolve. "We have tried to keep classroom observations in line with union recommendations but Ofsted clearly didn't agree with some of our own judgements. It could be that some teachers just didn't perform well when an inspector observed them or it could be that our own internal process was too generous. During the inspection some of our good teachers were not seen in their best light and may need some guidance on how to teach with confidence when an observer is in the room. I'm not suggesting that everyone has extra observations if they do not need them but we have a fair idea where problems lie and we will have to address them. Remember that not all staff were seen by Ofsted and I have a professional duty to get all our teachers to at least *Good*. We will have to target those members of staff who we believe are not up to a certain standard or who didn't perform well on the day."

Brian cut in. "I accept you'll need to show you're helping some members of staff to improve their performance but that can be achieved by developing them professionally and sending them on courses rather than just observing them."

"Yes, to an extent. There are all sorts of ways that we can help our colleagues but we need to know who needs help to start with and sometimes people don't ask for help or think they need it. If someone has to be formally observed again and it is above and beyond what's been agreed then we will make sure that this is reflected in the next twelve month period. That way we will support your members and all teachers without putting them under too much unnecessary stress. How does that sound Brian?"

Brian smugly nodded and backed off and down. He was sure he had won a public battle and gained ground for his members. Peter was equally pleased with himself. He had managed to compromise on the hoof and get the union rep to believe he had won the argument without Peter having to change his improvement strategy. He would worry about the medium and long term in the future!

Julie, sitting next to Peter and making short, sharp bullet points, jotted down the need to perform a miracle in order to keep everyone happy when she started the lesson observations campaign. Peter, sitting next to Julie and making it up as he went along, knew Julie was the one person who could make this miracle happen.

Peter fielded all manner of further questions. Some he found himself completely unable to answer but he assured them that answers would be found. The actual answers were probably waiting menacingly in the long grass somewhere just out of bounds from the short greens and the medium cut fairways.

Eventually the meeting, which should have lasted no more than forty minutes, was on its last legs. Sobia was staring at her watch and glaring at Peter. Neil was counting up his tally chart. Julie was hoping Peter had forgotten about the follow on meeting he wanted with her. Charlie was anxious to return to his office to stretch his own legs with the Head of Year 11. Jo just wanted to get home and Rick wanted to see Peter in his office before he went home.

The meeting broke up, the library chairs and tables were left scattered and the remaining biscuits were pocketed by starving underpaid middle leaders as they left and headed for their ageing Escorts or Mondeos.

Peter walked slowly back to his office. The secret army of Wombles had magically collected the school rubbish into different coloured plastic bags now lining the corridor. This street art was aesthetically more pleasing than the pupils' work displayed on the boards above the bags, Peter thought.

"Boss, I wonder if I could have a quick word?" Peter heard from behind as he was nearing his office. He turned to see *Call Me Rick* behind him and closing fast.

"I'm sorry. I have another meeting now. Can you arrange something tomorrow with Penny? I'll need to see you very soon to discuss the Maths department in any event. Tell her to schedule an hour for us in the next few days?"

"Okay, I'll do that. Good night," and Richard Perry was off.

Peter made for his office chair. He could really do with a recliner or a rocking chair and a warm mug of hot chocolate. He looked over tomorrow's diary entries. Endless meetings; endless talking. When would it ever end? Would it ever end?

In closing his diary on today, he remembered he needed to see Julie. He phoned her office and reminded her. She said that she'd pack away, close down her computer and drop in on the way to her car.

Putting down the phone, Julie wanted to say one of a few four letter words that came to mind. She refrained as her cleaner was just finishing up her office. *Why had she picked up the phone?* Now she'd be stuck for another hour. Her whole body ached and she just wanted to put her dressing gown and slippers on, have a drink, have something to eat, have something to drink, watch some TV, have a drink and then sleep until she could retire.

She arrived in Peter's office ten minutes later. He was at his desk tapping away on his laptop. *Was it his resignation letter?* She hoped so. She slumped as gracefully as she could into her usual chair.

"Long day?" asked Peter.

"Yeah, too long. Someone told me a long, long time ago that life gets easier as you get older. Seems like they told me a fairy tale."

"Look I won't keep you long but I saw Jo and she's agreed to help us out and take Ricard Perry under her wing for a while."

"I'm amazed she agreed" said Julie.

"My charm and good looks swung the deal."

"Yeah right," retorted Julie, rolling her heavy eyes. "It's your decision but I'm supposed to be line managing Maths. I can model how he should be working with his team. After all I was Head of Maths myself."

"And a very successful one but he seems to feel threatened by you. I'm sure he knows you could make a much better job of running the department. Anyway I want to ease your workload and good old Rick is enough to stress anyone out."

"What do you mean, ease my workload?" asked Julie.

"That's why I wanted to speak to you tonight. How do you fancy being a deputy head?"

PART 2
A Saucerful of Secrets

CHAPTER 7

The Piper at the Gates of Dawn played quietly in the background of Peter's mind. He sat at the desk in his study at home staring out of the window at the beautifully maintained and manicured back garden. The trimming of the lawn was assigned to Peter but everything else was Rachel's responsibility, domain and love. Rachel enjoyed working in her garden. Peter, on the other hand, enjoyed looking at Rachel's garden from the distance and height of his study. On Sunday mornings Peter would work on his laptop, only breaking the tedium by staring at plants and trees and listening to the favourite progressive rock bands of his youth.

Rachel was not working the soil this morning. She had decided to visit her daughter. Peter would hop in his car later to meet up with them once he had replied to all of the emails, read everything connected to education in the on-line newspapers and started to write his latest Head's report. As for most teachers, Sundays were for him more or less school days. Rachel knew this and kept herself busy on the day of rest as Peter was always pre-occupied and restless.

The first half of the weekend was a different matter. It had been agreed long ago that Friday nights and Saturdays were sacrosanct as non-school days to be timetabled by Rachel. Acting like a weekend PA she would fill Peter's diary with visits to friends, entertaining, shopping and DIY. The friends had been cultivated and grown through Rachel's various clubs and societies, Peter having few friends left of his own. Most had fallen by the wayside as he travelled his chosen career path. Now, as a Head teacher, it would be awkward to award any member of staff the status of friend. It would be easier, but more time consuming, to name his enemies.

Peter enjoyed Pink Floyd. They reminded him of a different time when the world seemed exciting and new. A time of long hair and no cares. A time when Syd Barrett was a living diamond, shining a light on the future. To Peter, today's world had lost its sparkle. Had it grown dim or was it him? Peter was old and wise enough to realise the world was still turning but it seemed to be getting ever faster and crazier. He longed for that time before the National Curriculum, SATs, Ofsted and league tables; before the internet, Google, Twitter and Facebook none of which Peter could see as improvements or progress. For him life wasn't better, it was shittier. People were more stressed and less happy; less pleasant and more aggressive; and he worried for the future of his pupils and their children.

Peter was feeling low. He knew it. It had been just over a week since the Ofsted inspection and the final report was staring at him from his laptop. It was one thing to hear the verbal feedback in a small office but another to read it plastered over the world-wide web. Admittedly, most people worldwide couldn't care less but a very small number of people would and he was one of them. The publication of the report should have been a minor event in life compared to the sad and devastating news of the death of Madiba or the thousands of flood victims in the Philippines but Peter was consumed by the nine page document. Only the first six pages detailed the findings of the inspection but as Peter read them over and over, the words burnt indelibly into his heart and soul.

"This is a school that requires improvement. It is not good because..." The opening statement was followed by a list of bullet points outlining the key areas for improvement followed by a much smaller section of friendly fire, highlighting the school's strengths.

To be fair to the lead inspector, Peter thought, in one of his few positive moments that morning, the verbal feedback matched the first three pages of the written report. There were no surprises, bad or good. Other than Charlie's pastoral care and Jo's area, it was a damning report.

Peter sat and waited for an epiphany. He desperately wanted the light to shine on him and give him a reason why he should not be taking pretty much full responsibility for the report's content. He couldn't blame the previous Head, the government, the school funds or the local community. They might be contributory factors but they were not plausible excuses for Whatmore not being a good school. The judgement was made on his watch and he would have to live with it or die by it. He alone.

He wondered about his senior leadership team. What would they all be doing right now?

Peter gazed out of the window as if he could see them all from his house. Sobia enjoying family life, Charlie playing squash with a buddy from his gym, Neil zapping aliens on another planet and Julie out socialising with friends. Peter re-focused on the screen in front of him and accepted that he was absolutely alone with all this.

Sobia would have liked some peace and quiet. She was expecting her husband's family and there was still so much to do. Only half of the food was prepared and less than half of her intended cleaning and tidying completed. Her husband had just left in the people carrier to collect his parents and other family members. It would take him less than an hour to collect the seven guests and return. If only his brother and sister had not agreed to come and then he could have taken the children with him. As it was, the terrible twosome was systematically untidying the freshly vacuumed living room and the hall. She felt like screaming along with her children. Her life was so orderly at work, everything in the right place, and her ladies doing what they were told.

Having the twins had thrown Sobia's life into chaos. She loved the kids and her husband but just occasionally she yearned for the single life and time for herself. Another tray of food was slipped into the oven and another toy was left abandoned in the middle of the hall. What would her mother-in-law say when she arrived? What would she think but not say? She dried the corner of her eye with a tea towel and looked forward to Monday and school.

Charlie was not at the gym. He would have been but his wife had decided to choose Sunday morning for a row with him. He had gone for a quick Sunday morning run, picking up a Sunday rag on the way back. He brought his wife a cup of tea in bed and had a shower. When he came back into the bedroom his wife had informed him she wanted to look for new lounge furniture. Charlie's casual mention of a pre-booked squash court had explosive consequences. In an instant the thoughtful gesture of tea in bed was forgotten and a red mist descended in the bedroom. The one-sided barrage quickly moved from simmering to boiling on topics and rhetorical questions ranging from time spent at home, to *Do you love me anymore*, through *Are you seeing someone else* and *I don't know why you married me*. Charlie's guilty conscience affected his offensive approach to the rallies, his quick wit and ready repartee was shot and he opted for the long game by adopting a defensive stance occasionally trying to make a telling point.

It took until half way through the afternoon before normal service had been resumed. They sat together on the worn out settee that needed replacing watching an old film. Through the magic of Hollywood everything again looked black and white.

Neil's screen was far from black and white. It was filled with a head and shoulders image of an attractive woman. She had long red hair, blue eyes, bright pink lipstick and a revealing yellow tee shirt. She lived in Russia and couldn't afford Skype but she could email Neil and had been for six months. They were in love and could talk to each other about anything. She loved gaming, learning new languages, cats and Great Britain. When she had saved up enough money for a one way flight and paid for a passport she would jump on the next plane and then jump into bed with Neil. She would also attach selfies from time to time and he would spend many a sticky night pawing over them. Neil would have given up his job in a second and flown to Russia but she had told him to wait. She wanted to be with him in England and after all, they needed his income so they could live together and have a family. Neil saw the sense in this and knew he had found a woman who would look after him for the rest of his life. He longed for a time when they could be together and today he had made a life-changing decision. He had told her he was going to send her enough money to fast track her passport, to buy a one-way flight to Heathrow and to afford some new clothes and a suitcase. He pressed send.

Julie on the other hand had pressed spend. She had spent Sunday morning shopping for clothes. She had made the decision late on Saturday night when she had finished crying at the end of watching a rom com on Netflix. She cried for a variety of reasons and her tears were born out of frustration and anger. If she could have focused on her note pad she would have listed the reasons.

Number 1 - she was upset by the content of the film. The stars had spent the majority of it being unhappy with each other's life styles, work, friends and family and yet by the end they had accepted each other, warts and vices and all.

Number 2 - she had not left her flat since arriving home from school on Friday night and had been wearing her pyjamas and dressing gown ever since.

Number 3 - she had not received a single text or phone call over the weekend; not a parent, a friend, or even a cold call.

Number 4 - she had eaten badly. Pizzas were the order of the day and night, accompanied by chocolate and the imminent possibility of an increase in inches and spots.

Number 5 - she had drunk wine as if it was going out of fashion from Friday until the early hours of Sunday.

Number 6 - she had still not decided how to respond to Peter's offer to promote her. She couldn't delay her decision any longer. It had been over a week and he was expecting gratitude and a positive acceptance by Monday.

Number 7 - she felt old and lonely.

So, taking off her frumpy dressing gown and looking at her blotchy face in the bathroom mirror, Julie decided to go for retail therapy in eight hours' time. She woke early, showered, and then spent time in front of several mirrors applying makeup and trying on various outfits until she was satisfied that she looked reasonably attractive without being tarty for a Sunday morning. Breakfast was black coffee and paracetamol and then she decided to walk to the shops to get some fresh air and kick start her latest fitness regime.

Three hours later and she had spent a small fortune on her credit cards, was flagging and had some of the characteristics of a bag lady. She needed to sit down and have something to eat. She ignored various cafes and sandwich shops and decided to go to her favourite place.

The pub-restaurant was open all day and attracted a wide variety of customers. She found a table, put her coat over the back of a chair and placed her carrier bags on the opposite seat. She ordered a Panini with salad and a drink from the bar. She had meant to ask for a diet coke but by the time the young barmaid asked her what table she was sitting at, the order had changed to a small red wine and then at the very last second to a large one.

She took her drink to the table and did what most single people do on their own in a public place; she scrolled through the old messages on her mobile. Exhausting that as entertainment, she opened her purse and examined the receipts for her purchases; a smart two piece suit for work or a possible future interview, a party dress that was a little tight and short but what the heck; some new underwear ranging from sensible to special occasions and a few pairs of tights and stockings. Her bank account would certainly require improvement but she'd be getting a pay rise if she accepted Peter's offer. The food arrived and the waitress kindly offered to get her another glass of wine. She would drink this second one slowly while eating and then walk home.

The restaurant was busy and loud. There were families ranging from 2.4 to 4.8 children, groups of older men who looked as if they had been drinking since first light and a couple of tables of younger men watching a live lunch time football match while drinking and swearing. Julie was beginning to be afflicted by an overwhelming sense of isolation when she became aware of someone standing beside her chair.

"Miss Osborne isn't it?" asked a young man.

Julie looked up at the tall, twenty-something man smiling sweetly at her. "Yes, that's right. Sorry do I know…I'm sorry but I don't…"

"It's Mark, erm Mark Dawson, you used to teach me years ago. I was in the sixth form at Light Hill School. You taught me A. level Maths for my last year."

The feeling of being isolated was replaced by feeling old. There was no denying his connection with her but she couldn't remember him. "I'm sorry, Mark. Forgive me for not remembering your name. It was a long time ago, but your face is familiar," Julie lied.

"That's okay. I don't expect you to remember me. I was in a large class of skinny, spotty youths who you probably hated."

"No, not at all. I loved my years at Light Hill. The pupils were great and were very kind to me."

"That's because most of the boys fancied you."

Julie felt her cheeks turn the colour of her last drop of wine. She laughed to cover her emotions. "Boys that age fancy anything in a skirt!" She changed the subject quickly and asked the normal questions teachers put to ex-pupils -what had he done since he left school, had he got a job and did he have a partner and family?

Julie learned that Mark had studied accountancy, was lucky enough to have a good job, was doing well in the firm, was a keen rugby player, had not had a regular girlfriend since university and lived locally in a flat with another guy from work. This should have been the end of the catching-up conversation with Julie saying something like "Well it's lovely to see you and I'm glad you are doing well." But Mark casually asked her if she wanted another drink.

While Mark was at the bar, Julie moved her bags from the seat opposite and straightened her clothes. Mark returned with a large red wine for Julie and a lager for himself and sat down across from her.

This seemingly confident, handsome young man was comfortable in the company of older women and was not afraid to ask Julie about herself. The wine had loosened her reticence and she told this total stranger all about her life since their paths had last crossed. Julie got the next round of drinks, this time opting for a smaller glass because she was beginning to feel the effects of the alcohol. Mark told her he had been walking to the shops and had seen her through the window as he passed the restaurant. He graphically demonstrated his double take, the three point turn he made in amongst the busy pedestrians and his nervous rehearsal before approaching his old teacher.

"I don't mean old, I mean ex-teacher," he said with a twinkle in his eye. They both laughed and when the laughter faded the smiles on their faces remained.

"What are you doing now?" asked Mark.

"I was going to stagger home with my shopping. I shouldn't have drunk those last two glasses of wine," Julie admitted.

"Let me help you. I don't think I ever carried your books when you were my teacher. Let me carry your bags now." They both laughed again as Julie's phone rang for the first time this weekend.

"I'm sorry Mark, I ought to take it. Hello...Oh hi Peter...I'm fine...Are you OK?...Good...yes....yes...Sorry it's a bit noisy here...Yes....No...I haven't made up my mind yet...There's a lot to consider...I'll speak to you tomorrow...Sorry, I've got company at the moment...Perhaps we can talk through things tomorrow...See you soon...Bye...Bye."

"Boyfriend?" asked Mark.

"My boss. Now what was that about being a chivalrous gentlemen and carrying my bags home?" They stood and Mark gathered Julie's carrier bags. He opened the door and in an exaggerated and mocking fashion gestured for Julie to go first. The rush of cold air hit them as they stepped on to the high street. Julie led the way back to her flat. It had been a very successful shopping trip.

Peter put down the phone. It had been a mistake to call Julie over the weekend. As he suspected and could hear, she was having a great time with people of her own age. She didn't want to be discussing school matters on a Sunday with him even if they involved her promotion. But he wanted to know one way or the other. He wanted something positive to think about. He wanted a plan that would make a difference and Julie was central to that. So why did she not seem interested or enthusiastic about being his second deputy?

Peter looked at his watch. He would work for another hour before driving to his daughter's house. He needed to think about the Senior Leadership Team meeting tomorrow night. There would be a lot to discuss and debate. Not least whether Jo had made any progress with helping Richard Perry and the Maths department. And he needed someone to lead on Numeracy across the curriculum and give it a new lease of life but each of them was carrying a great deal of baggage. Julie was ideal but was far too busy already; Sobia was brilliant with numbers but was not a teacher; Charlie was consumed with pastoral matters and was no longer seen as a classroom practitioner and Neil was Neil. Would any of them be interested in taking on this extra work? Could anyone be talked into doing the job? Was anyone interested in numeracy at all?

As he stared out of his study window all of his team were at that moment in the process of improving their Maths skills.

Sobia was close to tears in her kitchen. The rest of the family were sitting in the dining room enjoying each other's company while she was counting samosas and coming up short. She was sure she made more than this. Where had they gone? The house was untidy, the food was not ready and she would receive another black mark from her husband. Why couldn't she be a good wife?

Charlie was counting the cost of the argument. He had lost his deposit on the squash court but he had saved on the post-match drinks. However, as a peace offering he had promised his wife a new sofa and this put the day into negative equity. This was the price paid for being a devoted husband.

Neil was on-line looking at his bank statements to see how much surplus funds he had. Once his Russian doll had given him a ball park figure that she would need to fly to him, he could send her the money. That's what you do when you're in love.

Julie was multi-tasking. She was concentrating on walking in a straight line back to her flat and subtracting at the same time. The exam question that she was struggling with was entry level but never-the-less important in getting a pass. The problem was this. *If a qualified Maths teacher with X years of experience in education wants to sleep with a fit, handsome accountant that left university Y years ago, how many hours should she wait?* As an outstanding teacher she gave herself the following advice *Always attempt every question before time runs out.* Good advice. She would act on it as soon as possible.

Peter stared at the willows and considered the busy Monday ahead. Peter would have to meet Julie and Jo to discuss Maths. He had a planning meeting with Clive Howell to nail down the presentation that Clive would give to the staff. He had a conference call set up with Evelyn, the elusive School Improvement Advisor. This would be the first contact he had managed to have with her since Ofsted. He must arrange a time for Sobia to meet with him to discuss the action plan focus on leadership. Perhaps she could join him when Clive arrived? He also needed to speak with Charlie and Neil regarding pupils' outcomes and what they had planned so far. Perhaps they could join in with Evelyn's conference call?

His mind was spinning just like the plates he was trying to keep in the air. Perhaps he shouldn't do anymore school work today. The future was scaring him. He had not gone into teaching to feel like this. He did not want to be part of the name, blame and shame game. He wanted to be trusted to run his school the way he wanted and not have to compete with other schools across the country. He knew his local community, the parents and their children and he was only interested in his pupils as emerging adults and caring citizens not their grades on a particular random day in their brief lives. Peter knew his views would not go down well in the corridors of power. He would have to play their game on an uneven pitch.

These were the ramblings of a sad old man who was behind the times. He felt like Boxer in Animal Farm trying to build and re-build his school his way, only to be told by the pigs that all schools are equal but some schools are more equal than others. Peter accepted that he would be off to the knacker's yard soon. He closed his laptop and his eyes. He mentally travelled back and forth across his career and lived in past chapters for a while until it was time to leave. Fortunately, as Peter Pan woke, he was granted the gift of forgetfulness.

CHAPTER 8

Peter joined Charlie at the main doors as the first wave of pupils flooded into school. Some of the older pupils needed visual frisking as they entered the building. Peter, Charlie and the Heads of Year stood on guard checking uniform, adornments to uniform, foot wear, hair styles, make-up and eating habits. The guards were well drilled, welcoming the pupils with smiles on their faces but scanning each with the laser eyes of Homeland Security officers at a New York airport. The pupils were allowed into the canteen area for breakfast and hot drinks. Possibly the healthiest meal of the day for some of them. Only after the five minute staff briefing were pupils able to access their classrooms. As usual, the line of pupils grew at Reception as pupils remembered that they had forgotten various things and needed to ring home to get mum or dad to bring it in for them.

In five minutes time Peter would leave Charlie and his team to supervise the pupils while he conducted his briefing in the staffroom.

As was normal once Peter had returned to his office, Charlie followed him in to find out the current state of the nation.

"Good weekend?" asked Peter.

"Not bad," replied Charlie, yesterday's sofa incident forgotten. "What about you?"

"Fine, the usual stuff."

This was the extent of the exchange into each other's personal lives. Charlie was happy not to get touchy feely with other blokes and Peter found it difficult to talk to Charlie about anything other than school, sport and cars.

"Anything to report from the briefing?" asked Charlie.

"Not really. I decided not to mention Ofsted this morning. It seems to crop up in every sentence I speak at the moment."

"Not your fault. We're all totally consumed with it at present. I'll be glad when our first HMI visit is over and then at least we can expect a slightly easier time."

"God, I hope so. I did mention that next Monday Clive Howell is delivering the training on Leadership at our INSET session."

"You never know, he might surprise us but I'm not holding my breath."

"He's coming in later this morning to plan the day."

Charlie was just about to apologise that he was already committed to other meetings when Peter out-manoeuvred him.

"I know you're busy this morning but I would like you to spare an hour this afternoon. I want you and Neil to give me some feedback on what you've been working on for the action plan. Let's say two o'clock. Is that okay with you Charlie?"

"Yeah, I can make time. I'm seeing Neil this morning to prepare a few things." Charlie was lying and Peter knew it. *Still*, Peter thought, *two birds one stone. I've got a huddle for the conference call and given Charlie a reminder to get his finger out.*

"Great, I'll see you later. Will you tell Neil when you see him?"

"Sure will boss, have a good session with Clive."

Charlie's brief flirtation with Penny was cut short by her phone ringing.

"Morning Penny, did you have a nice weekend?" asked Peter.

"Yes thank you. You sound in a good mood this morning."

"I thought I always sounded like this. You know me, always looking on the bright side."

"I'll take your word on that. What can I do for you?"

"Can you come in; there are a few things I need you to arrange for me."

"No problem, I'll just finish this letter and then I'll be in."

"I'll put the kettle on."

"Thank you and I'll have a couple of your happy pills."

They sat at the meeting table, coffees to hand, Penny with her notepad, pen and shorthand at the ready.

"Still smiling," said Peter.

"Wait until the end of the day and I'll give you a check-up before I leave."

Just for a second they had forgotten the context of their relationship. Peter was supposed to be the down trodden cynical boss and Penny the straight faced and straight talking power behind the throne. There was a warmth between them this morning that rarely showed itself. It passed and they quickly reverted to type. Had Penny told Charlie that she'd give him a *check-up* at the end of the day, the conversation would undoubtedly have headed in a very different direction.

"Clive Howell is supposed to be here in five minutes or so but there are various people I want to get hold of today. First, if Clive is on time I want you to interrupt at eleven and say that my next meeting is ready. I could do with Sobia joining me for the Clive Howell show. I know she won't like it, but tough. Between eleven and two I need a session with Jo Slater and some time with Julie. Can you organise all that and remind Charlie and Neil that they're sitting in on my conference call with Evelyn at two o'clock sharp?"

"Of course. Don't you want to phone Julie yourself?"

"No, I'll leave it to you and can you type up and circulate the SLT agenda?" Peter passed across his hand written draft.

Clive Howell knocked but waltzed in without waiting for Penny to open it.

"Hi both. Are you well? Great! Is that coffee I can smell; a lovely Monday morning; I've woken up and I can smell the coffee. But seriously folks, how are things; have you cracked the action plan? I'll take a look at it if you like. Now what about this training next week? What do you want me to bring to the table?"

Feeling sorry for Peter, Penny glanced back as she headed for the door. He already had his head in his hands. She went back to her desk and phoned

Sobia. "I know this is short notice but Peter needs your advice and wondered if you were available to see him at the moment?"

"I'm in the middle of something but if he wants to come down to my office I can speak to him." replied Sobia.

"Peter will be most grateful but he asked if you would come up to his office." Penny managed to trick Sobia into saying yes without giving her the real story.

"Fine, I'll be with you in five minutes."

Sobia put the phone down and her mind started racing. What did he want to see her about? Good or bad? He hardly ever wanted her for anything that involved praise or reward, so she jumped to the natural conclusion that she had done something wrong. What had she done or not done? What had she said or not said? Well, she was not going to stand for it! She was doing the best she could under difficult circumstances. Her eyes watered and she swivelled her chair towards the wall. She was already in enough trouble from yesterday. The family meal had been a fiasco and her husband had made his dissatisfaction very clear. As she stood to walk to the Head's office Sobia checked the long sleeves of her blouse were covering the bruises on her arms.

Penny tried Julie on her phone but there was no reply so she decided to wander down to the English department to see Jo Slater. This had the advantage of taking her away from her desk when Sobia stormed in to see the Head. Penny's route to the English Department corridor would be circuitous and might happen to take her past the Pastoral Block.

When Sobia entered Peter's office, she was both on the offensive and the defensive, her guard up and armed with slings, arrows and a calculator. She was surprised to find Clive Howell in full flow across the table from the Head.

"Oh I thought you were free...Shall I come back when you've finished?"

"Hi Sobia. No, no, not at all. Thanks for popping in."

Peter motioned for Sobia to join them. As she sat down, refusing the offered drink, she realised she was not about to be accused of anything. She was merely the victim of a cunning plan by Peter to out-gun the enemy. Was she losing her touch? In less than twenty-four hours she had been cruelly mistreated by her husband and now manipulated by her boss. She sat there in silence listening to Clive's monologue, licking her wounds.

"Sobia, I was sharing with Peter, that I usually like the training I do to be hands-on. I don't want to talk at the staff and I don't want to weigh them down with paper work. I want them to leave the session with bite-size takeaways. What do you think guys?"

Peter turned to look at Sobia but her eyes would not make contact with the four male eyes pointing at her.

"I think it's important to make the training session interactive but I want the middle leaders to feel that they've learned how to improve their leadership skills," said Peter lamely.

"Peter, Peter; remember this is training for all leaders at whatever rung of the greasy ladder. In a school all teachers and pupils are leaders; they are all leaders of learning. The way I describe it in my training sessions is that the classroom is a microcosm of the real world outside and in that classroom everyone is both teacher and learner. I usually get them to do various roleplay activities to experience assertively leading others without having to lay down the law..."

At this point both Sobia and Peter had heard enough and needed to interrupt Clive. Sobia drew first and Peter un-cocked his tongue.

"Coming from a business background, I've spent many years thinking outside an imaginary box somewhere in a blue sky before falling to Earth and having to hit the ground running. Leadership is not about jargon and buzzwords. It's about getting the job done and making sure everyone is working towards the same ends. If it means laying down the law then that's what you have to do. It's not a democracy. People are paid at different levels to supervise the work of others who they are responsible for. Surely pupils are here to learn and they're taught by teachers paid to do the job. Their managers are paid to ensure that this is done properly and if they fail then they should be shown the door."

"I hear what you're saying Sobia but we're dealing with a school - a very different animal to the private sector. A school has to be led by buy-in and negotiation. It's an art rather than a science and the rules of the game are blurred," Clive responded.

"And perhaps that's why schools fail and are in chaos because no-one has any respect for the rules and no-one knows what they're supposed to be doing." Sobia made eye contact with Peter for the first time since sitting down but it was now Peter who couldn't meet her glare.

"It would be much simpler if everyone knew what they had to do and got on with it. There is no art to managing people. You just have to tell them straight what is expected of them. I managed a team of over twenty people in my last job and we were the top performing division of a successful company for three years running. We didn't have endless training on how to develop leadership styles. We just kept on top of things. If your workers are underperforming, then they should be told and warned. The fact is, some of the leaders at Whatmore are good and get results and some are inadequate. The ineffective managers may be reasonable teachers but they can't tell others what to do and so they haven't got the required authority or respect." This time Sobia caught and held Peter's gaze. "Why are you giving everyone the same training when some managers don't need it and some will never be any good?"

"Everyone deserves the same opportunities and chances and Ofsted like to see whole-school training but I take your point, Sobia. We could differentiate the training to cater for the needs of individual leaders..." Clive's head was now outside the box and he was breathing in pure blue sky. "I like your spirit and style Sobia. There is some mileage in this. I could get the staff working on different tables depending on their existing ability as leaders and we could set them different learning objectives for the session. I could set them real examples of leadership issues and then they could come up with possible solutions..."

For the next twenty-three minutes Clive talked out loud to an audience of two who had lost the thread and the will to live.

Clive rounded up by saying that he would peel the onion in the next week, that he hoped that his radical approach to this training session would not boil the ocean and that he had enjoyed the face time. Ironically there had been no need for Penny to interrupt as it had lasted less than the allotted two hours but it still felt to Peter and Sobia as if they dived head-first into a treacle-filled swimming pool.

After Clive had gone, Sobia made to follow him out but Peter asked her to sit down again. Sobia's brittle strength deserted her as she waited for her boss to dress her down for showing disloyalty to the school in front of an officer of the local authority (even one who was a total plonker).

In fact Peter had spent some of the meeting hating Sobia, much of it admiring her honesty and at the end feeling sorry for her. The session had visibly peeled back some of the metaphorical layers of Sobia's onion. For the first time he was aware of layers which seemed damaged, nervous and fragile. She had constantly adjusted her clothing and fidgeted. With an underused intuition, Peter could see her emptiness and hurt. He couldn't be a heartless fool looking through a glass onion.

"Are you okay?" he asked. "You seemed really up-tight when you came in at the beginning of the meeting and then you went for Clive in a big way…"

"He deserved it. He's an idiot. I don't know how that man got to be in that position in the authority."

"If it's any consolation, he'll probably be out of a job soon. The government is systematically reducing local authority powers. In two years' time there'll be more chance seeing a dodo walking along the local street than an education adviser." Sobia came close to smiling. "And I seemed to come in for some stick as well… I don't mind you having a go at me but I would like you to choose your moments more carefully. You know I really rate you and like your matter-of-fact way of doing things. It's a breath of fresh air compared to the way we all operate. I don't want you to change your views but I would ask you to choose your battlefields more carefully…"

Peter was expecting a grudging nod and a quick exit but what followed was something else.

"I'm…I'm sorry," whispered Sobia and burst into tears. For the next few minutes she sobbed and sobbed. Peter could do very little other than offer her his box of man-sized tissues. It was inappropriate to ask her anything until she had stopped crying and it was certainly not possible to comfort her by holding her hand or putting an arm around her shoulder - so he headed for the door. He was going to delegate the situation to Penny but then he stopped himself, opened his door slightly and poked his head through the gap.

"Penny. No calls or meetings until I say so please."

He closed the door again and sat down at Sobia's side.

"Take your time...no-one is waiting to see me. We can sit here for as long as we want."

"I'm sorry...I don't know why I started crying...It's not like me...I'm so sorry..."

"Don't apologise....the job gets to all of us at some point in our lives and life sometimes gets in the way of our jobs...." Peter said, not appreciating what he had just said. "Is there anything I can do?" He hoped for a simple *no* by way of an answer.

"How about finding me a husband who takes care of me...and children that do what they're told...and a family that doesn't think I'm a failure..."

"So it's not about work then?" asked Peter in a way that sounded caring and comforting to him and crass to anyone else.

Sobia started crying again. He decided to take the safe route. Say nothing and do nothing. How long could she carry on crying for anyway? It would be physically impossible to continue crying much longer. And how many tissues were left in that box?

Seven more tissues later, Sobia was ready to talk.

"I'm so sorry, It's not like me to get upset, particularly in front of...work colleagues. I suppose I've had a lot going on in my life recently and then we had Ofsted and it's all boiled over. My husband's family came round yesterday and it wasn't successful, so we had words last night. I'm not being a good mother or wife at the moment. There's too much to think about; too much to do. And I didn't get much sleep last night and today I'm snapping at everyone and saying the wrong things. I don't know if I can carry on with all of this...." She started crying again.

"Sobia, you are doing a fine job here. I value you and your strength and commitment. I want you to continue as Business Manager and if necessary we can get you extra support."

"Thank you but you know how hard it is for me to let go of my work. I find it difficult to trust anyone else with the school's finances. I admit I'm a bit of a perfectionist."

"I know you are." Peter assumed his most understanding and sympathetic facial expression. Behind this façade he was asking himself *At what point does perfectionism become autism?* and *If trust is a vital part of good leadership what does that say about Sobia?* He stopped himself answering either question.

"I'm the same at home but my husband expects the house to be perfect and the children are going through a difficult phase. Their behaviour at times is..."

"Unsatisfactory with occasional elements of good?" Peter finished Sobia's sentence.

"I've got so much to do on the budget at the moment and we have to start working up our target on leadership improvement for the action plan..." Her tears began again.

A germ of an idea came into Peter's head - a way of getting Sobia out of his office without seeming heartless.

"Sobia, we've all got a great deal to do in the next few weeks but we have to pace ourselves. The work you have on your desk can wait for a while. Nothing is that pressing. We can look at the leadership target later in the week. Right?"

"I...suppose...so..." Sobia sighed.

"Then I want you to follow my advice and I don't want an argument over this." For the first time in their working relationship Peter appeared to be in charge and assertive. Peter liked it and so did Sobia.

"Penny will get your handbag and coat from your office now and you will go home. You will do whatever you need to do there; vacuum the carpets, cook a meal, collect the kids from school or just watch day time television and spend the evening having quality time with your family. I will see you back in school tomorrow. And if you need a little longer to re-charge your batteries then give me a ring. You will have my permission. Is that okay?"

"Yes...but what about my team....what will they think...What will they do when I'm not there?"

"Penny will tell them that you're representing me at an urgent and sudden meeting. As for what'll they do today, how about trusting them to do their jobs?" As Peter finished speaking with real authority and purpose, he stood a few inches taller than usual. He again opened the door slightly to explain to Penny what he wanted her to do and then closed it and turned to face Sobia. She was staring at him in a new light.

"Thank you....P...Peter...I will be back tomorrow...You have my word. I'm so sorry about this. Thank you."

Penny brought Sobia her handbag and coat and saw her on her way to the car. Returning Penny made an observation. "Peter...and you thought today was going so well. Tears before lunch time! What did you or Clive say to cause such a sweet woman to use all your tissues?"

"It wasn't Clive. Not directly, I know he can make any right minded person hit the bottle or run screaming to the nearest mental hospital but he was just being his normal self. And then after he went I just asked Sobia if she was okay and without a flood warning the dam just burst."

"Maybe she was upset because you were being nice to her for a change," Penny delivered this message with just the right amount of sarcasm.

"I'm always nice Penny, I keep telling you this but you won't believe me. I've told her to have the rest of today off and tomorrow if necessary. We can cope short term."

"I'm sure Cathy and Diane could cope without Sobia in the longer term too."

"Now Mrs Hinks. We're all Godot's children; all waiting for something better to come along."

Penny didn't understand the aphorism which meant that for the second time in the space of twenty minutes or so he had said something very profound on the surface but left all parties baffled and bewildered.

"Anyway, I must get on." Penny got there before Peter could say the same thing. "I've sent the SLT agenda out and spoken to Jo. She should be here any minute."

"What about Julie?"

"I haven't been able to track her down. She's somewhere in the building, but not in her office. I'll try again in a few minutes. Do you want her to pop down when she can?"

"Yes, preferably before I talk to Evelyn. It doesn't matter if Jo's still with me."

"Alright but no more upsetting impressionable women today, thank you very much," said a brightly shining Penny as she left Peter's office.

Peter smiled back as she closed the door. The day wasn't going to plan but he was quite pleased with his handling of the Sobia incident. Perhaps the scenario could be used as an outstanding example of leadership by Clive at his training next week. *The Day Peter Slayed the Dragon*. The stuff of folklore - Sir Peter gallantly riding in full armour, a beautiful assistant head straddling his leather saddle, looking adoringly into his eyes through the thin slit of his visor.

His imagination came crashing down to earth, knocked into reality by the sound of knuckles on wood. Jo Slater was at the door and there were other battles to win and damsels to save.

"Come on in. Thanks for coming. Would you like a drink?"

"No thanks. I've just had a coffee but you go ahead if you need a shot of caffeine."

"I'm becoming far too reliant on caffeine recently. I need to wean myself off it before I become a Java junkie."

"There are worse things to get hooked on I suppose."

"And better things!" joked Peter.

"I wouldn't know Headmaster," Jo smiled at the smiling Head before their facial expressions defaulted back to serious and professional.

"I wanted to catch up with you regarding the meeting you had with Richard Perry last week. Was he receptive to you? Did you manage to get through to him?" asked Peter fearing Jo's response.

"I met him for an hour last Wednesday when we were both free. I had a word with Julie and she has agreed to keep us both off covering on a Wednesday afternoon period 5 for the foreseeable future. As for the reception I got...let's just say it could have been more positive but we both survived. Richard was naturally very defensive and quite happy to spend the hour explaining why leading a Maths Department is a very different proposition to my job. I steered clear of comparisons and tried to get him to outline all the issues he faces in leading his team. He listed the problems as new and inexperienced teachers; insufficient management time due to his own teaching load and... that SLT had not given him as much support as he would have liked." Jo paused, expecting Peter to come back at her defensively.

"So how did you move things forward? What advice did you give him?"

"By the time Richard had finished there wasn't much time for anything else! I said this Wednesday we would change the emphasis and concentrate on Richard himself; his strengths and where he thought he needs support as a leader. I told him Julie would be working with the rest of his team and I would be specifically assisting him. That's right isn't it?"

"Yes that's right. Just keep us informed of progress."

"Peter, you I both know a significant change to Richard's leadership is going to take time and careful handling. Presently, all I can spare for him is an hour a week. That's precious little time to affect a meaningful difference in his leadership style when he seems to feel he has nothing left to learn. If you want me to do this mentoring role properly I'll need more time and your assurance that you are not expecting instant results."

Peter made all of the right noises, including *This is a marathon not a sprint, Rome wasn't built in a day* and *Softly, softly wins the race*. He wasn't sure about the last quote but Jo was too polite to correct him and he fought shy of telling her the truth about how short a time she really had to turn Richard Perry around. He wanted to keep her sweet and hoped positive strokes would do the trick. In his dreams!

Jo left Peter's office reassured. It meant she could forget all about the Maths department for two whole days. Peter was equally satisfied; he could make Jo the *person responsible* for improving the leadership of Maths. The problem was that following publication of the inspection report he had about six weeks to demonstrate progress. The clock was ticking.

Almost lunch time. Peter could get a sandwich and show his face in the school canteen for a few minutes or he could summon Julie to see whether she was minded to accept the promotion. There was a third option of course.

"Penny?" Peter rang through to her desk. "Do you fancy a working lunch?"

"Are you asking me on a date?" Penny at her most mischievous.

"Well, if twenty minutes over sarnies in my office constitutes a date, I suppose I am."

"Alright then. I just want to check on Cathy and Diane first."

"Thank you for that. I suppose we should just trust them to get on with their work but they'll probably be feeling a little rudderless without Captain Sobia at the helm. It may do them some good you know, Big Sister not watching them for a whole afternoon."

"They may be in the middle of a party when I walk in."

"Can you do me another favour? Stop off and get me a sandwich and one for yourself. School funds can pay. Don't tell Sobia when she returns."

"So, just to confirm, you've invited me for lunch, no candle light or mood music but I have to fetch the sandwiches and the poor pupils and their parents will indirectly be paying for them?"

"Sounds about right. How can you refuse?"

"See you in five minutes. I'll put my best frock on!"

On days like this Peter couldn't ask for a better PA. He was on top of his game and she was playing along wonderfully. He had just enough time to phone Julie in her office. No reply. No matter, he would catch her later. He felt guilty for not showing his face in the canteen but was comforted to know his deputy would be doing his duty and that all would be peace and harmony.

Unfortunately, all was not peace and harmony. Penny had dashed to pick up the sandwiches as most of the pupils arrived in the canteen. Other than a couple of well-meaning dinner ladies there was no-one in authority supervising. Mr Briggs wasn't there. Neither was Ms Osborne.

Charlie had a legitimate excuse. He was in Middle Earth talking a lot of Gollums with Neil. Charlie had discovered the hidden door to Neil's lair and bravely entered, bringing warnings of an impending battle between the Head and the other male members of his senior team. Charlie and Neil had done nothing in the last week on their part of the action plan. They had neither spoken nor emailed each other. They had been too busy. Now, with only a few hours to go before the conference call which would, no doubt, focus on pupil attainment and progress, Charlie had panicked not because he was scared of Peter's reaction but from a seldom tapped sense of loyalty. As Peter's deputy he should try to set a good example whenever possible.

So Charlie entered the Kingdom of the Nerd and explained to Neil that they would have to come up with a cunning plan before 2.00 pm. Charlie, sitting half on and half off the work surface supporting several gizmos and gadgets that looked live and dangerous, reminded Neil that they had been tasked with coming up with ideas for an internal league table to map pupil performance across the different subjects.

Neil's brain re-engaged on the new matter in hand and his fingers started to weave their magic. Numbers, grids, charts and graphs flashed up on the screen. Charlie watched mesmerised and bemused in equal measure. Neil vainly tried to explain what he was doing. Charlie, nodded and made encouraging noises, not wishing to reveal his total ignorance and indifference for man-made machines and the mad men who serve them.

All Charlie knew was that, on balance, all things electronic were more trouble than they were worth. Some years before he had mislaid a mobile phone only for it to be found by his first wife replete with passionately incriminating texts from the woman destined eventually to become his second wife and then his second ex-wife. Apart from gambling with his sex life he had also accidently entered the dark and risky world of on-line gambling, regularly lightening his wallet over several years before he was able to stem his addiction and replace it with the healthier thrills of the squash, badminton or tennis court.

Here amongst Neil's toys, Charlie felt old and more than a little jealous. His main playthings were now only shuttlecocks and balls. Neil's solutions looked and sounded impressive and would certainly give them some breathing space at this afternoon's meeting. Now, it was time for Charlie to find a reason for leaving this dungeon for the fresh air and natural light of the real world. *Blimey, was it really half way through lunch time?* Charlie hoped Julie or Peter had made it to the dining hall to prevent any risk of World War Three or even Custard's last stand. Charlie thanked Neil and rode out into a metaphorical sunset. His hopes that the cavalry would not be needed were doomed to disappointment. The canteen was Chilli Con Carnage.

While Charlie was assisting the battered and bruised dinner ladies to clear debris and detritus off the dining hall floor, ceilings and walls, Peter and Penny were enjoying a leisurely lunch in the safety of the Head's office and were checking a letter Peter had drafted to be sent home with pupils. Perhaps a third of the letters would make it home and of those a quarter might be read by a parent. Penny had to admit the letter sounded convincing, managing a measure of positivity and optimism with a slight twist of realism and truth.

"Sounds a great school, we ought to work there," said Penny.

"I agree. Wonder if there are any jobs going?"

"I hear the Head and his PA's jobs may be advertised soon."

"I'll definitely go for the PA if you apply for the Headship," said Peter. They both laughed, sipping coffee. Peter knew Penny was safe. In truth Penny wasn't so sure about either of them.

"Can you get that typed up and out by the end of the day? It'd be better if parents read my side of the story rather than going on to the website."

"You don't want a reply slip at the bottom of the page do you?" asked Penny.

"No thanks. I can live without parental venting. Perhaps we ought to put at the top in large type *It is vital that this letter gets home in one piece'. T*hen we could be fairly certain we wouldn't be getting any come back tomorrow. "

"Perhaps instead of a tear off slip I could put dotted lines on the page so they can all fold the letter up and make paper planes." It was a suggestion worth consideration.

"Quite a few will do that anyway."

"What a waste of time and money."

"Are we talking about the letter or Ofsted generally?" There was a glint in Peter's eye.

"I couldn't possibly say. Remember, I might be the next Head of Whatmore, so I have to remain professional at all times."

"It's never stopped me."

"No comment! Right, your conference call is fast approaching. I'll send Charlie and Neil in as soon as they arrive."

"Thanks Penny. I just want to try to speak to Julie first."

"She's probably chatting to Charlie after lunch duty or observing someone's lesson."

"I'm sure you're right. Thanks for the date. We must do it again sometime."

"Perhaps we could have Chinese or Indian next time or take in a movie."

They both laughed again. It had taken a couple of years and the ice was not fully broken but it had thawed and was now slowly melting. Strangely, since Ofsted, they had become closer, Penny sympathising with Peter's position and he realising he felt more comfortable with Penny than anybody else in school. Or at home.

Still no reply from Julie's phone. A knock on the door heralded Neil, struggling in, carrying his laptop and dropping various sheets of paper across the floor.

"Sorry, sorry. Charlie thought it would be useful to show you what we have been working on this.....recently."

"Here let me." Peter shot up to help Neil recover from his Colombo-style entrance. Not that Neil would get the comparison with the chaotically brilliant crime solver.

"Is Charlie here yet or is he chatting up Penny?"

"I haven't seen him since....for a while." Neil stammered as Peter helped him pick up the papers. "He knows we're speaking with Evelyn Chadbourne at two."

The phone rang and it was Evelyn. Peter put his phone on speaker mode and introduced Neil to Evelyn.

"Good afternoon. Is the rest of your team joining us, Peter?"

"Charlie will be but Sobia's not well and Julie's observing lessons."

"That's a pity but not to worry. I've got an hour between commitments so I'm hoping we can make best use of the time."

"So do I," replied Peter wondering if this hour would end up being invoiced to Whatmore as well as the school she was phoning from.

"So fill me in on where you are since Ofsted reported. Has the report been published? Is it what you expected? What have you been doing in the meantime?"

"The report was published last Friday and I'm sending a letter out to parents explaining the judgement and the start we've made on the action plan."

"Good...and your actions are based around the key areas for improvement?"

What else would they be based on? "Yes."

"And...remind me...those are...?"

"Quality of teaching, standards, progress in some subjects and leadership."

"So everything other than behaviour and safety....?"

"I wouldn't say everything. There were areas of the school that weren't inspected or acknowledged during Ofsted's visit. They came in to look at specific things and didn't take a global account of the school." Peter sounded defensive, even to himself.

"As you know, they follow a framework and three of the four inspection categories were below standard."

Peter decided to get his real grievance out of the way immediately. "Yet your report on the school just over five months ago judged us as *Good* in all four…"

"Yes but if you recall I was only in Whatmore for a day and had to make a judgement based on what I saw and what you told me. The lessons I sat in on were generally good and your predictions for the summer exams were positive. Based on that I felt you were moving forward and were just about edging into the *Good* quartile. As you said, it was over five months ago and a lot can happen in that time."

Peter looked at Neil and Neil looked at Peter.

The Head broke the deafening silence. "Yes, we could have improved in that time! So let me get this right, Evelyn. Are you saying you were wrong to judge us as *Good* because we gave you misleading information or that the school was good then and now it isn't or that you didn't have enough time to make an accurate judgement?"

"Peter, I came in for a day at your request and tried to get a feel for the school and from my experience and knowledge of how Ofsted work I came to the conclusion that if progress continued you would be a good school."

"But you didn't," interjected Neil. "You said it was a good school. I have your report in front of me. You didn't say that it could or would be a good school if everything continues to improve. You said in your opinion we were a good school."

As Neil stuck the knife in, Charlie walked in to Peter's office and took a seat, mouthing his apologies and stuck his thumb up in support of what he'd caught Neil saying.

"Evelyn, Charlie has now joined us." Peter, out of courtesy, broke the tension momentarily. "Anyway, so we are now a school requiring improvement having deteriorated since you saw us earlier in the year at which point we didn't require improvement. Is that what you're saying?"

"It may be difficult to accept but it's how you have to interpret it."

"Hi Evelyn, Charlie here."

"Hello Charlie."

"I don't think we have to interpret it that way at all. It could fairly be said that either you or Ofsted got it wrong. Earlier this year we put our faith in your opinion and based our self- evaluation partly on your views..."

"But Charlie, remember, I was only seeing a snapshot of the school. You're there day in day out. I came in to validate your evaluation..." Evelyn was sounding increasingly desperate.

Peter spoke again. "What you're saying is that we were paying you to rubber stamp our judgements. Whereas I thought we were employing you for your experience and skill."

"I work as a critical friend to challenge you and the staff."

There was a lull. Not so much a truce in this phoney war as a chance for all four to catch breath. All of them knew that Evelyn's relationship with Whatmore was coming to an end.

"Can I move on to the action plan, Evelyn? I'd like to spend a little time going through it and hear what you have to say." said Peter.

"Of course...go ahead."

Peter did so before handing over to Neil improving the monitoring of pupil progress. Neil's lengthy exposition left no-one the wiser but nobody dared say so.

There followed a long pause. Peter wasn't sure if Evelyn was still conscious so he cleared his throat and thanked Neil which gave her the cue to speak.

"That sounds impressive. Both useful and user-friendly. You must send me a copy of the spreadsheet."

Charlie intervened to stop Neil sending it to her straight away from his laptop. "Once we've trialled it, we'll gladly send you a copy without any kids names on it."

"Oh, of course. Well, it sounds as if you're moving in the right direction. Do send me the draft action plan and I'll take a look at it for you...and if you want me to speak to the HMI just let me know and I'll find the time if I possibly can."

"Thanks. We'll be in touch. Take care." With that Evelyn became the newest member of Whatmore's *Consigned-to-History department*. The School Improvement Partner was recognised as a false prophet not to be worshipped or followed ever again.

"Boss, we can do without her!" observed Charlie. "She's an expensive luxury; a waste of money. Typical woman!"

"It's a good job Sobia or Julie didn't hear you say that. It'd get you a verbal kick in the balls. I'm sorry I dragged you into that but I'm getting fed up with other people telling us what we're doing wrong. We're perfectly capable of being crap on our own without any help!"

At Neil's command his laptop delivered the Titanic theme song. Charlie and Neil acted out playing the instruments on deck as Peter saluted and sank below his table.

Penny, walked straight in on them. For a second she didn't know whether to laugh or to laugh loudly but Charlie grabbed her and started spinning her around, a la DiCaprio and Winslet, so she lost the option of being merely an aloof observer of the general foolishness.

A modicum of sanity was restored eventually and a degree of embarrassment settled over the whole crew. Penny tried to remember why she'd come into the Head's office and resorted to telling them that Peter's letter had been printed off.

Neil and Charlie followed Penny out.

"What was that all about?" she asked.

"Just male bonding. It's how alpha males celebrate plucking up courage to gang up on a poor defenceless female. We've decided to dispense with Evelyn Chadbourne's services."

"Oh I see. Shouldn't you pass this by the governors before officially casting her aside?"

"Fair point, well made. Although we didn't actually tell her during the phone call. We made the decision afterwards. Who do you think we are...real men?"

"Not for a second!" said Penny.

Peter looked at the clock. There was less than half an hour before the SLT meeting and he needed some down time. He'd coped with Sobia's tears, Jo's obstinacy, Penny's jokes, Evelyn signing her own death warrant, Charlie and Neil behaving badly and the raising of the Titanic. All within the comfort and security of his own office. He needed to clear his mind.

He still hadn't spoken to Julie and belatedly it occurred to him that he'd not considered Charlie in all of this. Would he feel slighted if another deputy head was appointed? Perhaps he should speak to Charlie after SLT and then see Julie in the morning.

Peter's mind moved on to the matter of his wife. She deserved a card and some flowers for putting up with him in his currently distracted and disengaged state. Rachel had not said anything. She hadn't screamed or shouted at him for putting the school first in their marriage. Nor had she filed for divorce citing Whatmore as the third party. But things were not at all rosy in her garden. He would stop off at a supermarket on the way home tonight and try to repair the damage. Peter was adding flowers onto his to-do list when the ever-punctual Neil, knocked the door and normal hectic service resumed.

Amazingly, Charlie was next to arrive and it was Julie, walking in a few minutes late, who needed to apologise. Charlie grinned at her and she blushed.

"Julie, I was just saying to Neil and Charlie that Sobia can't be here so it's just us tonight. We were also light on lunch time supervision and we had a few problems I gather. Now we don't have a formal rota for that but I think we need one. Charlie, you do it usually, don't you?"

"Yes, I try to get down there every day but sometimes I'm caught up in pupil issues."

"What about you, Julie? How often do you supervise in the canteen?"

"I suppose twice a week. Charlie sometimes rings me on other days to see if I can show my face."

"What about you Neil? Peter knew the answer even before Neil started stuttering. "Well you are on the Leadership team and paid accordingly and I think it would be good for you to be more of a presence around the school."

"Does that mean you're going to ask Sobia as well?"

"Yes....I will I think it would be good for her too. The five of us can spread the supervision across the week so Charlie doesn't have to do every day. We'll all commit to three days a week. Remember, it's free food if you supervise...not much of a selling point, eh?"

"The sandwiches are okay," said Julie.

"Three duties a week each. I think it's only fair, Neil."

Charlie perked up. "I tell you what Neil, I'll do my duties on the same day as you. The kids are usually fine when I'm in there. I'll let you stand by the hot new dinner lady if you want."

"Thanks, but I'm not that interested any more..."

All eyes suddenly were on Neil. Brain cells started to fire up as Peter, Charlie and Julie began to deconstruct Neil's last statement. The trouble was that they had so little previous history or personal information to go on. Thoughts running wild in their heads ranged from *Neil has been left broken hearted by a girl and wants nothing to do with women anymore*.'(Julie) through *Neil was heterosexual but is now gay* (Peter) to *So Neil bats for the other side* (Charlie).

Peter attempted to change the subject. "I would quite like to discuss the action plan. No-one's got to leave early tonight, have they?"

"Actually…" Both Charlie and Julie started to answer at the same time.

"Sorry….after you," said Charlie.

"I need to leave at five. I've got to get back to the flat. I'm having a quote for some work and the builder could only make tonight." Julie thought she'd sounded convincing.

"And I have to leave at about the same time…it's my wife's birthday and I said I'd take her out," said Charlie, less convincingly.

"I guess we can cut things short tonight," said Peter. He wasn't so much disappointed at the meeting finishing early as not being able to speak to Charlie about the notion of having a second deputy head. Still at least it meant he could surprise Rachel by coming home early and a bunch of flowers would score bonus points.

"Well we'd better get started then. While I think about it, I need to see you for a few minutes tomorrow morning, Charlie and you Julie after that. Can you make that a priority please?" He said it with a pinch of grit in his voice.

They managed to discuss the action plan but none of them could truthfully swear they had made enough progress. They also filled Julie in on the Evelyn situation. Peter suggested seeking Ann Brown's approval to finding a Head teacher from a similar school who could give more practical and realistic advice. There was full agreement with this suggestion, particularly since it was 4.58pm.

Peter closed the meeting and reminded Charlie and Julie to see him in the morning. They both felt like naughty school pupils as they packed away, put their coats on and pushed their chairs under the table. Leaving the office, Neil went one way, while Julie and Charlie headed for the car park.

"How's your day been Jules?"

"Busy. You know, out and about. Peter was in a funny mood tonight, don't you think?"

"He wasn't happy with cutting things short tonight. Still, I promised my wife and you've got a man with dirty hands and mind to entertain."

"I should be so lucky," smiled Julie.

Charlie's car was in its usual spot, next to the Head's. Julie's was some distance away. Her usual spot had been taken when she sneaked back into school. As she started the engine she looked at her face in the mirror to check her make-up. She was blushing again.

CHAPTER 9

Julie looked at the alarm clock again. The green LED numerals now read 4.29 am. She had slept but was now in between trying to go back to sleep and admitting defeat and getting up. She was physically tired but her mind was racing. She eased herself up to a forty-five degree angle so she was no longer just looking at the dark ceiling. She felt cold and pulled the quilt up to cover her body. Normally she would be wearing pyjamas but not the last two nights.

She glanced sideways at her sleeping stud. When he was awake her body temperature was permanently in the red zone but since their last heated encounter around midnight she had cooled down. Her body ached. She was sore in some unusual places. She couldn't remember the last time she'd had as much exercise or as much fun doing it. She had learnt new moves from Mark and practice was making her perfect. If her sex education had been observed and graded, she might well be achieving *Outstanding*!

Julie was aware that she had the advantages of age and experience. She was at her peak and in her prime, but just now at this ungodly hour she felt more like Miss Brodie than the crème de la crème. The fit young thing lying next to her, sleeping peacefully, would stir in a couple of hours' time and be up and ready to start again on his ex-teacher's new fitness regime. She looked forward to it in one sense. In fact, there was part of her that would like to wake Mark up and begin the warm up now but she needed time to think and that would be difficult, if not impossible, with a strapping rugby player on top of her, by the side of her and underneath her as she knew he soon would be.

Julie was confused. She felt ancient comparing herself with Mark's trim and young body but she also felt like a Year 11 tart, willing to let her modesty slip at a touch or the tug of a button. *Was this just a casual fling or could it or should it develop further?* She was happy not to answer presently and be ruled by the moment. These last two days had done her the world of good and she was happy to seek further improvement.

Mark, however, might get bored and trade her in for a new sporting year's model. One thing was certain, she wouldn't be ending this relationship while she was enjoying it so much. Mark wasn't just a body. He was caring, considerate and funny. If she could, she would display him on her bedroom wall as a teaching aid. Just at the moment keeping him caged in her flat seemed to be the sensible option. *Could she go to the pub with him, could they go for a meal or the movies? Would it be possible for either of them to show off the other to their friends?* As much as she would like to tweet and Facebook her news to the world, she couldn't. Not yet. Not for a good while.

One of Julie's university friends had said back then that she could always tell when Julie had enjoyed rumpy-pumpy the night before because she'd walk around all day with a smile on her face. Julie had been very aware of this when she walked in to school yesterday. She had walked as quickly as her aching legs could go, after very little sleep and far too much sex.

Once all the pupils were in their classrooms and all the teachers were executing their lesson plans, she had slowly and guiltily driven out of school and back to her flat to be with Mark. She had never played hooky before. She smiled at the realisation that the person in charge of absences had had a day off to have it off over and over again.

But now the guilt had set in. *Had anyone noticed her come and go? What gave her the right to play fast and loose with the school rules*? But on the other hand, she had always struggled in every day, come rain, shine or hangover and she was sure the school would have coped without her for the day. It wouldn't have gone into special measures while she was missing, presumed observing lessons for most of the day.

But then there was the matter of Peter and his 64 million dollar question. Did she want to be considered for the post of Deputy Head? The question had been spinning round in her head for days and she was no nearer coming up with an answer. All she seemed able to do was generate loads more questions of her own. *Would Peter's offer have been made if the school had been judged by Ofsted as Good? Would accepting the position mean that she was stuck at Whatmore for another two years, if not longer? Was her job consuming too much of her life? Could she find satisfaction and happiness in another school? Did she not need a change of direction in her life? Was she a career woman or a woman that wanted a reliable man in her life and a couple of kids? Was she drinking too much? Was she putting on weight? Was she getting old?*

Julie looked at Mark. She was tempted to touch him but thought better of it.

She needed more thinking time. *Could she play for time? She could say she was interested and let the ball start rolling. This would give her a couple of months for the advert in the Times Educational Supplement and for shortlisting. She could show willing while looking around for other jobs and seeing how things developed with Mark. Better that than deflating Peter's expectations in a few hours' time. The poor bloke seemed under enough stress as it was. But what about if she went for the job, only to be beaten by someone else on the day? How would she cope with that?*

Her mind was spinning and she knew she couldn't go back to sleep. She moved down the bed and gently groped for Mark's wake-up button.

Charlie was also awake. He had quietly left the marital bed to relieve himself, returning with an empty bladder without disturbing his wife. While he was playing with his own wake-up button he was addressing some strangely philosophical concerns of his own. His full bladder in the middle of the night was telling him he was no longer young and he was worrying about his prostate. The women in his life were all telling him, *It doesn't matter; you're just tired. Next time it will be okay*. The more he heard this, the more he worried and the less well he performed. *Was he moving towards inadequate? Should he really be having a bit on the side at his age? Even a great looking bit with all the bits in the right places? She was a colleague with her own life and family. What in God's name did she need him for? Other than the obvious, which was not quite as obvious as it used to be. Why was he being so unfair on his wife? She was a lovely person. She put up with him and accepted him for what he was - a grown-up kid who hadn't really ever grown up. She made very few demands. All she wanted was an occasional new stick of furniture and occasional sex. Surely he could manage that?*

While trying to clumsily measure his erection under the duvet he also thought about his length of service. *When should he retire? Should he go now? Would he have enough pension to pay for golf clubs, tennis games and new settees? How long did he want to carry on doing this job? Should the school be looking for younger blood? Should he step down while he was on top of his game? He had had a great innings and the job would only get more difficult wouldn't it? Was this something he and his wife should discuss tonight?*

They had had a really pleasant evening. They'd talked and laughed across a restaurant table; had cuddled and held hands in the cinema like two teenagers on their first or second date and had fallen asleep having shared a bottle of wine and some long and loving kisses.

Charlie lay prone, quite impressed by his height and length at this time in the morning particularly after all the alcohol. *Was it a personal best? Perhaps it would be a good time to get a second opinion.* There were two possible approaches - the flattering salesman at the front door or the sneaky thief in through the back. He decided to slip in without knocking. He could be out again in three minutes without raising the alarm.

Neil hadn't heard from his Russian girl for a few days now but he was sure that she was too busy or too excited to contact him. It was 8.39am in Kubinka and she would be walking to work. She worked in a coffee bar in the city centre. She hated it and couldn't wait to leave the job and the country behind. She had the money Neil sent and would now be making plans to escape her dull life and live their dream. Sometimes, over the months, communication had been difficult so Neil wasn't worried. He was sure she wouldn't change her mind. He tossed and turned unable to get back to sleep.

Yesterday he had almost let slip that he was seeing someone. His excitement had almost got the better of him. It wasn't that he didn't trust Charlie, but he knew that once Charlie found out he was going to marry a Russian beauty the jokes would never stop. He have to be very careful not to give Charlie any hint of his plans when they were doing lunch duties together. Neil admired Charlie greatly. If he had created a virtual teacher on Sim School, it would be someone like Charlie Briggs. Confident, amusing, good looking and a magnet for the opposite sex. But Neil was hiding away in a world of secrets and mystery, never allowing his real self to be revealed to the giants who walk upright and breathe fresh air. Their worlds were very different and must be kept apart.

It was 4.48am and Sobia woke from a beautiful world in which she was married to an adoring husband, had two wonderful children and had given up her job because her husband wanted her to be happy and free from the day-to-day drudgery of life. In that dream-world her only action plan had been to grow old happily, protected and loved by all her family.

She opened her eyes and looked around her. She could just begin to pick out various landmarks in her bedroom. The wardrobe bought with wedding gift vouchers, the chest-of-drawers inherited some years ago and a set of ornate curtains that her mother-in-law made for her without consultation. She could hear the heavy breathing of her husband lying motionless on the bed that used to belong to his grandparents. Her life was not her own and neither was her bedroom. She wasn't sure where and when things had started to unravel but lying in a darkened room full of other people's memories Sobia knew it was too late to mend things.

She ought to talk to her husband about how she was feeling but that was never going to happen. She should go into school today and pick up where she had left off. She wasn't too sure if that was going to happen either.

Yesterday she had arrived home from school in the middle of the day, undetected, and lived her dream for a few hours. She had sat down for an hour with a cup of tea and some biscuits watching mindless television. It was wonderful. She then cooked a few things and tidied a few rooms. Then she sat down and watched some more TV and drank more tea with more biscuits. She was uninterrupted, peaceful and calm. She was able to spend a happy hour with her children when they came home from school and then her husband arrived, armed with flowers to assuage his guilty conscience. The night was pleasant - no cross words or corporal punishment and the twins were well behaved and she wanted more of this life. She wanted her dream. What would it take for it all to come true for ever and a day? Well, perhaps not forever but perhaps for one more day. She could legitimately have one more day at home. Once her husband had left for work she could run the children to school and then have a sudden bout of sickness. If her neighbours saw her return she would hold her stomach as she walked slowly to the front door. She could then shut the door and have the house to herself for six or seven hours. She could watch more television, cook and clean a little and drink tea and eat biscuits a lot. She deserved this. School could manage without her. She was determined not to feel guilty about lying to her husband. He was a mean bully. She would have a day to herself to spite him.

The room started to get lighter and Sobia started to make out the detail on the wooden bedroom furniture and curtains. She wondered if in her husband's beloved shed she would be able to find a sharp axe or a can of petrol.

Peter, unlike the rest of his senior team, was not tossing or turning in bed at 5.00am. He was in his study in what had become a routine he couldn't shake off. He was averaging four to five hours sleep a night and yet always felt wide awake until evening when, having finished his paperwork, he would start watching a documentary or an episode from a detective series only to be woken by the theme music over the end credits or by Rachel nudging him and telling him to go to bed.

He sat at his desk. The room was lit by the computer screen, a table lamp and the red light of the coffee percolator. He would sit there for an hour before jumping in the shower. He rather enjoyed this time of day. His study was filled with the gentle and witty sounds of his favourite rock band of all time – Caravan – and with the smell of simmering coffee. He loved the smell of percolation in the morning.

Peter wasn't thinking much about the day ahead. The meetings with Charlie and Julie. The fall-out from the parents who'd received his Ofsted letter. The assembly message he was going to give. What he needed to say to *Call Me Rick*. This could all wait until the school day began. Instead he sat there with his music and his coffee, in splendid isolation, thinking profound thoughts about his life in teaching, secretly relishing the fear that his entire profession was heading down the tubes to oblivion.

Perhaps, he ought to do something with all of the pent up emotion he couldn't display in any classroom. Perhaps he ought to write a book about Ofsted and the effect it had on a school. He could write it anonymously and publish it on the day he retired or was fired. Perhaps he needed to start fairly soon.

CHAPTER 10

The main hall was silent momentarily as Mr Burlington finished reading Charles Causley's poem about Timothy Winters, bringing to a conclusion his assembly message. It was doubtful that the theme of good fortune versus real poverty and starvation had reached the majority of the pupils condemned to sit through it. Most had switched off pretty much as soon as he started, plunging gormlessly into a zombie state, re-charging their teenage batteries.

At the end of the daily ritual of a formal assembly the pupils would be let loose to cause some form of havoc in any number of school sporting events involving the Olympic disciplines of throwing, hitting, chasing, screaming, swearing and farting. The boys were no better either. The first lesson buzzer sounded and World War Z began for the day.

"That's a piece from my past," Charlie announced as he caught up with Peter in the corridor.

"I hadn't got you down as the poetic type Mr Briggs."

"No. It's true it wouldn't be in my top ten of things to do with a spare afternoon!"

As they walked to Peter's office they punctuated their own conversation with helpful observations for some of the straggling zombies.

"You really shouldn't be doing that!" and "I don't think you should be doing that!" "Do you think you should be doing that?" and simplest of all, "Stop doing that!"

They both acknowledged Penny at her work station, Charlie, less formally than Peter.

"Penny, no calls for a while, thanks." Peter said.

Charlie winked at Penny behind Peter's back and passed his hand across his neck, as if to suggest that he was a condemned man, before closing the door.

"Coffee, Charlie?"

"I'll have a hot black one thanks."

They settled with their coffee in two of the comfier chairs.

"I wanted to speak to you about a possible structure change in the SLT."

"No problem." Charlie tried to stay calm. Below the surface his mind raced.

"You lead a pastoral team that works really well but we don't have an equivalent for teaching and learning. Julie is the nearest we've got but her time is spent on cover, curriculum and timetable matters. Neil and Sobia have very specific roles and clearly have their work cut out with IT and finances. I think we need another deputy head to lead on improving pupil and teacher performance. How would you feel about that? Obviously you would be the senior and first to sit in my chair if I was run over by a bus one day..."

"I think it's a really sensible idea...not the bus thing...I mean. If the school can afford it. I'm not precious about my status. But...be honest with me, Peter. Is this your way of trying to replace me? Is the bus heading in my direction?"

"No, not at all. I want you to work here until you are ready to go. You do a brilliant job, I know that, the staff know that and Ofsted recognised that. Why would I want you to go?"

"The thing is I'm not sure how long I want to carry on. There is part of me that wants to go fairly soon but I want it to be when I'm ready and not when others think I should."

"I know exactly how you feel. I've had real serious doubts about my future since Ofsted. I'm sure Ann Brown would like me gone so that she could bring some new young blood in. But why should I give her the satisfaction of falling on my own sword?"

"The job will only get tougher from now on and I don't want to be one of those teachers that hang on and on and then keel over and die in their first week of retirement. I suppose... don't quote me on this, I may think of going at the end of the year or more likely next...unless I was given a massive golden goodbye and then I'd walk away on Friday."

"I think you only get a pay off if you're doing a bad job."

"So what are you saying? Shall I start being bad from now on?"

"You've always been a bad boy, Charlie, but you seem to always get away with it!"

"Not always. Ask my ex-wives!"

"Hah. Well you'll probably outlast me."

"So when do you want to move on this second deputy idea?"

"As quickly as I can. It will be good for the school and a smart addition to the Ofsted action plan."

"I expect Julie will apply."

"I'll have a quiet word with her this morning about the possibility. See if she would be interested."

"I bet she'd snap your hand off if you offered her the position."

Peter felt himself blushing slightly as he agreed.

The revolving door magically transformed Charlie into Penny who then ushered in Julie who had been hovering outside.

Julie sat in her usual chair with her usual notepad beside her and composed herself, rehearsing in her mind the various responses she could give to Peter's questions.

Peter eased himself down into his chair and began to drink his fourth mug of coffee of the day. He felt obliged to start with preliminary small talk as Julie was not forthcoming. He stared at her for a moment and detected a change in her appearance but couldn't put his finger on it, although he would have liked to.

"We don't seem to have had a chance to catch up recently but I do need to fill you in on my thinking regarding the second deputy head position. As I said the other day, I'd be very interested in knowing if you wanted to apply for it."

"Sorry Peter, I haven't been avoiding you. I've been up to my ears in work and I needed time to consider." Julie moved into her prepared speech effortlessly. She told him how flattered she was to be considered for the post.

Peter nodded, bracing himself for the *BUT* from Julie. He could sense she was about to turn him down but the coup-de-gras did not come. Instead, Julie said she would certainly be applying for the post. Peter smiled and nodded some more. In some bizarre way it was as if Peter had won the first round of a reality TV show. He assumed Julie was telling him she'd be happy to work for him and stay until she retired.

Julie's view from across the table was myopic in comparison and didn't extend further than the next few days. Her future vision revolved around sharing a bed with Mark in the evenings until the weekend and then sharing a bed with Mark until Monday morning. Her loyalty and commitment to her job had gone, her need for wine was drying up and her addiction was changing, from grape to grope.

Her tactics had fooled Peter completely. He had not a clue just how far apart their thought processes were and happily launched into a detailed discussion about the improvement agenda and the action plan, failing to spot Julie's successful masking of how little by way of lesson observations she had carried out.

Peter brought the conversation around to the place it had launched from. "So if you were to apply and get the deputy's post, would you see that as a stepping stone to being a Head or don't you fancy the big chair?"

"To be honest I haven't really thought that far ahead. What I do know is that I want to enjoy my life and not spend every waking hour marking, planning lessons and telling pupils and other teachers that they could do better." Julie had been caught off guard.

"It sounds as if you are not too happy with life at the moment. Would this possible promotion make things any better?"

"I don't know. I might decide to go for a complete change of direction. Get married, bring up three adorable kids and live in a little cottage in Dreamland."

"I see. Any sign of Prince Charming as yet?"

"One or two frogs and…nothing to speak about…really. I'll make sure you're the first to know if I get hit by Cupid's arrow."

"I don't suppose its easy meeting people after long days at work?"

"Tell me about it. I'm too tired to go out in the week. I try to socialise at weekends but most of my mates are in long-term relationships and that can be a bit awkward."

"Apparently the internet is the new way to meet people. These dating sites are supposed to be safe and relatively successful," said Peter, sounding as if he knew what he was talking about.

Julie was feeling a little uncomfortable herself. She hadn't wanted to admit to Peter that she'd become lonely and desperate over the last few months. She also didn't want the world to know about the young frog she was trying to turn into a prince. And she certainly didn't want to reveal anything else of her new undercover life wearing Victoria's Secrets.

They sat there for a few moments sharing thoughts and emotions without speaking. Julie felt sad for Peter. He was over the hill, possibly in a loveless marriage and having to take pleasure in conversing with and looking at younger women on the staff. In turn Peter felt sad for Julie as a thirty-something without a partner, climbing the hill on her own and her only companions seemed to be father figures.

They mutually realised their meeting was over and agreed to catch up in a couple of days' time.

The revolving door turned yet again and this time Penny sat briefly in front of Peter before he could catch breath.

"Just thought I'd let you know some parents have been on the phone, worried about their children's education, bless them. I tried to say all of the right things but a couple of them would like to hear the bull from the horse's mouth. I said you would ring them later on this morning. Here are their phone numbers. And you ought to know that Sobia rang earlier on to say she's not coming in today. She sounded a little strange but she didn't seem to want to talk."

"Thanks Penny. I will ring the parents now - get it out of the way. I don't think I'll ring Sobia. Maybe she just needs a little time away from this hell hole."

"Don't we all?"

Once Penny left Peter made the calls to the parents. In less than twenty minutes he'd managed to convince both anxious mums that the school was fine and dandy and that they shouldn't transfer their children elsewhere. A pity really as Peter would have loved to see the back of one of the boys.

Peter then tried to phone his chair of governors.

Ann Brown, along with a coach-load of other sixty and seventy somethings, was listening to a talk by a well-travelled elderly gentlemen on the wildlife encountered in his three month educational trip to South America. Ann's interest in the Brazilian rain forest was waning after the first hour of his talk and the umpteenth slide of native birds that all looked similar to the ones she saw every morning in her back garden. She was quite relieved when her muted mobile informed her of a missed call from Peter Burlington.

"Hi, sorry I missed you. I've been bird watching," she announced.

"Do you want to talk later? It can wait."

"No please don't, I need a reason to be away from a lecture on lesser spotted tits by an overly spotted twit."

"Sounds like being back at school, Ann. Anyway, I just wanted to get back to you on a couple of things. First, the letter about Ofsted went out last night. We've had a handful of concerned parents but we seem to have allayed their fears. As we speak World War Three hasn't broken out."

"Good. What about the local rag?" asked Ann.

"Nothing as yet but I expect someone from The Gazette will be phoning us up soon. I think I'll ask them to meet me and then I can give them a tour of the best elements of the school."

"I think you're right. It's harder for them to write a damning article if you're seen to be the good guy doing a good job..."

"Even if it's not a good school?"

"Well yes, even then."

"Well we have to be on alert if we do get the call. By the way I'm at the Heads' conference tomorrow but I'll make sure Charlie is briefed if the Gazette phones up. And talking of Charlie, I've shared the notion of a second deputy with him and Julie…both supported the idea."

"What was Julie's response?"

"I'm fairly certain she'll apply for the position. She seems happy here and it may do her good to have a new challenge - re-invent herself."

"Anyone else on SLT feeling the pressure at the moment?"

Peter paused. He didn't want to mention Sobia's tears or Neil coming out of the closet the other night. Nor that Charlie might be leaving at the end of the year.

"No, we're all busy doing nothing, trying not to find lots of things not to do…"

"What is it with you and Disney?"

"I think I've been very restrained recently. But one day, when I retire, I want to take the whole family out to Orlando for a month and live the dream with Mickey and Minnie. Do you know, if I could raise the funds, I'd take all of our pupils on a two week educational school trip out to Disney World. Walt Disney certainly knew how to inspire children far more than any wicked secretary of state for education could."

"Peter, I've got to go, it looks like the bird man from Brazil is finishing off and I have to say something complimentary about him. I think we ought to mention the second deputy position at the next staffing committee meeting don't you?"

"Yes. We need to start the ball rolling quickly. Give me a ring later in the week and we can sort out the next steps. Have a good day." Peter finished in a mock American accent.

Penny broke into his good mood. Richard Perry wanted to see him urgently. Peter said that it would be fine for Richard to come down up to his office in the next fifteen minutes. Seconds after Peter put the phone down, *Call Me*

Rick walked straight in. He'd been waiting outside for the go ahead from Penny.

"Hello...what can I do for you?" asked Peter unsmiling. Mickey Mouse had gone, heading for a dark hole in the skirting board.

"I don't think I can do this anymore. I've got Ms Osborne and Mrs Slater putting me under the microscope and questioning everything I do. The department is complaining that they're being treated as if they were all amateurs and I feel my position is being compromised. I can't magically turn this all around. I'm a good teacher and I can lead a good team but this isn't what I expected to take on. I can get another job, somewhere I feel happy and appreciated and not have to put up with all of this hassle."

Richard was holding his head in his hands and didn't hear Peter's mouthed reply. "Perhaps you can you find me a job like that too."

If Peter hadn't handled Sobia as well as he wished, he was even worse now with Richard. He could empathise somewhat but couldn't find the right words to say. Glib utterances, *Never-mind* or *Worse things happen at sea* wouldn't cut it. In fact it was just another character flaw like all the others his wife Rachel was forever reminding him about.

So Peter sat there waiting for the hissy fit to fade before attempting the sort of practical conversation he could cope with.

"Richard...Rick...it's a difficult time. Jo and Julie have been put in place to support you, not to undermine you. In six months or so the department will have been turned around and we'll look back at this as a blip. I will give you this advice free of charge. One of the attributes you'll always need to do this mad job is self-belief. There is one person who will consistently need convincing that you can do the job of teaching kids and leading adults, and that person is you. And if others can help you improve, then let them help you. On a personal note, try to be positive in the classroom, in the corridors and in the staff room even when you feel like crap. Somebody told me once that to be an effective teacher, first you have to be an effective actor. We have to convince our audiences we know what we're doing and are enjoying it..."

Peter's Churchillian speech fizzled out before he got to fighting on the beaches. He was generally happy with it however, because he'd relayed several important subliminal messages. *Stop whinging, grow a pair, don't think you can have any time off and maybe, just maybe, one day I will give you a decent reference!*

Richard Perry seemed to take in the speech and assured Peter that he would try to be a better man, teacher and head of department. Peter made such supportive noises as he could stomach to utter and Richard left feeling better for venting. Within a couple of hours Richard had forgotten most of the important elements of the conversation and regained his self-belief that he was right and everybody else was wrong.

It was roughly lunchtime, give or take a few minutes. School lunch was a moveable feast. Not because the teachers couldn't tell the time. Peter was fairly convinced that almost all of his staff could do that and tie their own shoelaces. It was that the end of Period 3 was often dependent on the behaviour of the class. Good-behaviour meant they got out of the classroom on the buzzer but a badly behaved class could be anything from five minutes early to five minutes late. Stronger teachers would keep the little darlings in for the extra moments after as an immediate punishment while weaker ones could be subject to early abandonment by the cleverest and naughtiest pupils.

Peter told Penny that he was going outside and might be some time. He made his way along the icy corridors to the dining hall. As Peter approached, he could smell the inviting and heady combination of cottage bolognaise, battered custard, sponge sausages, tikka donuts, French pies and spaghetti fingers. He decided to stand and deliver his lunch duty, grab a take away sandwich and devour it back in his den once the masses had had their fill. As he approached the counter to greet the red-faced and frazzled cooks and servers he realised he was not alone. Behind him in a neat orderly single line were Charlie, Neil and Julie.

"All present and correct, Sir!" joked Charlie saluting in military fashion. "Where would you like us Captain?"

"I suggest you and Neil man the machine gun turret and Julie and I will take the high ground over by the water fountain with our bazookas."

"And very nice bazookas they are....." Charlie quipped glancing in the general direction of Julie's ribs.

"Charlie!!!" was the chorus from the other three senior leaders. Charlie was incorrigible: PE not PC. But everyone loved him, accepting him for what he was without taking offence. All he need do was smile to get away with anything.

And so the four brave senior leaders positioned themselves for a long, hot encounter and ultimately won the battle of the Little Big Corn, recapturing the dining facilities from the food fighters. During the mayhem Peter hoped he'd managed to communicate to Charlie that he would be at a conference tomorrow and that the Gazette might be in contact over the Ofsted inspection.

Peter made his way back to his office to find Brian Green talking to Penny. His heart sank. *Could he eat his sandwich while discussing important union matters or would he have to wait until after the meeting was over?*

"Good to see you Brian. Come on in."

Coffees poured, Peter offered Brian a biscuit which he accepted. This meant Peter could legitimately eat his sandwich after explaining he had been on duty through the lunch break. Brian was happy for Peter to eat but less sympathetic about him having missed lunch time. Brian believed that it was the duty of senior leaders to cover breaks so his members could have their hard-earned respite from the rigours of teaching. *After all*, Brian thought, *SLT don't do anything else all day.*

The discussion took a couple of minutes to get underway as the union rep had to digest a mouthful of stale Hob Nob and the Head was deploying his teeth to penetrate the sandwich wrapping.

"Perhaps we ought to meet on a regular basis while we're being monitored by the HMI. It would be helpful to pre-empt any staff issues." Peter started in his usual conciliatory fashion.

"That would be useful. Staff welfare is my main concern and it's important in this difficult time that SLT and the teacher unions work together to protect the workforce. I've attended several union meetings recently and the common issue with so-called failing schools is that the staff have been made to work harder and longer without any compensation or recognition. Of course the Department for Education has set this impossibly short time line to improve all these failing schools and yet they offer very little financial or personnel support to help them. So the NUT is monitoring the actions taken by Heads and trying to make sure that the decisions taken are in the interests of staff as well as pupils. I'll be particularly interested in the lesson observation strategy. As I said at the department meeting the other day, this could be a knee jerk reaction. Staff shouldn't be continuously observed. That shouldn't and can't happen…"

Peter nodded and took another bite of his sandwich, expecting Brian to continue his speech, but he didn't. Indeed he seemed to expect a meaningful response.

Peter cleared his throat and said "I think the NUT are right to monitor the whole Ofsted process. We know for sure that the Department for Education is desperate to prove to the world that our education system is improving and improving quickly. So they're fixated with quick wins and if that causes casualties along the way, so be it. Like you, I want a sustainable and sensible solution to the predicament we are facing. However, if a teacher isn't meeting the required standard then I have to take action against him or her…and I will. Our classroom monitoring system will have to be more robust but we're not observing for the sake of it. I was talking with Julie Osborne this morning and she is going to put emphasis on teachers who are not consistently *Good* or better. Is that a problem for you?"

"So what you're saying is that your judgments on the teachers before Ofsted came in were inaccurate and now you're going to start all over again?" stated Brian provocatively.

"The problems with our assessments is only part of the story. Some teachers didn't perform as well as usual when an inspector saw them. Some of our high performing teachers won't need to be seen again because they're consistently effective in the classroom. So to answer your question, we're not starting again from scratch."

"Glad to hear it. What about departments that were criticised in the report?"

"I suppose you mean Maths. We're helping Richard Perry with his team. It's not easy for him to do it on his own and so we've got Jo Slater to act as critical friend and Julie is supporting the other team members. I spoke with Richard today. I'll be honest with you, he's feeling the pressure but we're trying all we can to support him."

Brian nodded and made a few scribbled notes. "And what about leadership training?"

"We have Clive Howell from the local authority doing Monday night's twilight training session as a starting point. We'll follow that up with specific training for middle or indeed senior leaders who require development."

Brian Green rolled his eyes at the mention of Clive Howell but thought better than to criticise the school for providing training even if it was going to be led by a buffoon.

Peter continued, "Brian, I'd like you to be involved in the action plan, perhaps at our next meeting I can show you a draft…I'd welcome your thoughts."

"I'd be happy to help." The union rep didn't realise that he'd been played.

"And by the way, I'll be observing the History department in the next two weeks and union reps aren't exempt. Make sure your pupils' books are marked up-to-date."

"Thanks."

The meeting finished with a date put in the diary for later in the month and Peter's door stopped revolving for the first time in the day. He tackled his in-tray, signed various letters, wrote a few emails, made a few phone calls and drank several mugs of coffee. The pupils left for the day and staff gradually drained from the building. Penny poked her head around the door and wished him luck at the Heads' conference and said that she'd be sure to speak to Sobia if she returned to school.

An hour or so later Peter looked up from his desk and noticed Neil leaving the building carrying various bits of technology and Julie walking to her car. *Was that a short skirt she was wearing?*

Some ten minutes later Charlie, carrying his gym bag, breezed by Peter's office to confirm that he wouldn't spend all the school's reserves while Peter was at the conference.

After that the only signs of life in the corridors were the cleaners trying to erase all evidence of the madness of the day without working too hard.

Peter wondered why he wasn't going home yet. There was no reason to stay and yet he didn't feel he could go home. *Did he feel the need to stay at school longer than anyone else on the staff? Was it his self-imposed detention for doing badly in the Ofsted inspection? Was he setting a good example to the rest of the staff? Perhaps he was setting a bad example...they all needed to leave the school as soon as they could and get a life.*

He should be on his way home to Rachel to excitedly tell her the events of the day. But the days of enthusiastic engagement at home were over. He could manage the act at school but at night his façade folded and his character slumped onto the couch. When Peter talked to Rachel about his working day it was usually edited low lights of issues that she couldn't understand or help him solve. Over the years Rachel had learnt to listen and sympathise and then move the conversation away from Whatmore. That's what he needed, he supposed, distraction and escape. She fulfilled the necessary role of making Peter feel human, after a fashion.

Peter decided to make a move. Just a small, undramatic move; shutting down his computer, putting various folders into his briefcase and standing up. The blood went to his head.

CHAPTER 11

At 8.15 am Julie pinned the cover list on the staff noticeboard. By the time she had pushed in the last drawing pin she was aware of a group of teachers massing behind her. They were not interested at all in their colleagues' health but their own free periods. If Julie did manage to get the deputy position then arranging cover would be the first job she would jettison.

Turning to walk out the door, she remembered she hadn't included the Head on the cover list. In one sense there was no need. He didn't teach any classes, but the staff ought to know he was absent and that Charlie would be conducting the staff briefing and handling any emergencies. She fought her way back through the scrum to scribble a note on the bottom of the cover sheet.

As she turned away for a second time Julie noticed Corinne Peckett, a fairly recent addition to the teaching staff, working on a computer at the back of the staff room. Julie made her way over.

"Hi Corinne," said Julie, deliberately bright and breezy. There was no response. Corinne was wearing headphones under her long brunette hair. Julie touched Corinne's shoulder and made her jump. "Hi Corinne," Julie repeated herself.

"Sorry, I was miles away."

"I just wanted to remind you that I'm coming in to see you teach period 2 today. Charlie Briggs will be with me as the Head's out today."

"I hadn't forgotten. It's kept me awake most of the night, worrying about how the class is going to behave and if they can make progress in the time you are observing..."

"Look, just do the best you can. We don't expect things to be perfect, you have only been teaching for a few months..."

"I've got some difficult boys in my Year 9 class and I don't want to fail my observation."

"Corinne, there is no failing here. We're coming in to see if we can suggest ways to improve your teaching. Please don't worry."

"Thanks Ms Osborne." Corinne returned to her power points.

Ms Osborne, thought Julie. *She's clearly placed me into the next generation, the generation that doesn't party, the generation that wears Marks and Sparks clothes and the generation that likes to be called by their last names. When did I get moved up? It's not fair. I'm dating a man much younger than me. Surely that makes me an honorary member of the twenties club? And another thing...maybe I won't be Ms Osborne forever; perhaps my last name may change one day...* Julie headed for the door and was met by Charlie laughing and joking with a couple of teachers as he walked into the staff room.

"Morning gorgeous," Charlie said as his eyes met Julie's.

"Good morning, Mr Briggs. I might as well stay here and give you moral support at the briefing."

"My morals need all the support they can get!"

"So I've been told by half the women in the local community."

"Only half? But thanks, Julie, I'd appreciate it...in case anybody asks a question with words of two syllables or more."

Charlie's briefing was brief, sharp and to the point but still about ten times more engaging and funnier than Peter delivering similar material. Julie stood next to Charlie showing support and indicating a bond that was slowly growing in strength. Once the messages were given and any questions answered, the teachers headed out to their assigned classrooms.

"Can you spare some time before we observe Corinne?" asked Charlie.

"Yes, sure."

"Do you mind if we meet in my office. I want to check on a few pastoral issues first. Can you pop down at about 9.30?"

"No problem. See you in a bit." Julie expecting a rude rejoinder but none came. Julie was a little disappointed.

When Julie knocked on Charlie's office door and walked in, Charlie and the Head of Year 11 were in the middle of a lively discussion. "Sorry, do you want me to come back in five minutes?"

"No come on in. We were finished," replied Charlie. As the other woman got up to leave Charlie's office, Julie caught the look on her face and the hint of tears in her eyes. The door closed rather too forcefully.

"Everything okay?" asked Julie.

"Difference of opinion over a pastoral matter."

Charlie volunteered this without looking directly at Julie. He was almost blushing and she decided not to push it.

"You wanted a quick word before we observe?"

"Yes. Not about Corinne, I want to talk about you, so you don't need to make any notes."

"Sounds ominous, Charlie. What have I done?"

"Julie, stop thinking you're in the wrong all the time. You're one of only a few members of staff who's pretty much faultless whatever they do."

It was Julie's turn to blush.

"I wanted a chat about your position here. You may have already made your mind up about the new deputy's job but I wanted to just say a couple of things. Is that okay?"

"Fine, Charlie, but this might be a bit difficult."

"Why's that?"

"Because I've never ever had a serious conversation with you and I'm going to be wondering when the punch line's coming."

"Am I that bad? The class clown with no heart or soul?" Charlie looked down at his desk and Julie started to get worried.

"No I didn't mean it like that. All I meant was....." She stopped mid-sentence glimpsing Charlie's beaming smile. "You are impossible. Did you just ask me along to your office to make fun of me or was it to make some more inappropriate sexual innuendos or worse try to lure me into bed?" She reached despairingly for a tissue and dabbed at her eyes.

"No. God no. Sorry Julie, I didn't mean....no I really wanted to talk to you about...." It was Charlie's turn to break off, realising that he too had been had. Julie had removed the tissue to produce a full beam that dazzled the deputy.

"Touché!" That moment of intimacy was stronger and more sincere than Charlie had ever experienced in any of his one-to-ones with the Head of Year 11.

Once they had both composed themselves Charlie continued with his serious attempt to put Julie's mind at ease.

"Not only do I support having a second deputy I'd also support you being it. The other thing I want you to know is that I am considering retirement at the end of this academic year or next, so that could mean you becoming the senior deputy quite quickly. That's got to help if you want to go for headships. I know I'm planning your career for you, so tell me to butt out if you want to, but I thought it would be useful to know what my plans are."

"Thanks Charlie. I've told Peter I'll apply. I just wasn't sure if I should move to another school to be a deputy, perhaps a different type of school before considering headship. What do you think?" asked Julie.

"Look, you're great with the kids here and when you apply for headships you can say you played a major role in getting the school to *Good*...You are happy here?"

"Most of the time. I have my down days, like everyone else."

"Then go for the position here, stay two or three years and then apply somewhere else for a headship. Simples!"

"Yeah, thanks. That's good advice, Charlie but I'm not sure if I want to carry on in teaching for the rest of my life."

"Why ever not? You're just the sort of person the profession needs."

"But there's part of me that wants to do something different."

"Like what?"

"I don't know. Back pack around South America, set up my own business, have kids and live off the state."

"Sounds like you've got more thinking to do but it doesn't stop you applying."

"No. I assure you I will apply. And what about you, retiring so early? What's that about?" Julie needed to vacate the spotlight.

"There are lots of golf courses and sandy beaches on my bucket list and the only major item on the fuckit list is Whatmore. Excuse my French! So I may go this year, or if not, definitely next year. I don't want to have a heart attack or stroke at my desk."

It was Julie who found it almost impossible to suppress any attempt at sexual innuendo at this last remark.

"Is it scary....the thought of stopping work?"

"No, I'm looking forward to doing what I want to do and at my pace."

"How about your wife?"

"Mrs Briggs the Third will have a lot of jobs for me to do, I'm sure. It'll have to be a trade-off between screw driver and golf driver. But it will be good to take Mrs B on holidays and play some tennis together from time to time."

"It sounds great. If only I could find my own sugar daddy who would take me away from all of this." Julie could feel her cheeks warm up again as the two of them sat imagining future days.

"I think it's time to observe Corinne," said Charlie.

They both left the dreamy realm of romantic sunny beaches and headed for Room 147.

An hour and ten minutes later Julie returned to her office, having observed Corinne's lesson and briefly discussed her view with Charlie. Now her immediate priorities were to make a drink and text Mark. Both hot and steamy. She sat down to gather her thoughts before Corinne arrived for her feedback only to be interrupted by Jo Slater.

"Hi Julie, can I have a quick word?"

"Come in. Have a seat. Would you like a drink?" Julie was already sounding like a deputy.

"I've just had one. I like your dress. The colour really suits you."

"Thank you. I'm updating my wardrobe from frumpy to less-frumpy!"

"More like eye-catching into hot! Is this because you fancied a change or because you fancy a fella?"

Julie, caught slightly off-guard hesitated. "Erm...a little of both I suppose." To add to her embarrassment her personal mobile, lying on her coffee table pinged an X-rated reply. Julie made a grab for it, afraid that Jo would pick it up and confiscate it or worse, read the message.

"On cue. Please feel free to reply. I don't want to come between true love."

"No it's fine. He can wait." A mistake but it was too late to correct herself. Before she knew it, Julie was telling Jo about the gorgeous man she'd met and how young he'd made her feel again. Hence the new clothes.

Jo had intended to talk about Richard Perry but this was much more interesting territory. With the flood gates open, Julie's pent up secrets spilled out and without being too explicit she let Jo know that her man was like a young, wild animal in her bedroom. Jo, ever the English teacher, appreciated the imagery and wanted detail. The knock on Julie's door brought them both back to the reality of a school life more ordinary. There had been no mention of Maths and they had only just dipped their toes into Julie's enticingly murky pool of secrets. They decided to continue at lunch time...there was so much to talk about.

Corinne Peckett stood waiting until Jo took her leave and Julie invited her in.

"Now before I tell you what Charlie...Mr Briggs and I observed, why don't you tell me what you thought of that lesson." It would be easier if Corinne also thought the lesson was bad. If she thought it was good then it was going to be a difficult feedback session.

It took twenty three minutes and two tissues to prove that Corinne might not be much good as a teacher but she was a rather better judge of lessons.

Julie's task was to pick Corinne up off the floor and try to find positives from a sixty minute lesson that felt as if it had lasted a day.

Corinne was a product of the Teach First system, a clever idea in a long line of clever initiatives from the Department for Education, to make teaching a desirable and easy career path by fast tracking brainy students from fancy universities into brainless schools. Six weeks and a crash course in how to teach, and they were standing in front of thirty pupils who couldn't tell their left wing from their right. Corinne might not be posh but she wasn't part of today's suburban society. Her cloistered and protected life so far made it difficult to cope with street wise kids who could and would strip her of confidence, credibility and car tyres while she was looking the other way. To be fair to Corinne, she knew she had a lot to learn but now a rain of criticism was pouring and she no longer owned a brolly - it had been stolen from her classroom.

Julie fundamentally disagreed with the Teach First system. She couldn't see that this new breed of super teachers were so intelligent that they could learn how to teach during the summer holidays. But the school had been desperate for another Maths teacher and they had to work to get Corinne to make the grade.

Julie tried to tease out the few positives of an awful lesson. She exaggerated the brief moments that were satisfactory before she gave Corinne three action points to work on over the next week before her next observation.

"But how would Ofsted have graded my lesson? Would I have passed?" Corinne asked in all innocence with a double helping of naivety.

Julie so wanted to be positive, to encourage Corinne and make her feel it was all worthwhile. If she told Corinne the truth about her teaching she might not come into school tomorrow or ever again. So Julie did what Peter would have done. She told half-truths. "They would have picked up the better elements of the lesson. Overall I don't think we're a secure *Good* yet but I can see green shoots and you're certainly getting better."

Corinne started to perk up as the long range forecast seemed to suggest some sunnier days ahead. The stark reality for Julie was that Whatmore needed a Maths teacher standing up in front of six or seven classes of pupils and Corinne was the body they had. Julie had sold her soul and become pragmatic and Machiavellian overnight. A Deputy Head in waiting.

As Corinne left Julie's office to recuperate over lunch time Jo reappeared clutching sandwiches. "I thought we might need to feed our hunger."

Meanwhile, in Peter's office, Penny was breaking bread with Sobia. Sobia had returned to work that morning and Penny arranged for the cook to bring her a plate of vegetarian sandwiches and some fruit juice.

"That's very nice of you. I know you and Peter are worried about me but I'm alright. Really I am." The expression on her face told a different story.

"That would make you the only person at Whatmore who is. Look you can tell me to mind my own business but something's bothering you and I want to know if there's anything I can do to help."

"I suppose that's the problem, Penny, I never have time off, I work too hard and take things too seriously and exhaustion just got the better of me. I just needed to re-charge my batteries and I feel much better now." Sobia was trying hard to convince Penny and herself that she was now charged and ever ready.

"So how are you going to stop this happening again?"

"I don't think it will. I just needed to be normal for a day without the pressures of work and...home."

"Are Peter and the governors putting you under too much pressure or are you putting yourself under undue pressure?" asked Penny.

"I'm pretty sure it's me. I want everything just right. I want the books to balance and I want my life..."

"Straight?"

"Yes, I suppose so."

"Does your husband think you work too hard?"

"He's more concerned about how I'm failing as a wife and mother. He gets very cross with me."

"Have you talked to him about your feelings? Perhaps you could sit down together and see if there are changes you can make."

"I never get time to sit. Once I get home, I'm cooking, cleaning and looking after the children."

"So what does your husband do in the evenings?"

"He comes home later than me and then he's quite tired and needs some peace and quiet..."

"So the children are mostly your responsibility?"

"He does help out at weekends sometimes..."

"That's good of him. How does he treat you, if you don't mind me asking?"

"He's fine." Sobia's manner became more defensive.

"He needs to take care of you if you're feeling down. I'm sure he'll be more thoughtful since you had to go home."

"I don't expect so."

"Why ever not?"

"Because...because he doesn't know I had the day off yesterday and was home early the day before!" Sobia's demeanour changed again and her eyes darkened like a storm cloud.

"Why didn't you tell him? You can't expect him to be sympathetic if he doesn't know you're struggling."

"I don't want to cause another argument so it's easier for me to stay silent."

"I don't understand, Sobia. You're such a strong and formidable woman at work and yet you're worried about what your husband will say..."

"And do..." As Sobia uttered these two powerful words the heavens opened and the two women held each other tight sheltering from the storm for the remainder of their lunchtime. Very little else was said or needed to be said.

As the bell sounded for the end of lunch time Charlie and Neil were encouraging the pupils to leave the dining hall and return their trays.

"I wonder where Julie got to today, I saw her earlier and she didn't say she couldn't help out. Still, we managed heroically, didn't we?"

"I'm not sure I'd cope if you weren't here," said Neil.

"I'm sure you would. The more you're seen around the school the more the pupils will accept you. Just doing this dinner duty will help you because they'll realise you're an important player in the life of the school - not just the guy who fixes computers."

"I admit it's good to get out of my office occasionally."

"So shadow me for a day and see how the pastoral system works. It can't be much fun just spending your time in a darkened room."

"You forget, I'm surrounded by Windows!" Neil's techie joke almost backfired because Charlie didn't immediately get it.

"Sorry, bit slow on the uptake there."

"Okay. I will pop down to the pastoral offices to see what goes on sometime."

"No problem."

With that Charlie headed for Peter's office. He found Sobia and Penny in the act of vacating it. Sobia walked straight past without acknowledging him.

"How goes it Mrs Hinks?"

"Okay, Mr Briggs. Do you want to use the Head's office?"

"No I was just coming to see if The Gazette's made contact?"

"Not a word. Have you eaten, Charlie?"

"Why are you proposing to cook me a meal tonight?"

"Not unless Mr Hinks and Mrs Briggs are invited! It's just that there are some spare sandwiches left. Do you want them or you could take them for your poor suffering team."

"I'll take you up on that. And I've freed myself up this afternoon to walk around poking my deputy head into lessons. Everything alright with Sobia?"

"Yes, fine." With this lie the conversation was over. Charlie scooped up the sandwiches and headed for the classroom maze. Penny smiled to herself. Charlie was so obviously trying desperately to act as a Head would. She knew his good intentions would be side-tracked on his travels by sporty, youngish, male teachers who were free and willing to talk about football and sporty, youngish, female teachers who were free and attractive. He probably wouldn't actually set foot inside a classroom but he would walk the team talk and keepy-uppy the spirits. Penny didn't know if she should ring Peter or wait until tomorrow morning to tell him about Sobia. She had to tell him. It was just a question of when.

CHAPTER 12

Peter had driven away from the flashy conference hotel early, claiming the need to go back to school for various meetings. He had put some petrol in the car and bought some comfort food from the garage. He was in the familiar lane he normally took as a short cut home. He reversed his car into the gateway to a farmer's field, turned the ignition off, unwrapped a chocolate bar and sat looking blankly around at the countryside.

There were no vital meetings commanding his attendance. In reality, he just needed to leave. He wasn't certain what the collective noun for Head teachers was but he had some unflattering suggestions if anyone ever needed to know. No-one was expecting him back at school but then again, Rachel wasn't expecting him home for a while either.

He could sit ignoring his mobile phone, eating chocolate and watching a different world go by. At this time of day, Peter perhaps looked like a travelling salesman, taking a break between appointments. If he was still here in six hours' time, he would have been taken for a dodgy dealer or even a dogger.

Peter didn't care how it looked. He needed time to release the pressure that had simmered and then boiled after lunch. The morning sessions had been unexceptional. There had been presentations on various educational topics and sales pitches by a couple of companies who were trying to get schools to part with some of their budgets on ground-breaking initiatives that would supposedly revolutionise teaching.

After choosing the chicken casserole over the vegetable lasagne and the cheesecake rather than the fruit cocktail, he was required to sit in a circle to discuss local issues and developments. It was only when Peter sat down and started looking around the group that he realised how old he was in comparison to his peers. They were Heads of primary, secondary, special schools and academies and they all looked younger and healthier than him. Some of them could have passed as students themselves. *How the hell did they become Head teachers at that age? What was wrong with slowly gaining experience, credibility and respect as you worked your way up the ladder?*

What was worse than them looking so young was the fact that all of them sounded worldly wise and so certain in their beliefs. They sounded like the world was theirs, everything was black and white and they owned all of the paint brushes.

As the discussion developed, Peter felt himself shrinking further and further into his shell. The more any of God's gifts to England's leading schools talked, the more he wished he had stayed away and sent Julie as his representative. She would have coped much better.

When the subject turned to school self-evaluation and Ofsted, the young bloods couldn't resist telling the rest of the group how marvellous they were and how *Outstanding* their schools were or would be judged. It was at this point that Peter started to look at his watch every two minutes and then when the pressure cooker got to full steam he mimed to the organiser that he had to leave and go back to his school.

And so here he was. Sitting in his car feeling old and useless and eating chocolate after consuming a full meal only two hours earlier.

Peter Pan had got old, fat and weary. Too stiff, heavy and disillusioned to fly. He had spent his whole life leading lost boys and girls and now he wanted some Smee time. He couldn't take a flying jump now, even if he wanted to. The windows in his sensible car were too small and the bedroom windows at home were all UPVC sealed units. He had abandoned his dreams of being a famous rock guitarist as he lost his hair, gained weight and abandoned all pretence at learning to read music. After today he would retire his air guitar for good and sit off stage in the twilight zone somewhere between middle age and doolally.

It didn't feel fair. If he was sacked now, that would be the end of his career. If he'd been a football manager he would have kept getting sacked from under-performing teams and rehired by other desperate clubs. Peter sighed. It was not right but it was no good moaning, nothing would change. The football managers were human beings after all. It's not as if they were bankers.

Two of the three chocolate bars remained, teasing him with a taste of paradise. *What should he do? Go to school or go home?* He would make a decision on the direction of travel once he had re-fuelled with sweets.

Peter wanted to wave a magic wand and make everything better immediately. He wanted to wield the stick to make rapid improvements but knew deep down that he was a carrot man. He was from the co-operation society not the corporate punishment camp. He remembered a quote from some film or other...*Beatings will continue until morale improves*...and wondered if he would be a good pirate captain or if even on the high seas he would still require improvement.

Peter made a decision...not to do anything for a while; not to turn left or right or even to turn on the ignition. He was safe and happy here. He had a full tank, a full stomach and a spare chocolate bar if he became desperate. *Dear God. He was a grown man in his fifties. He had a good life. He had done well for himself. He was a good husband, wasn't he? He was a good dad, wasn't he? He was a goodish Head teacher, wasn't he? What more did he want? What else could he have done with his life?*

His dream of riffing with Eric Clapton on stage in front of thousands of adoring fans had always been sheer fantasy but he once had a talent for writing. As an angst-riddled teenager he wrote poems in his bedroom about love and death and into his twenties he wrote short stories about love and death. He even remembered writing a poem to Rachel after their first date. She was taken with his light, sensitive and romantic touch which gained him entry into her heart and underwear far quicker than her other suitors. Somewhere and somehow the creative muse dried up. He had spent a lifetime since writing lesson plans, pupil reports, letters to parents and ever-increasing lists using bullet points and highlighter pens. There was no original thought or word play, it was all matter of fact that turned the grey matter into pulp fiction.

Peter sat there and made a promise to himself that he would start the book he had always wanted to write. Not so much about him or his life but about Ofsted and schools. It would be a warning for others who followed him. He only wished someone had written a book about the problems facing schools when he was wondering what to do with his life. Would reading one book written by some hard bitten old cynic have stopped him from training to be a teacher? Perhaps not. But he might have picked up the guitar and practised every day instead of being duped into teaching by its promises of long holidays and short hours.

In his head he composed a raft of advice to his younger self:

> Listen to your parents – once in a blue moon they make sense
> Tell your sister you love her
> Keep a record of all your friends - you will lose contact with so many over the years
> If you are not sure about something - take a risk and go for it
> Don't be shy of new people and new situations - particularly new girls who show an interest
> Practise playing a guitar for two hours every day - a real one made out of wood
> Don't smoke so that you have to kick the habit later - and put on a lot of weight
> Don't watch soap operas – you will lose the will to live
> Support a football team from Manchester - to avoid years of trauma and heartache
> Keep writing for you own pleasure - not to please and appease everyone else
> Keep all your old stuff - it will all become fashionable again and may be worth a fortune
> Look after your teeth - stay out of fights in pubs
> Don't trust academics when they talk about the right foods to eat
> Don't trust politicians - ever

If only he had a pen handy he could have written these pearls of wisdom down and driven them back in time in his sensible five door DeLorean. After all, he did have over thirty years to kill and he could be back to the present before Rachel had started cooking tea. Or perhaps she wouldn't be there at all if he managed to change his past. His brain and heart started to ache. *Was it the conference, past regrets and present tensions or was it too much chocolate?* There was only one way to know for certain. He slowly reached for the last chocolate bar sitting seductively on his passenger seat. There was once a time when he would have been attempting to unwrap something far more rewarding sitting next to him in a country lane. That was in a time when his Ford Cortina was a finely tuned instrument and a babe magnet to boot. At least, Peter thought, as he lunged for the treat, the chocolate bar didn't coyly protest or claim to have a headache.

The sky was darkening now and Peter was getting cold. It was time to make a decision, his second major decision of the day. He had left the conference early and he was not going to school today, he was going to drive home. What powerful and decisive leadership skills he had exercised. He was sure the National College of Teaching and Leadership would be proud of him.

As he started the engine and put the heater on, his mobile phone rang. It was Penny. She was one of the few colleagues who had his mobile number. This could only be bad news. He turned the ignition off and pressed the green button on his phone to take the call.

CHAPTER 13

Peter hadn't slept well.

After the phone call from Penny, Peter's journey back to the present had occurred more quickly than he would have liked. He drove home thinking about Sobia and her situation and realised his problems paled into insignificance compared to being scared in your own home.

He was met at the door by his ecstatic wife with news of a pregnancy. They were to be grandparents for a second time. She had invited their daughter, son-in-law and grandson around to celebrate. Rachel had cooked and they would be arriving within the hour.

Peter was pleased for everyone concerned, especially Rachel who loved being a grandma. For himself, it was hard trying to get excited by the prospect of more baby-sitting duties and conversations revolving around nappies and gripe water but he couldn't get past the celebratory meal. He had already eaten enough today to last him for a week but he still had another three courses to negotiate before bed time.

When he did get to bed the odd moments of sleep interrupted his waking thoughts of babies and women screaming in pain. He wondered if his stomach ache was stress, a ghost pregnancy or just over-indulgence. He spent a good deal of the night sitting on the loo in the en-suite contemplating the day ahead.

He knew that he would have to talk to Sobia and the Gazette reporter who had contacted the school yesterday afternoon. He also decided to hold a short senior team meeting to up the ante on the action plan and inform them about the proposed changes to the leadership team.

On his final visit to the toilet at 5:16, about half an hour after the last one, he decided to take a notepad and pen with him to record his thoughts for the day. Three pages of notepad and half a roll of toilet paper later he returned to bed slowly slipping under the sheets, trying not to disturb Rachel who was dreaming of opening a shop called Grandmother Care. The bedroom was still dark but Peter could see and sense that Rachel was sleeping like a baby. Peter consoled himself that if he could not make Rachel content and complete then at least their daughter could.

At 5:58 Peter conceded he wouldn't get any more sleep. The only positive was that during the night he must have lost about three pounds in weight. This would normally have seemed like a moral victory but he was sure he'd added double that amount during yesterday's non-stop eating marathon. During the final course of last night's meal and the draining of his second glass of cheap bubbly, Peter had re-branded his consumption as discomfort eating. He knew he was a heart attack waiting to happen...the stresses of work, being overweight, lack of exercise, and paranoia at being old and bald. It dawned on him that his body as well as his mind required improvement. He decided not to step on to the scales before he had a shower. If they could talk to him they'd say *Just one at a time, please*. So he opted for *ignorance is bliss*. He would wait and wait until he knew he was lighter than yesterday before weighing himself.

In the shower Peter was pleased to discover that he could still see most of his feet over his stomach when he looked down but a little disappointed that that was about all he could see. So as not to disturb his wife, he grabbed his clothes from the dark wardrobe and dressed on the landing. He struggled with his suit trousers and decided he definitely did not need a belt today. Peter's shirt, tie and suit were different colours and he looked and felt a real mess. He hoped The Gazette wouldn't want a photograph for their piece on Whatmore. *Shabby Head teacher sets poor example for shoddy school*.

Breakfast was just a cup of coffee and Peter was parked and in school before some members of staff had even woken up. He dumped his briefcase on his desk and hunted in his top drawer for the more suitably coloured spare tie he was sure was lurking at the back. It was, so he went to the nearest toilet and stared at himself in the mirror, doing the best he could with his appearance.

In the last half an hour or so all of Peter's team had stared at themselves in the mirror before facing the day.

Sobia had liberally applied make-up to cover as many cracks as possible. She would take a repair kit with her to school in case of further eye leakage.

Charlie had looked for his looks and wondered whether his eye sight was starting to fail. It was time to make some decisions about his future before they were taken for him.

Neil stared at the stupid, naïve, gullible man who had lost his heart and a considerable amount of money to a non-existent dream and decided that today was the beginning of a new chapter in his life. He would power up.

Julie had tried to apply her make-up, but it was both a difficult and pleasurable experience for her as she was being manhandled from behind. She would need to finish her face off when she got to work. The weekend was fast approaching and with it came nervous excitement at the prospect of key stage two in the relationship.

All of them were present and reasonably correct in advance of the bell for the start of the pupils' day.

Penny was also in early. She hung up her coat, locked her handbag away in her filing cabinet and knocked on Peter's door. Peter was on his third coffee of the day and he made Penny one without asking her. The conversation they were about to have needed caffeine.

"I didn't get much sleep last night," Peter admitted.

"Neither did I," replied Penny. "What do you think we ought to do?"

"All we can do is talk to Sobia. It's not our place to contact the police. Surely with domestic violence it has to come from the victim. It's not our place to interfere and if we go in all guns blazing, we could make matters a whole lot worse for her."

"Are matters not bad enough already? Knowing Sobia, she'll be embarrassed and not want to discuss it any more. But it doesn't mean we should forget it." Penny was determined to stop Peter defaulting to his *do nothing* approach.

"You seem to know her pretty well. I didn't think she got on with anyone."

"I don't know her well, but I'm trying to put myself in her place and think how someone might react in the cold light of day after admitting she's being abused by her own husband. She might be frightened to let this go further. So we have to be really careful how we deal with this."

"I agree. We'll have a follow-up conversation today. Even if it's just a pleasant *How are you feeling today?*"

"I think we have to be stronger than that."

"Okay, I'll see her this morning..."

"I ought to see her not you. She confided in me yesterday so we don't have to go over old ground and I'm not her boss. And you'd much rather me do it, anyway," said Penny.

"You're a star, bless you. Do you want me to be there when you speak to her?"

"Absolutely not but I'd like to see her somewhere quiet...say... in here."

"No problem. You could do it while I take the reporter from The *Gazette* for a guided tour?"

"Sounds like a plan." As she reached the door, Penny looked back and asked "Are you okay?"

"Yeah, good thanks. I forgot to tell you I'm going to be a granddad again!"

"Congratulations. I bet Rachel's thrilled."

"Tell me about it...and Penny..."

"Yes?"

"Thanks for doing this and all the other things you bail me out on. I do appreciate it."

"Just part of the low paid job...I'll see you later."

At 9.30 am. Neil decided to take the plunge and leave his office. As usual he had hidden away for the last hour or so avoiding pupils, staff and any other strange beings lurking in the corridors. He had remained cocooned in his hidey hole until the pupils had all found their way to the first lessons. The school would now be relatively quiet and settled. Most classes would start the day in a state of drowsy acquiescence and it was the best time of the day for teachers to get the little darlings to conform and hopefully learn something.

After a gigabyte of umming and ahhing Neil had decided to speak to someone about his love life or lack of it. He had had his heart and wallet emptied in the last couple of weeks and he could no longer trust his best friend - the internet. He wanted to try a new, different and radical approach. To date a real woman in the real world. To wine and dine someone who would be interested in him, to hold her hand and kiss her and to make her laugh – to actually laugh out loud rather than resorting to *LOL*. He knew what he wanted but he didn't have a clue how to get there. He was navigating virgin territory without a Help screen. His pathetically short list of people who he could talk to threw up only one name…Charlie Briggs.

Neil found himself walking towards the pastoral block like a naughty little boy about to have his ear bent by the deputy head. He hadn't formulated what to say but he knew he'd have to divulge a fair amount of personal stuff if he was hoping to get back some good advice and guidance on his own pastoral concerns.

If Neil had been sitting at a screen pressing buttons, his avatar would be chuckling, and moving along the corridor towards the door of discovery. Behind the door would be Briggadoom who would cast his spell on the poor mortal causing him to give away his secrets. As it was Neil's avatar would be smiling at the irony of the real Neil asking for an audience with the legendary Casanova of Whatmore.

The urban myth about Charlie was that over the years he had sampled most of the females on the staff who had a pulse. Charlie would have been delighted with the rumour but disappointed that it was far from true, apart from the odd fling while trying desperately to stay faithful to his wives. So there he was, an aging and over-rated stallion, being asked to advise the stable boy how to get women in the hay.

Once Neil had waited for Charlie to tell off two boys for saying politically incorrect things to their Geography teacher and then a group of girls who were being horrible to one of their best friends, it was his time.

The meeting didn't start well. Erroneously Charlie had assumed Neil wanted to talk about Ofsted matters and was expecting to be able to put his brain into neutral for half an hour while Neil talked another language. When he raised the subject of women, Charlie was shocked into life. Neil started talking and talking the language of love and could not be shut down. Charlie listened to the saga of the virtual Russian, managing to nod sympathetically in all of the right places.

"I'm sorry your love life isn't going the way you want it to," interjected Charlie who wanted to say *Whose love life is?* but stopped himself. "How can I help?"

"I suppose I needed to get it all off my chest. I've been an absolute idiot in the last few weeks. I am the person on the staff who keeps banging on about computer security and here I am conned out of thousands of pounds by a bunch of crooks who played me for a fool?"

"Well, we all get shafted from time to time but we have to move on and learn from it. I might as well say this and you can tell me to shut up if you want but I think you need to re-brand yourself. Most people on the staff don't really know you because you don't mix. You stay in your office and communicate through the network if you can get away with it. Most people think you're a loner. You need to get out there. Go in the staff room at break times. Go and ask teachers about their IT problems face-to-face. Find a few like-minded colleagues and get to know them and you need to do the same when you go home at night. Do you go out much in the evenings?"

"No, not really…" replied Neil, shrinking in his chair.

"You have to start somewhere and you're young enough to change. If you want me to suggest a few tactics I will, but you might not like my suggestions."

"No. I came for advice and I value your opinion. Go ahead and don't hold back. I couldn't feel any worse than I do already."

"This isn't about making you feel worse. You have to feel better about yourself and when you feel more positive then you'll be more attractive to the opposite sex." Charlie relaxed into his swivel chair and into the unaccustomed role of Agony Uncle. "If I were you I'd start with my appearance. Lose the apology for a beard and get your hair cut shorter. Then I'd go into town and lash out on some new clothes; jacket, trousers, shirts, ties… BUT don't buy them off the internet. Try them on in the shop and ask for advice, preferably from a young, attractive shop assistant. And while you're at the shops, walk around and look at all the women shopping - they're real and some of them are single and some of the single ones just might like you if you gave them a chance."

"Come on, Charlie. I'm not going to get a haircut and buy a new shirt on Saturday and then have a line of women queuing up outside Top Man in the town centre waiting to go on a date with me. It's not going to happen."

"Of course it's not going to happen just like that. I'm afraid you'll need to make other changes before you're really ready to sell yourself in the market place. You have to wean yourself off your computer addiction. Try limiting yourself on how much screen time you do every day and spend more time talking to real people and looking them in the eye. You've a good sense of humour but most people at Whatmore wouldn't know that. But once you feel comfortable talking to your colleagues here you'll be able to face the world of strangers outside. Come out on some of the staff social events. We go out every half term and it usually involves beers and a few laughs. I'll make sure you know when the next social is, and you can come with me if that helps. Once you get your confidence sorted you'll be able to start chatting up some of the younger women on the staff..."

"There's probably no single women on the staff anyway..." Neil muttered.

"I think you'll find there are. Remember my role is dealing with all things pastoral and part of my remit is to get to know the current status of all of the young women on the staff." Charlie winked just in case Neil had taken him seriously. "There's a certain teacher I observed the other day who could definitely do with a knight in shining armour to rescue her from the evils of the interactive whiteboard. But let's not rush things. Your action plan for the next week is to go shopping on Saturday and start using the staff room next week. Is that an achievable plan?"

"I think so. Thanks Charlie. This has been really helpful." Neil stood and held out his hand to shake Charlie's. The gesture seemed overly formal but Charlie went along with it knowing it meant this awkward counselling session was at an end.

Charlie slumped back, emotionally drained; saddened by Neil's predicament but rather pleased at managing to give him some reasonably hard messages without destroying him. Perhaps he should quit teaching, become a priest and take confessionals. Unfortunately, it was only thirty seconds later and two skips of his fertile imagination before Charlie was fantasising about naughty young nuns kneeling before him asking for redemption. He smiled to himself. Clearly there was still hope for the old todger yet!

Julie Osborne, meanwhile, was preparing for a long session with Richard Perry by continuing discussions with her new best friend, Jo Slater. She was trying hard to convince herself that the meeting was about Maths and Ofsted but she knew deep down that she wanted to chat with Jo about other matters entirely and her personal action plan.

Jo knew enough to close the door behind her. "I've brought chocolate," she announced. "I thought we might need the sugar rush."

"Thanks, Jo. Would you like caffeine as well? White, no sugar?"

"That would be good. What time is Rick Perry coming over?"

"In about half an hour. I wanted to see if you could add anything to the conversation. Peter needs feedback on how we think things are going with Maths and he's putting some heat on me to perform miracles with the department."

"Yes, I had something similar from him the other day so I had to tell him that I can't make Rick an effective leader overnight."

"And what was Peter's reaction?"

"Between you and me, he said the right things but he's still expecting an immediate turn around. Here, have a chocolate bar. It's the best substitute for a man and sometimes a lot more satisfying."

They smiled knowingly at each other across the coffee table and these two intelligent women realised that this was the cue to start in on non-mathematical, non-educational and non-professional matters. Twenty years before, they could have had this conversation behind the bike sheds, sharing a cheap cigarette and lipstick. Now they could sit in comfort and share coffee, chocolate and confidences without risk of authoritarian reprimand.

"How are things going?" Jo asked.

This was all the invitation Julie needed to compare notes on a range of topics that would have made even Charlie Briggs blush. If this had been the starter activity in a Biology lesson, Ofsted would have had to assess it as *Outstanding* as both girls were fully engaged and showing hunger for further knowledge.

"So if Mark is so good and bad at the same time, if you know what I mean, what's stopping you letting friends and family know the two of you are an item. You can't keep him locked away in your flat forever…it's like a social chastity belt."

"I know, but the problem is I taught him and he's so much younger than me."

"But do you feel so much older than him? I'm not trying to sound clever but it sounds to me as if he's making you feel young. It's not like he's tweeted all of his mates that he's bagged one of his old teachers. He's respected your privacy and been discreet about your relationship so far."

"As far as I know he has but he wants to take the relationship to the next level. He's been invited to a party on Saturday and he wants me to go."

"That's great. He wants to show you off to his friends."

"I know and I am really excited at the prospect of holding hands with a bloke in public. It's been ages since I snogged someone on a dance floor or had to stop wandering hands in a dark corner of a party. But I'm so scared what others might think."

"Do they need to know you're older? I'm sure you won't look it dressed up to the nines. You're looking younger recently anyway - wearing heels, dresses, skirts instead of trousers and sensible shoes. You're looking great now…if a little tired in the mornings!"

They both giggled. "That's the result of trying to look good! You don't get your eight hours sleep!"

"That will change with time but my advice is milk it while you can. Be the cat that has the full cream while it's fresh!"

They both laughed even louder this time.

"So you think I should go to the party?"

"Definitely. Wear something sexy and show yourself off. Make him feel good in front of his mates. Make yourself feel good and hold glands all night."

Their laughter was uncontrollable. Their mascara was running down their reddened cheeks and their minds were bright blue. Fortunately, they managed to steady the ship before the knock on the door announced the poor unfortunate specimen who neither of them found in the least attractive. Rick was obliviously entering the heat of a lioness's den.

Rick walked in prepared to admit that his team of maths teachers were not up to standard but unwilling if not unable to take in a bad word against himself. Sitting down, Rick completed a concentric triangle around the remains of the previous meeting - two coffee cups with lipstick smears adorning the top of each and two chocolate bar wrappers. He waited to be offered refreshments but Julie pounced before he could compose himself and his excuses.

"Thanks for coming, Richard. I'm sorry it's fairly short notice but I need to get your views on progress. I've asked Jo to sit in because she has been working with you on leadership issues and we've just had a very interesting discussion on that before you came in." Julie glanced at Jo and Jo glanced back at Julie.

"I can also report back on some of the lessons I've seen recently but I wanted to hear what you have been doing as Head of Maths in the last couple of weeks…" Julie left the last words of her opening speech hanging in the air.

Richard Perry took the next five minutes and thirty-seven seconds to demonstrate all the leadership characteristics of an isolated and injured wildebeest under the spotlight of a savannah sun. His approach to survival was to divert and misdirect. His diatribe blamed, yet again, the world and his wife and anyone else that he could think to name. He blamed systems and communications and threw in an insult or two about Ofsted, the Department for Education and the Secretary of State.

They waited until Richard Perry had burnt himself out before Julie very calmly posed her question again. "So what have you been working on in the last couple of weeks to improve the performance of the students in Maths?"

"Well…I've been trying to make myself more available to my team and I've asked them to come to see me if they have any problems. The trouble is I have precious little free time for the team during the day…I have a full timetable and then there are meetings like this and with Jo that I'm supposed to attend."

Feeling uncomfortable and slightly sorry for him, Jo tried to rescue him. "We know improvement will take a while but you have plans in place don't you? Perhaps you could go through those with us?"

"Yes, absolutely. I haven't finalised them yet. I need to share them with the team first, once I have time to type them up."

"So could you talk us through them?" said Julie losing patience.

"Of course…….my plans so far are to improve teaching in the department and analyse the pupils' performance so we have a better idea of what's going wrong and then we can move forward. Jo's helping me and supporting me and as I have said already I am there for everyone else…"

"Thank you Richard," said Julie, pushing the knife in deeper. "I wonder if you could write your plan up as soon as possible and then I can share it with SLT. Do you need any help in producing the plan quickly?"

"No. It'll be fine. I'll…cut and paste a template and then just bang it off for you…you should have it tomorrow…"

"Good. Well thanks for popping in and I'll be interested to see the plan tomorrow."

"Yep, no problems." Rick hurriedly left the scene.

Neither Julie nor Jo could find immediately words to express the inadequacy of Rick's attempts to satisfy them.

"Have you got time for another drink?" asked Julie.

"Have you got any gin?" said Jo.

"Sorry, I finished off my last full bottle the last time I met Rick!" She put the kettle back on.

Jo summed things up rather well. "What are we going to do with him? He's clearly in denial and he won't accept any responsibility."

"You're right. He doesn't seem to know what to do to help himself. He seems to be doing precious little. All he appears to do is turn up to meetings and get defensive. It doesn't feel as if he has the qualities to lead the department forward. What do you think, Jo?"

"I agree but we owe it to him to keep supporting him. I wonder how he'd be if he had a strong team of Maths teachers around him or if the GCSE grades in Maths were better…would his leadership still be in question?"

"Perhaps not, but we are where we are and Rick hasn't grasped the nettle. I don't feel his heart is in the battle. He seems a defeated man. It was sad to see."

Jo lightened the mood by remarking that it wouldn't be the first time she had come across a man without a plan. "Men, hey? You can live without them most of the time and you can live without them all of the time! So what are you going to say at SLT? And do you want me to carry on trying to positively stroke him…and I don't mean his ego!"

They shared a second drink and Julie rationalised not painting too despairing a picture of Rick and his department just yet. She was prepared to give him more time. Time for Jo and Julie to keep working on him. There was another reason to keep this arrangement going: it provided an excuse to keep meeting Jo. They agreed to meet next week and Jo whispered that she expected a blow by blow account of the weekend. Smiles and affection all round.

At Reception, Penny gathered up the reporter from The Gazette. Kevin Shaw was armed with a thin briefcase, a smartphone and little or no background research. Penny's aim was to remove him as quickly as possible from the pressure point at which the general public meet the lazy, part-time, over-paid professionals. This was the war zone where parents, believing every word their child said, sparred with teachers who believed in nothing other than what they had seen or heard. This was the place where fuses were short and most days you could rely on a display of public fireworks.

"Nice to meet you, Kevin. Mr. Burlington is expecting you."

"Thanks…Penny. I wonder if you could fill in some gaps for me. I've only recently joined The Gazette and I don't know the area well. What sort of school is this?"

"What do you mean? Do you mean is it a secondary school or primary? Or do you mean is it an academy or a state school? Or do you mean is Whatmore a good school?"

"Err….yes….I suppose all of those."

"I'll let Mr Burlington answer your questions."

She used what she'd heard to pass a coded message to Peter. "This is Kevin Shaw. He's new to The Gazette and the area and doesn't know too much about Whatmore."

Over the essential coffee and biscuits, Peter seized on the young man's heaven-sent ignorance "I thought I'd give you some context about Whatmore before we have a tour of the school and then I could take you to meet some of our pupils who will serve you some lunch. Would that work for you, Kevin?"

"That would be great. I didn't have enough time to make myself any sandwiches this morning."

"I think we can do better than sandwiches."

"I ought to say that I'm a vegetarian though."

"No problem. Excuse me a moment."

Peter closed the door behind him. "Penny, I need the cook to come up with an edible hot vegetarian main course in the next hour and can we have it served in the conference room by a couple of nice kids who look relatively normal and healthy. Give me twenty minutes or so to ply him with propaganda and chocolate biscuits and then we'll start the tour and you can have my office for your chat with Sobia."

Kevin was messing with his phone when Peter returned. He looked younger than many of the pupils. Perhaps, Peter thought, he could help Kevin write the article or at least proof read and correct his first draft.

Twenty nine minutes later Peter led Kevin past Penny's desk. Kevin held his phone in one hand and a half-eaten biscuit in the other. Peter winked at Penny and she sprang into action. Her plan for Sobia was to fetch her and play it by ear. Sometimes not having a plan is the best plan of all.

In Sobia's lair, Penny found a jaw-dropping sight. Sobia, Diane and Cathy were sitting in the centre of the room eating cream cakes and chatting. They all looked up guiltily.

"Hello ladies. Sorry to interrupt. I wonder if I could have a quick word, Sobia?"

"Of course. I was coming to see you once we'd finished our cakes."

"Somebody's birthday?" asked Penny as they walked back to Peter's office.

"No, I just wanted to treat Diane and Cathy and thank them for working so hard and covering in the office while I was away."

"That's a really nice touch, Sobia."

"I'm a really nice person, Penny."

"You are. Peter's giving a local newspaper reporter a guided tour so we can use his office again."

"I promise I won't get upset today."

"So why do you feel different today?"

"I made some decisions in the middle of the night when I couldn't sleep. I want to stay married. I love my husband and my children. Compared to a lot of women I'm very lucky."

"You sure you mean that? Are you really content…happy…with your life?"

"I am. Yes I am. It's not really my husband's fault. It's me that's got to change. I need to be more thoughtful and considerate at home and at work too."

"Please don't put all of the blame on yourself. You don't deserve to live in fear of your husband. I know it's your choice what you do but promise that if things get bad again you'll come and talk to me. I will always listen."

"Thank you."

There was nothing else to be said. Both women knew Sobia's determination was all show but it was a very convincing show.

The Senior Leadership Team meeting began almost half an hour later than scheduled following another convincing show – Peter's sales pitch to Kevin Shaw and The Gazette. Even so Charlie was late and walked in on a bunch of smiling faces.

"I was explaining to the team that I wined and dined Kevin Shaw from The Gazette earlier today," said Peter.

"How did it go?"

"I ended up practically writing his article for him so we may just have got away with it."

"That's a relief," Charlie replied realising why the team were feeling happy.

"That doesn't stop the editor writing a very different story when this Kevin chap goes back to the office," pointed out Neil.

"You're absolutely right, Neil. We could get a doom and gloom article next week, but let's hope not."

"Let's just face the problem if or when the story comes out," said Sobia in a considered way.

The team's body language told Peter to move on to other matters. Unfortunately for the team the other matters were both pressing and depressing.

"Ann Brown is giving me some heat on our action plan and she wants to see a rough draft by next weekend. I think we need to make this a major priority. We can't meet after school on Monday because Clive Howell is leading a training session and we are expected to be there. How about Tuesday after lunch and we will just stay here until it's finished?"

Not one of them could quickly and imaginatively create a legitimate reason why they could not attend this vital meeting so the date and time were agreed.

Peter's next move was to reinforce the need for all of them to be at Clive's training session, smiling and enthusiastic. Peter looked specifically at Charlie as he made the point.

"What're you suggesting boss? You know I'm a great fan of Clive Howell and I've been looking forward to this session for some time now." Charlie's sarcasm hit a chord with most of the team.

"I know. The chances are the session will be awful but we just have to see it through."

"Let's make the best of it," Sobia offered to the meeting. Some of her colleagues were not sure how to take her second such interjection in the meeting. Some thought that she was just hurrying along the meeting because she was fed up, but Julie could see that Sobia was trying to be conciliatory.

The male members had their minds and eyes elsewhere. Neil was looking at his IPad. Peter was looking at his diary. Charlie was staring at the wall. All three were trying hard not to look at Julie's blouse and the unbuttoned button divulging the colour of her bra.

They moved on to the matter of national strike action that could be hitting the school in the next month. Even Whatmore would have its quota of teachers sacrificing a day's wages to have a day off school and to make their feelings known by sitting in front of their flat screen TVs all day, perhaps even watching the news.

They moved from impending strike action to the re-structuring of the senior leadership team. Julie was expecting most of the team to be looking at her at this stage as they were probably all aware or could guess that she would be applying for the second deputy position. Strangely, no-one was other than Sobia. Julie looked down at the table to escape Sobia's strained glare, saw the gaping hole in her blouse and re-fastened it, red-cheeked.

"Well I think it's the right thing to do," said Charlie. "Teaching and Learning has to be at the centre of what we do here and having a deputy who is responsible and accountable for moving it forward makes absolute sense."

Neil asked how the post would be advertised and Sobia led a discussion on salary point and scale. Peter made it clear that the salary would be equitable with the existing deputy post but that Charlie would be regarded as first deputy based on experience and status at the school.

"You mean because Charlie's an old codger, we have to respect him?" asked Neil playfully.

"Well to his face, at least," replied Peter.

"Thank you fans," Charlie smiled, "it's good to know how much you like and admire me…"

They all laughed and Peter wrapped up the meeting with some social news. "Oh, and by the way, it's at home with the Burlingtons two weeks this Saturday. You can come on your own or bring a plus one. Attendance and bringing a bottle are compulsory."

The team all nodded acceptance knowing that it was an obligatory obligation that not even a doctor's note could out-trump.

As they moved to the door, Charlie whispered in Julie's ear. She was expecting some comment about the deputy head position but instead blushed again as he said "Hope you're going to wear that bra to Peter's bash!"

Julie thumped him playfully on the arm and they made their separate ways to their cars.

CHAPTER 14

Weekends and nights were the best times to appreciate the design and structure of Whatmore School. It was a 60s build that had passed its fiftieth birthday. It had survived into middle age because the buildings were only occupied for about a third of the time. It wasn't like schools in China where the pupils seemed to be permanently taught, day and night, awake or asleep.

On this Saturday morning Michael could sneak around the main building without fear of detection. The alarms were set on the external doors and there was a concentration of movement detectors around the school safe, but he wasn't interested in school funds. Michael's needs were more fundamental and he liked to explore and search the corridors and classrooms systematically without disturbance and distraction.

Michael had to admit that the school was certainly showing signs of age. Apparently, there had been a promise from the local authority some years ago of razing it to the ground and replacing the school with a building fit for the future. It would have been a fabulous design by a fabulous architect. The new school would have been made of glass and shiny plastic with a huge atrium. Everyone would have looked at it from the outside and admired the architect's bold statement standing proud within the local community. And once the designers and builders had been and gone then the school would have been bequeathed to future pupils and teachers to make some sense of the castle made of sand. As with all of the Buildings Schools For The Future designs, it would have taken several years to design and build it properly, followed by several more years for the teachers and pupils to make it work properly by altering as much as they could, followed by a rapid ageing process that meant the school, in ten years' time, would be unfit for purpose. At best, the new shiny schools of the 21st century would last half of the time of the existing buildings. Whatmore was overlooked and unloved but for fifty years it had stood the test of term times.

Michael was loyal to the school. No matter what others said about Whatmore, he was a huge fan and supporter. He had attended the school for a couple of years now, along with his small group of mates. The rooms were spacious, the corridors were long and the food was good. What more could a rat need?

On Saturday morning, Peter the Head and Rachel the Wife were mid-journey between their home and their daughter's house. Normally Rachel would be making this journey on her own and Peter would follow on later in the day. However, last night, in between *Eastenders* and *Masterchef*, Peter had suggested they could drive over to their daughter's house together and spend some quality time with their ever growing family.

Rachel seemed happy and relieved. It appeared Peter was beginning to re-surface from the depression consuming him since the dreaded Ofsted inspection. She had tried to talk him out of his black mood on several occasions without success and she felt it was better to give him some space and time while he worked through his issues.

Peter was also feeling happier. He was slowly putting things into perspective and his school plans were being actioned. The two teams that he nominally headed, Team Whatmore and Team Burlington, were strong and supportive and made him proud. Maybe others would say his man management of his two teams was questionable but despite the flaws he was happy with both.

Charlie, meanwhile, was dutifully following his wife around a maze of self-assembly Swedish furniture in the middle of town. Each piece of furniture, with an unpronounceable name, stared at Charlie as he slowly walked by. Each piece of particleboard challenged him to buy it and then spend a glorious day attempting to construct it to look like the item displayed in the shop, without swearing in Anglo-Saxon. For a man who liked to voice his grumpiness at every opportunity, Charlie was keeping calm and biting his lip to demonstrate to his wife that he was a good husband. He would not complain about the quality of the furniture, the price of the sticks of flimsy wood, the fact that he had to single-handedly load the flat packs on to a trolley, join a mile-long queue to pay for the products and then attempt to load the awkward shaped boxes into the car without assistance. He would smile outwardly and be content in the knowledge that he would be rewarded later for good behaviour.

Sobia, on the other hand, was taking the lead. During Friday, while at her desk at work, she had created an action plan for the next seven days.

The first two days of the plan were dedicated entirely to her immediate family. Last night, Sobia had delicately explained her proposals for the weekend to her husband while they enjoyed a late evening meal, once she had got the twins off to bed.

Sobia had left Whatmore as early as she could last night, collected the twins from her sister and then let them watch videos while she cooked the boys their favourite meals: chicken nuggets and chips for the youngsters and chicken curry and chips for her old man. During the meal she had suggested they could take the boys to the cinema to see the latest Disney film.

As Sobia served her husband his dessert, he admitted it had been a long time since he had been to the cinema. She quickly followed up by telling him that afterwards her sister had agreed to have the boys overnight so that they could have some quality time together.

After winning both rounds, Sobia played her ace of trumps - she had invited his family around on Sunday for lunch. She would cook all of their favourite food fresh that morning and the house would be spotless because the boys would be dropped back home only after her in-laws had arrived.

The plan had been well-received by her husband. He appreciated her careful planning and thoughtfulness and he offered to help. On Saturday morning he broke the surprise to the excited twins that they were off to see a movie and then stay the night at their auntie's.

Sobia was packing the boot of the car with two small overnight bags when her husband joined her on the driveway and stroked her shoulder. It was the sort of romantic, intimate public gesture Sobia had not experienced for some time. Things were improving.

It was now 12:51 and Neil had four minutes to get to the pay machine at the car park. Any longer than four minutes and he would have to pay an extra £3.50 and he had already spent a relative fortune this morning. He moved apace up the ramp to the third floor, unencumbered by long hair flowing in the wind.

Neil had asked the barber for a short, modern style and to do something with his beard. He left with his hair gelled and his beard stubbled. He hardly recognised himself when the barber offered him the mirror and asked if the look was okay. Neil was pleased but less so with the cost of applying a pair of scissors and a razor around his head.

Once fleeced, Neil bought three new shirts, two ties and a smart jacket at various fashion outlets. By the time Neil handed over his credit card at the last trendy shop he was holding his breath, hoping that the card machine managed to find some money lurking at the bottom of his bank account. With most of his funds lost somewhere in Russia, Neil was now existing by selling prized possessions on Ebay. Several bits of kit that he was painstakingly and lovingly restoring were now open to bids on-line. He had enough loose change in his pocket to pay for the car park and enough petrol fumes in the tank to drive home. He would certainly have to stay in for the rest of the weekend.

As Neil approached the pay machine there were still two minutes on the clock. He would make it comfortably to the machine and pay the tariff if the couple ahead of him would stop messing about. They were too busy clowning around, giving each other various carrier bags to hold and groping around each other's bodies for change. They were clearly, very selfishly, in love.

As Neil approached them, they looked round and the woman said "Neil?"

"Julie?"

"Is that really you Neil? You've had a haircut."

"I know…" said Neil feeling very uncomfortable.

"Of course. Sorry," said Julie feeling even more uncomfortable.

Neil looked at Julie and then at the man with his arm around her shoulder. Julie looked at Neil and then at the man at her shoulder. The man with the arm looked at both of them in turn waiting to be introduced or acknowledged by Julie.

After seconds of endless awkwardness, Julie summoned up her courage and broke the silence.

"Neil, this is Mark...my...my boyfriend."

PART 3
Close To The Edge

CHAPTER 15

Peter needed some cave time. Last Saturday he had dutifully accompanied Rachel to their daughter's house and immersed himself in pregnancy and baby talk. He couldn't face another Saturday with a day-long single item agenda meeting so he had asked Rachel if he could be excused because of school stuff. Rachel accepted his apologies. She had acknowledged and appreciated his commitment to the family recently and secretly she was as pleased about today's arrangement as Peter was. She had her daughter to herself for the day and Peter could sit in his study and occupy his time with reading, writing, music and snacks.

Peter, with the whole house to himself, still headed for his office as soon as he had waved Rachel off the drive. He took supplies with him upstairs - a mug of coffee and a packet of biscuits. This would keep him going for a couple of hours. After that he would have to stretch his legs and get some exercise by going down to the kitchen to make another coffee and hunt and gather more food.

He sat at his desk, fired up his laptop, sorted out some music to listen to and stared out of the window waiting for Bill Gates to tell him that his technology was ready and safe to use.

It had been an interesting few weeks at Whatmore. Mind you, when wasn't it interesting? There had been highs and lows. The school was still standing and so were most of the staff. Staff attendance had improved recently and the pupils were generally playing ball. The dining hall had been incident free and Charlie had only excluded four pupils in the last three weeks, only one of them for more than a single day. The exception was a boy heading inexorably towards gardening leave if his behaviour didn't improve. Sad to say, he was a lad who was never going to be a grade C or above in any subject and so gardening leave was probably good preparation for the rest of his life. Peter could have wept when Charlie showed him the boy's record, captured in a school file. He could also have sworn at the system that meant that this boy would never have an opportunity to discover what could make him a valued member of society.

Peter moved on to another low. Clive Howell's twilight training session had been an unmitigated disaster. The staff behaved themselves very well and kept their pent up resentment under control as Clive managed to patronise and antagonise pretty much every one of them.

By the end of the hour long session Peter had to intervene to stop Clive handing out anonymous evaluation forms for everyone to fill in. That would have been asking for trouble. So Peter publically thanked Clive and told the staff that they could fill in the form later. Charlie took the cue to speak to the staff about a pastoral matter while Peter showed Clive to the main door.

Peter was unsurprised to learn that Clive had thought that his training session had gone down well and Peter, with a generous heart, agreed with him. This was one of those moments when Peter knew that he was a half-decent bloke and his self-evaluation skills were more than half-decent. He knew Clive's session was poor but what was the point of telling him. Clive probably wouldn't listen or accept his judgement anyway. After all, Peter Burlington was the Head of a school that required improvement.

The action plan in preparation for the HMI visit was progressing well. The SLT had spent a long but ultimately productive meeting finishing a draft. The matrix included actions, success criteria, named leads taking responsibility, impact measures and timelines. It also had a commentary box for each action so the HMI could see where and how progress was happening. It was, of course, all nonsense and a huge waste of everybody's time but it was a hoop that had to be jumped through. The draft had been shown to Ann Brown, as Chair of Governors, first and then to the full governing board for approval. Peter had then shared it with the Heads of Department and after that to the whole staff and their extended families and friends

It was a painstaking process but Peter didn't want anyone to say they hadn't been consulted. Of course, that would never happen. There were always people who you could shove a document under their nose and five minutes later they would claim they had never seen the paper work. It was also a frustration for Peter that certain people would gladly spend twenty minutes nit-picking at a document, a document that had taken twenty tiring days to prepare without any attempt at input from the nit-picker.

Still, it was done now and apart from the odd amendment or correction, it was ready to fool the world.

The governors had also given the go-ahead to appoint a second deputy head. Charlie, Sobia, Penny and Peter had worked on the advert, the timeline and the process. Peter had decided that for very good reasons that the process of appointing a second deputy, once approved by the governors, should not be discussed by the full SLT as it would put Julie in a difficult position.

There had not been any articles featuring Whatmore in The Gazette for the last two Fridays and it was now the received wisdom of all those who were very concerned that the school's inspection result was yesterday's news and would not be run further by the local paper.

The Maths department continued to be an issue and in particular the Head of Maths. Julie was observing and coaching some of the team and Jo was meeting regularly with Richard Perry. Julie and Jo met most days in Julie's office to discuss matters and were taking the situation very seriously. Peter was sure that these two strong and trusted women would soon be in a position to share their findings and the progress they had made.

As far as the SLT was concerned they were generally in fine fettle.

Neil had smartened himself up and looked and seemed different. He was in the staff room more and Peter had noticed that he was interacting much better now with pupils during lunch times in the dining hall.

Sobia seemed in better spirits and was less negative in meetings. Penny was keeping an eye on things from a distance and she saw signs of hope. Peter realised it was sensible not to interfere if things were moving in the right direction.

Julie looked well and continued to work hard. She hadn't popped in to his office much recently for one-to-ones, but Peter understood that she was keeping a professional distance as the impending interview approached. He had heard there might be a new man in her life but that was from a secondary source - Year 10 girls gossiping at lunch time.

Charlie was Charlie. He had had a few problems with one of his team recently. The Head of Year 11 had been working through some personal issues which had meant that she had been off school for a couple of days and in tears in Charlie's office. Peter didn't ask Charlie for details but was sure Charlie was on top of the situation.

Four biscuits later and Peter was ready to do some homework. He would just make himself another coffee then he would begin. Perhaps before he went down stairs he would make a list of what he needed to do, prioritise it, and write it out again in order of importance. If he then made that coffee, he could really start working.

He looked at his diary. This was a good starting point to work out what needed to be done. First, Peter took out all of the loose sheets of paper he had collected during the last week. He had shoved them in between next week's pages to read later. Now was later so he ought to read these first and see which sheets could be shoved into the following weeks' pages. Once he had done that and cleared a path to look at the forthcoming commitments in his diary, he was ready for a break.

CHAPTER 16

Corinne Peckett was the first teacher to arrive at Whatmore on Monday soon after six in the morning. She was let in by the tired and unhelpful assistant site manager who was just beginning the process of disarming the alarms before unlocking the external doors.

Corinne had woken up on Sunday morning expecting to spend most of the day marking and preparing for the week ahead. She had made some tea and toast and settled down on her rented sofa in her pyjamas and switched on her laptop. Corinne thought she knew her way around computers but two hours later she had still not managed to get the machine to behave.

The screen in front of her flashed and flickered, pop-up messages kept appearing telling her that there was a problem with her device and by lunch time she was ready to throw the device out of the window, followed by the cold tea and toast and finally herself. How could she operate at school tomorrow without her laptop and without her power points? She started to shiver with fright. It must be a virus. Should she take the laptop into *PCs r US* to see if they could give the computer a course of anti-virus tablets or perhaps she should just have tomorrow off school and pretend she was ill rather than the laptop. Maybe she could drive to her mom and dad's house in three hours and borrow their laptop but then she wouldn't have any time for marking all of her Maths books for Monday.

Eventually Corinne had decided on a plan of action. She would mark all of her classes' books during the afternoon and find some activities to do with the pupils that didn't involve the interactive whiteboard. There must be things she could do with the kids. After all, that's what teachers did in the old days before IT.

By early evening on Sunday, Corinne had marked all of the books. She had written something positive and encouraging and a *next steps* comment inside each book. Ofsted and her line managers would appreciate this even if the pupils, wouldn't bother to read any of it! It then dawned on Corinne that if she got into school early the next morning she could use one of the computers wired up to the intranet in the staff room and produce her power points and send them to the fixed computer in her classroom. That would work. For the first time that day Corinne managed to breathe steadily and she calmed herself down by making another mug of tea. *Had she actually eaten anything?* She couldn't remember. She was still in her pyjamas and a nervous wreck. *What sort of life was this?* She knew she had a lot to learn but one day she was going to be a great teacher like Ms Osborne or Mr Briggs. Then she would have a life.

So Corinne arrived in the staff room excessively early on Monday morning and started typing out her power points for the day. She had perhaps a good hour before the others would come in to ruin the peace and tranquillity. She was calmer than any other time in the last twenty hours or so but she was suffering from a lack of quality sleep.

At 7.08 am Neil walked into the staff room amazed that he was not alone.

"Oh, hi…You're in early," he said, stating the obvious.

"Oh, hello Mr Turner. Yes I'm just doing some preparation for my lessons. I had a major problem with my laptop yesterday, I think it was a virus or something and I couldn't access my files or get on the web. I'll have to work here each night and early in the morning until I can get a replacement lap top. I can produce my slides here and send them through the intranet."

"Good idea…and it's Neil…Neil Turner. I'm the person to speak to if you have a problem with IT. Have you got your lap top with you? I could have a look at it today if you want."

"That would be brilliant…Neil. To be honest I didn't know who to ask. I was going to see Rick Perry later and see if he could give me any advice."

"He would only pass it on to me any way. You're Corinne aren't you?"

"Yes, Corinne Peckett. I started in September. I'm in the dreaded Maths department. I sort of keep myself to myself mainly. I seem to be too busy to socialise outside the department. I'm hoping it will get easier soon but I have my doubts."

"What do you mean, doubts?"

"Well some of my university friends who are a year ahead of me said that they hoped the second year of teaching would be easier but it hasn't worked out like that for them. They still have no life to speak of. Perhaps I should have stuck with accountancy. I had a few years seeing the world before I went to university and then half way through the course I decided I didn't want to be a bean counter and at the end I jumped onto the Teach First programme."

"So you're one of the students who left university with a first class degree from a redbrick college?"

"Well yes, but I don't feel very clever now when I can't get my classes or my laptop to behave."

"Let me have a look at it during the day. I'll meet you back here at the end of school. Okay?"

"Thank you Neil. I appreciate it," replied Corinne warmly, handing Neil her laptop and then turning back to the screen in front of her.

Neil headed for the door, forgetting why he went into the staff room in the first place and headed for his office.

The staffroom started to fill up slowly with teachers and teaching assistants over the next hour so that by ten past eight, staff were struggling to find a seat ready for the briefing.

There was some movement when Julie Osborne arrived with the cover list and one or two teachers followed her out of the staff room only to return later with miserable or angry faces.

Richard Perry and Jo Slater entered the staff room together, Richard appeared serious and animated while Jo was calm and cool.

Charlie Briggs was making Brian Green laugh to the point of crying about something rude or unrepeatable. Charlie perched on the edge of a table strewn with age-old documents that were vital at one stage but now remained gathering dust because the cleaners were not sure if they could or should bin them.

Most of the school personnel were holding a strong hot drink and passing the time while they waited for their illustrious Head to arrive and deliver his briefing.

On time, Peter, minus a fanfare, walked into the dragons' den and read from his list of things he had scribbled in his study yesterday. Charlie and Julie said a few things, Brian Green asked to meet with his union members on Tuesday night and the performance was brought to a close with the usual "Let's be careful out there!" which still flew above the heads of everyone under the age of fifty.

The staff room turned into an empty, untidy cupboard within the next few minutes. Half-drunk mugs were left waiting to be washed up by the sweet old lady who was paid a pittance to clear and clean up for these highly paid and important professionals.

At break time the staff room filled up with Educational Psychologists, visitors and university students who were on placement at Whatmore. Very few teachers made the trip to the staff room. They were either on duty around the school or in their departments, marking, preparing, photocopying or gossiping unprofessionally.

At lunch time it was a more leisurely arrangement. Teachers had time to microwave something that had been prepared the day before and eat it while still gossiping unprofessionally to colleagues across a wider curriculum. Apart from the SLT, only impoverished teachers volunteered for paid lunch time duty. It was seen by the staff as their duty not to do a duty and to let the highest paid among them put up with the pupils at lunch time since they didn't have to put up with them for the rest of the day.

Between these key points in the day, the odd teacher who was free, would stray into the staffroom and pick up their mail from their pigeon hole or make a quick coffee and then return to use the peace and quiet of a vacant classroom.

The end of the day saw the same professionals pop in to the staffroom in dribs and drabs to collect coats, lunch boxes and documents that may or may not be important. By quarter to five the staffroom was empty other than the cleaner who made it known to the four walls and the other human being in the room what messy thoughtless tramps teachers were.

Corinne nodded and tried to smile in sympathy but she was too absorbed with work to really connect with a woman old enough to have been her grandmother.

"Hi Corinne. I thought I would find you here. Here's your laptop back," said Neil.

"No luck Neil?" asked Corinne.

"Oh yes, it's sorted. There was a virus on the machine so I cleaned your files and defragged your systems." Had Charlie delivered this line it would have taken on a whole new meaning. As it was, Corinne understood what he was talking about and felt so grateful for his help.

"Thank you so much. That's brilliant. I can't tell you how relieved I am. I thought I'd have to do this here in the staff room every night and every morning for the next few weeks."

"Glad I could help but remember it's my job here to sort out IT problems and you can always get hold of me. I'm here usually between seven am and six pm."

"So you don't have much of a life either?"

"Well the IT systems keep me quite busy and I like helping people out if I can. I suppose I'd better let you get back to your work."

"That's okay, I've finished all I needed to do tonight and now that I have my laptop working I feel better about the rest of the week. I can relax a bit."

"Good. It sounds as if you could do with switching off from school for a few hours before you try to get some sleep tonight…I don't suppose…no…never mind."

"What?"

"I was wondering…if you fancied going for a drink before you went home?"

"Oh, thanks but no…Thank you for asking but I don't really do pubs."

"Okay, that's fine, no problem, never mind…" jabbered Neil.

There was a ten second pause that lasted ten minutes.

"How about we go for a bite to eat instead?" asked Corinne, smiling for the first time in weeks.

CHAPTER 17

Peter was ready for bed and it was only ten in the morning. He was too tired to focus on the office clock or to read the face of his watch. Even when his eye sight was 20/20 he found it difficult to tell the time on his wrist watch. It was one of those without anything helpful on it, like sensible hands or numbers, but he had to wear it as it was a fiftieth birthday present from either his daughter or his wife....he was too tired to remember which it was or what their names were.

Perhaps if he told Penny to hold all calls and shoot anyone approaching his office door, he could have a power nap for the rest of the day. No, that wouldn't work. Penny could deflect all phone calls for the rest of the day and Peter was pretty sure she possessed a selection of fire arms in the bottom drawer of her desk, but he would feel guilty sleeping on the job and a little embarrassed that he could probably get away with it for a bit without anyone noticing. Why was it he felt he could sleep at his desk right now but ten hours ago, lying horizontal on his comfy king size bed, he couldn't even see one single sheep to count in his field of dreams.

He had laid there in bed going through various things in his mind. The various things were a series of questions that became a to-do list which he mentally started to draft, then re-arrange and prioritise with actions, time limits and success criteria.

First: How many people were coming to the get-together on Saturday? He didn't know for certain. Consequently Rachel had chewed his ear off because she needed to know numbers for catering purposes. He would ask his SLT in the next 24 hours and a definitive number would be reported back to his wife by the following evening.

Second: *Was the Ofsted Action Plan okay? Had everyone who needed to see it, seen it? What would the HMI think of it?* He would check with Penny and Charlie to see if they had forgotten to show it to anyone important. He would do this in the morning and task Penny with the job of listing all parties who had seen the latest draft of the plan. The problem was that there were so many iterations that Peter was not sure if everyone was working from the same version anymore. He set himself the target that by next Monday he would have a final definitive draft and circulate it to everyone. Well, perhaps not everyone. Certain tribes along the Amazon might not receive the document because of the cost of postage.

Third: When would he see any improvement in the Maths department? Was there ever going to be any real progress with Richard Perry in charge? Should he have another one-to-one with Mr Perry or should he talk to Julie and Jo first and get their take on the situation? It was one thing writing in the action plan that a series of strategies were under way but if the HMI couldn't see any tangible results from the school's efforts, then the plan was worthless. A meeting was needed with Jo and Julie. Some hard decisions needed to be taken and Peter was almost certain that he was hard enough to make them. Perhaps he would ask Charlie what he thought first. He would definitely do that tomorrow, once he had thought about it some more.

Peter kept on thinking, planning and trying to sleep. At certain times during the night he was sure that he had slept and managed to dream. He remembered being at the bottom of a dam and looking up as the wall started to crack. He also remembered teaching sex education to a group of Year 10 girls buck naked. He also remembered swapping places at birth with Jimi Hendrix - Jimi went on to be an outstanding Head teacher and Peter became a third rate backing guitarist in a band at a holiday camp. There was also the recurring dream that had haunted him for weeks now. It involved Peter waking up late every morning, deciding not to go to work and going down to a video store to hire *Groundhog Day*.

Peter knew he was going mad. It was just the rate of progress of his madness that alarmed him. *Could he last until he retired or was sacked? What was the time line?*

The phone rang on his desk and his madness scuttled back into the dark recesses of his mind for a break. Peter re-gained some sanity and drowned his sleepiness with a swig of cold coffee before picking up the phone.

"Brian Green wants to see you. He says it's urgent," said Penny apologetically.

Peter felt like instructing her to shoot him on sight but thought better of it. After all he could be standing right next to Penny at her desk.

"Is he with you now?"

"Yes he is."

"Okay, thanks Penny. Send him in please."

Peter came around his desk so they could sit across a coffee table rather than at his desk. The move suggested a meeting on equal terms with nothing to hide but was in fact because Peter had cramp in one of his legs.

"Brian, what can I help you with?" asked Peter, hoping Brian had come in to ask for some dinner money because his wife had forgotten to pack his sandwiches today. Alas, that was never going to be the issue.

"I wanted you to hear the news as soon as possible. I just opened my emails and the NUT have called a national strike for the week after next, on the Wednesday. Pretty much all of the NUT members will be out that day. We met last week as you know and they all voted for strike action and are all prepared to lose a day's pay."

"What's your guesstimate on numbers?"

"I think between thirty-six and forty teachers. Now, of course, it is not my place to discuss with you the course of action that you take but the NUT's line is that members from other unions cannot cover or substitute for striking colleagues," said Brian, towing the party line.

"I understand that. It's just a messy situation when teachers belong to different unions. It looks as if I'll have to close the school for the day and that means that striking teachers will lose a day's pay and the teachers in the other unions will get paid for doing nothing. That seems very unfair to me."

"I agree. I would be the first to admit this type of strike isn't ideal. It makes the profession look as if we don't or can't agree on the fundamentals such as pay, conditions and performance management. It would have been far more powerful if all the unions could agree on the same course of action."

"Or inaction, I suppose. Well thanks for letting me know, Brian. I appreciate that. I'll have to take advice from my union and discuss the situation with the Chair of Governors and the SLT. It was only a few years ago that I was in your union and would have supported the strike. Now I'm supposed to frown and tell you strike action is counter-productive and will only make more and more members of the public, and parents in particular, anti-teachers. As Head I have to say the timing of this strike isn't good but I suppose there never is a good time," admitted Peter.

"If we waited for the general public to decide on a good time then they would probably opt for half way through the summer holidays when it doesn't affect them."

"True. Can you give me a list of all of your members?"

"Why?"

"Don't panic, I'm not going to bully or harass them. But I will need a record of which teachers won't be at work that day as I have to notify the Local Authority for payment purposes. If you prefer, you can go round and canvas each of your members and supply me with a list of those who are striking. Would that be more acceptable?"

"I think so. Some teachers may find it a little intimidating to be asked the question by you."

"I understand. I'm such an ogre!"

"Shit, shit, shit!" exclaimed Peter once Brian had disappeared. Steam poured from the kettle and his ears.

"A three shit meeting, sounds bad," said Penny standing behind Peter. "Want to tell your Auntie Penny all about it."

"What would I do without you?" said Peter as he flopped back into his warm chair.

It took twenty minutes and another thirteen expletives to vent all poisonous gases from his body and render Peter calm enough to work with Penny on yet another piece of crisis management. This one involved several phone calls, several meetings and several drafts of a letter to parents explaining how very sorry he was to have to inform them that they would need to take responsibility for their own children as the school would be closed on the day of a planned teacher strike. Following this notification there would be several, to the power of ten, complaints from parents levelled at him. He would have to sit and listen to them slagging off teachers and threatening to send them to school anyway.

Many things at Whatmore were his fault or responsibility, but not this. For once, he was blameless. Not that that mattered to his more vocal parents. They needed a target to aim at and Peter was the biggest around. *Oh the joy of being a Head teacher!*

CHAPTER 18

"Wow!" It was all that Charlie could say after all that exertion. He was sweating profusely. Certain parts of his body were numb, other parts were stiff and he was in desperate need of a drink of water.

That was a really long session he thought but he'd enjoyed every minute of it until he stopped through exhaustion and aching feet. He slowed right down and walked the last few paces before sitting down on his favourite park bench. The late afternoon had faded into early evening and he told himself that he should be making his way homeward or at least to the club for a quick pint.

Charlie had left school as early as he could after spending most of the day in meetings about either teachers taking strike action or pupils striking each other. He had sat with Peter and Penny for a good portion of the day to work out the strategy for the NUT's strike day and to create a letter to parents in an attempt to limit damage and safeguard reputations. He had been invited into meetings with Brian Green and then separately with reps from the other unions who were not striking.

Penny, on Charlie's advice, had minuted all of the meetings, so there could be no confusion when it came to what was said and what was agreed. *Some hope* thought Charlie but it did formalise the meetings and cover backs. He couldn't help notice, even with his limited emotional intelligence, that Peter looked and sounded somewhere between scared and pissed off. With that in mind Charlie was happy to provide support in all the meetings.

By the end of the day all parties knew who was on strike next week and would be formally notified that they would be docked a day's pay. The non-striking brand of teachers would be formally notified of the employer's expectation that they would attend school and work the statutory hours.

A whole lot of formal notifications and expectations were discussed and, Charlie couldn't stop thinking as the day went on, they were wasting a great deal of time over a dispute that would not be resolved until the country had spare money again to spend on teachers. That wouldn't be happening during his career or, come to that, during his lifetime.

By the end of the morning a letter had been generated that would be sent out via pupil post. The same letter would go on the school's website, which gave parents two golden opportunities not to read the vital information it contained.

After lunch duty, Charlie had spent two hours seeing parents and their beloved and totally innocent children who were guilty of all sorts of crimes against Whatmore. One or two of the crimes involved physical altercations and almost all the offences involved verbal assault. When it came to meetings that involved child, parent, tutor and Year Head, Charlie was cast in the role of judge, jury, policeman, social worker and referee. He tried to restrict the use of un-pleasantries in the room but by the end of the session it was often the parents who were given a warning by Charlie because of their verbal or physical threats to their own kids. Of course there were always parents who adopted the same tactics as their offspring, claiming *It wasn't him - it was someone else* or *You're all picking on her*...but Charlie had heard it all before and knew how to deal with deaf, dumb and blind parents who wouldn't take responsibility. The parents never won in a game refereed by Mr Briggs. Over the last ten years he couldn't remember a meeting where he had to settle for a score draw. Unless Charlie was certain of the facts he wouldn't bother arranging a meeting with parents and by and large the parents knew that.

After four wins and some post-match de-briefing with his staff, Charlie was ready to leave school. He changed into his running kit, jumped in the car and ran around the local park seven times before coming to a halt at the bench overlooking the small, ornamental lake. On most circuits he said *Hello* back to kids who were playing football, skateboarding or hiding cigarettes behind their backs. This was his time now and he wasn't going to stop for anyone, even if they were smoking themselves to death in school uniform.

It had been a busy few days at work and in his personal life and he was tired and stressed, so Charlie put on his trainers to run away from it all. He had done a lot of thinking during his run, reflecting on some things he had done already and some things he was close to doing.

He had called it a day with the Head of Year 11. That hadn't gone down well. Through her tears in his office, she had pleaded for their exercise regime to continue in any shape or form. Charlie couldn't quite work out if she was really upset because he was such a catch or if she was offended that he had been the one to end the affair.

On a second stormy encounter she had demanded to know why he wanted to end their relationship. For Charlie this was the most difficult part of the puzzle to complete. He didn't want to say to this attractive youngish amazon that he was getting too old or that he had decided he loved his wife more or that he preferred to play golf rather than indulge in office rumpy-pumpy. A stereotypical cad and hypocrite to the end, he had fed her something along the lines that he was falling in love with her and he couldn't take the next step because they were both married. It sounded a load of rubbish and it was, but it went down better than he expected. This form of rejection didn't hurt her pride and they had managed to be professional with each other in the main office. She had not ventured into his private office at the end of the day for a while now.

Charlie sat on the bench, regaining his breath, knowing that he was developing his own action plan. The draft plan was something along the lines of:

a) Become a one-woman man
b) Stop working as a deputy head
c) Pay more attention to his wife
d) Stop looking at young attractive women walking by
e) Pay more attention to his wife.

Charlie could do this. The plan was manageable and achievable. *But what would be the time parameters? Who was the person responsible or more importantly who was the responsible person?* That would have to be moi, Charlie supposed.

He looked across the darkening lake and decided it was time to go. If he stayed out here any longer he could get mugged or worse, be mistaken for an old person wanting to feed the ducks.

He had one decision left as he hobbled back to the car, mobile phone in hand. Should he phone his wife and tell her that he was on his way home after a run or tell her that he was leaving school in about thirty minutes and then nip round to the sports club for a quick pint.

The new, improved Charlie Briggs sat in his car and made the call. He would be home in five minutes.

CHAPTER 19

The following day Julie quietly approached Penny and asked her when the advertisement was going in the Times Education Supplement. The answer was tomorrow's edition and that it was already available on-line.

"I've sorted out hard copies of everything you'll need and put it into a folder for you. I knew you'd be asking me some time soon."

"Thanks, Penny. I've tried to keep out of the way recently because it's awkward for everyone."

"Honestly, Julie, it's not awkward for me. I'm glad you're applying and I hope you get the post...if that's what you want. On the other hand, if you're feeling pressurised into applying for a job you don't really know if you want..."

There was a pause until Julie filled the gap. "Oh God Penny, is it that obvious? To be honest I'm in two minds. I'm not sure I want to be here much longer. The school is going through a rough patch and I'm still relatively young and..."

"And your personal life should take priority?"

"Well, yes. That as well..."

"There will always be other jobs for someone as good as you, but the right person to share your life with is a different matter. Finding someone who will look after you and treat you well is far more important than any job, don't you think? Or am I just an old romantic?"

"You're not old and if you're a romantic, then so am I."

"Peter wouldn't be happy if he heard me saying this but I think you need to give it some thought before you apply or certainly before you accept the position, if it's offered to you. Most people at Whatmore would like you to get the job but if you don't think it's right for you, don't sign on the dotted line..."

Penny handed Julie the pack and the counselling session was over. Penny returned to her screen and her austere façade while Julie walked back to her office clutching the pack tightly but almost wanting to throw it in the nearest bin.

When she got home that night Mark had cooked and laid the table. He met her by the door so obviously pleased to see her. He put his arms around her and kissed her passionately. This was a gentleman who would look after her. This was a man who would make a great dad.

He had proved himself thoughtful and considerate so many times since that wonderful day when they met but last Saturday was the real eye-opener for Julie. He was so amazingly kind and caring all that day. First of all he was so nice when they accidentally bumped into Neil Turner in the car park after they'd been shopping. While Julie and Neil had been so awkward they'd hardly been able to string two words together, Mark had taken charge and befriended Neil. He had kept the conversation going for twenty minutes in the car park and made both of them feel at ease. He'd even recognised Neil's anxiety about overrunning on the car park charge and insisted on giving him the extra money. Then on the way home, Mark had made it clear to Julie that it was really good to meet someone connected to her other life.

Later on that afternoon Julie had started to feel nauseous. It was Mark's friend's party in a few hours' time and she was already a nervous wreck. She was going to officially announce herself to Mark's friends as his older woman. She spent three hours getting ready and then aimed a series of impossible questions at Mark such as: *Don't I look like mutton dressed up like lamb in this?* and *Shouldn't I wear my hair up?* and *What do you think of these earrings?* and *Are you sure I don't look like a tart in this?* After being bombarded with these and many more questions, Mark just walked over to Julie and held her as closely as he dared without messing up her make-up and hair and told her she was *Perfect*. Her knees wobbled and if they hadn't been going out that night she would have ravaged him there and then.

At the party, he didn't leave Julie's side all night, except to fetch them drinks, and he made a point of introducing her as his girlfriend to anyone and everyone. They danced both fast and slow, pleasantly drunk and paid for a taxi back to her flat at three in the morning. An hour or so later they went to sleep in each other's arms. The perfect day and night. *Outstanding*!

Now, a few days' later, Julie wanted to ask Mark a couple of important questions. She waited until they had finished the meal, loaded the dishwasher and made a mug of tea and had snuggled up next to each other on the settee. Mark was flicking through the television channels with the remote control.

"Mark, before we watch anything on the box, can I ask you something?"

"Sure. What is it sweetheart? Are you okay?"

"Yes I'm fine but there are a couple of work things I want to discuss."

"Are you sure I'm the right person to talk to? What about the people in your team?"

"No, it's about the senior team, so I can't really ask them."

"Oh, okay." Mark switched the TV off, put down the remote and took Julie's hand in his. "You have my full attention for half an hour and then I'll have to start unbuttoning your blouse."

"In that case I'll be as quick as I can…You remember I said that I would have to go to Peter Burlington's house this Saturday afternoon. It's a sort of bonding session for his senior team. I'm not looking forward to it but I have to go."

"I know, but you can probably make excuses and come away early if you're not enjoying it," said Mark.

"Well, that's the thing. I won't enjoy it because I won't be with you." She kissed him and he thought that was the signal to start in on the unbuttoning. Julie playfully slapped his hand and moved slightly away from his clutches.

"What I'm trying to say is…would you come with me on Saturday? I know it will be awful and you won't know anyone and they'll be talking about school all of the time and they'll all be staring at us and it will be terrible. God, I'm sorry I shouldn't have mentioned it. I'll go by myself and get away as quickly as possible. We can go for a meal as soon as I get back." Julie was jabbering in her anxiety.

"No need," said Mark.

"Why not?"

"Because I'm coming with you to the party. I want to meet your colleagues and I don't want to be apart from you."

Julie's face burst into smiles. "Thank you. I love you Mark." She said it without considering the implications.

"And I love you too..." replied Mark genuinely. He moved in for the kill and Julie decided not to mention the application for deputy headship because he was already half way through the essential process of undoing her buttons.

CHAPTER 20

Peter had worked his way down his to-do list and he was feeling rather pleased with himself. He had managed to tick off several quick wins. He was ready for the more active part of his list. He needed to conduct a learning walk, which was the current jargon for walking around and making yourself noticed by the pupils and teachers. While poking his head into a few well-behaved classrooms and avoiding some of the more unruly classes he would attempt to track down his SLT. The number one priority on his list was now to get a yes or no out of all of them for tomorrow's get together at his house. Peter was under strict instruction from Rachel to get a definitive list of people attending so she could make sure there was enough food.

Peter made his way into the Pastoral block where he could see Charlie in the main office in discussion with another teacher. The man in question had an unfortunate way with his classes and unfortunately for the school was on a permanent contract. Whatever advice was given, it always ended up with the teacher claiming it was the pupils' fault. The kindest and most charitable words Peter could use to describe him were self-opinionated, pompous, obnoxious and arrogant. Charlie, Peter knew, might choose his words less carefully. Peter could see Charlie was fighting hard to control his tongue and his temper in dealing with Mr Wonderful. The man seemed to hate in equal measures, teaching and children but for some reason he managed to get good results out of the pupils, mainly because most of the kids were afraid of him. So although this teacher had no business working in any school, he fulfilled the Teachers' Standards.

Peter had often thought *Why on Earth did Mr Wonderful decide to teach?* and *How on Earth did he gain any satisfaction in doing the job?* In an ideal world Peter would have really enjoyed calling Wonderful into his office and sacking him on the spot or even better, in an alternative universe, he would have got even greater pleasure beating him up. Perhaps this wasn't something to be found in the leadership and management manuals but it ought to be in there filed under the heading *How to deal with difficult people.*

Peter peering through the glass section of the door, caught Charlie's eye. He mimed: *Are you coming to the party tomorrow?* and then *How many?* Charlie indicated two…or at least Peter hoped that's what he meant.

Next stop was Neil's office but knocking on the solid wooden door yielded no reply. Peter tried the door but it was locked.

The next part of the mystery tour was Julie's office. She was on the phone but indicated Peter should sit down. She told the person on the other end of the phone that she would call back later.

"Sorry Julie, I didn't mean to interrupt."

"That's okay, not a problem."

"I just wanted to ask you a couple of things as I was passing. First, the deputy job is in the TES today. Are you still going to apply?"

"Yes."

Peter was expecting a less abrupt response. "Ah…Good…Well if you need any help…I know I should be neutral in all this but if I can help please ask me or Charlie…In fact Charlie won't be involved in the interview process so he could certainly help you."

"Thanks…Do you think I need help?" asked Julie, playfully.

"No…no…of course not…" It was only after stammering his way through these five words that Peter realised that Julie was enjoying watching him squirm. He smiled at a Head teacher of the future.

"Peter, I appreciate the offer and that you're in a difficult position but it's okay. I'll apply and hope to get the job but if I don't I'm not going to slash my wrists. I'm a big girl."

Peter concentrated on staring at Julie's face for thirty seconds after this comment. It would be so easy to take it the wrong way.

"I know you can cope with the pressure but it'll seem weird when you see me showing other keen and enthusiastic applicants round – trying to sell them the school and throwing in mats and a spare wheel to boot, so to speak."

"I know the protocol. I'll diplomatically keep out of their way until the day of the interview and then I'll be Xena Warrior Princess going for their throats. Can you tell me what the party games will be?"

"You mean tomorrow at our bonding session or the interview process?" It was Peter's turn to be flippant.

"No, Mr B. On the day of the interview."

"There'll be a presentation, some small group interviews and a main interview in front of the world and her husband. I can't say more than that but I can tell you I'm not a believer in psychometric tests and silly games. I like to look someone in the eye to see if they are telling the truth, not hook them up to a lie detector."

"Blimey, Peter. I might as well quit now. My whole career has been based on blagging and bullshit!"

"I know the feeling. I'm really an eight stone, thirty seven year old woman but many years ago I decided to dress like this to climb the career ladder."

They grinned at each other, a warmth reviving between them that had been missing recently.

"Look, I'll let you go. I can see Jo hovering outside. More discussions on Maths I suppose? Perhaps next week the two of you can meet me to go through your discussions and plans?"

"Oh, sure. Happy to do that," said Julie feeling a touch of the heat rising in her face.

"And you'll be at the party tomorrow? No party games - just food, drink and unprofessional conversation."

"Yes, I will...Is it okay if I bring someone...a friend...of the male persuasion?" Julie's cheeks could almost activate the sprinklers in the office ceiling.

"Wow...of course it is...Yes...Brilliant...Look forward to meeting him. What's his name?"

"Mark."

"Have you warned Mark what he's letting himself in for…Neil the Nerd, Sobia the Ice Queen, Charlie the Clown and Peter the Buffoon."

"Don't worry. I've painted the worst picture possible. I've told him to wear bullet proof armour and ear protectors. Seriously, though, don't frighten him away. I'm only just getting my claws into him."

"Don't worry Xena, I'll be the perfect gentleman and diplomat…but I can't vouch for Charlie."

Peter left with a "Hi" to Jo and wishing the women *Good luck* with their Maths discussion.

"Thank you" said Jo, becoming the latest member of the glowing cheeks brigade and concealing her chocolate bars behind her back.

Wandering along the corridors towards Sobia's office, Peter spotted Neil in a seemingly empty classroom. He stopped in his tracks as if he'd espied a rare species he wanted to capture with a camera, a net or a gun. For Neil wasn't alone. He was talking to another member of the human race and both he and the other human were smiling. Surprised, he gave it a few seconds before knocking and disturbing them mid laugh. They looked up and froze.

"Sorry to disturb you…could I have a quick word, Neil?"

"Sure…yes…fine. I was just helping Miss Peckett with an IT issue. She's had a real problem with her…"

"Sorry Corinne, I didn't mean to disturb you both but it won't take a minute. I was just passing…" He didn't need to explain - he was the Head after all - but somehow he felt he ought to.

"It's not a problem, Mr Burlington. I mean the laptop is a problem but you interrupting isn't a problem, if you see what I mean," said Corinne.

Neil left the classroom with Peter who closed the door behind them. Corinne was safely encaged in her own room and Neil was now freed up to return to his own den if he wished.

"I just wanted to confirm that you're still coming tomorrow."

"Yes, I'll be there," said Neil.

"Good." Peter continued. "Some of the team are bringing someone but you don't have to. It'll be good to see you tomorrow"

"No, I'll be on my own but thanks."

"Good, glad you can come. About three o'clock" and with that Peter started to move away. Neil remained rooted to the spot.

Sobia was easy to track down. She rarely left her office unless summoned to a meeting. She was, as predicted, in her office but not at her desk. She was sitting with Cathy and Diane on either side of her. They were examining the contents of a folder together. They all looked up as Peter entered.

"Oh, hello Mr Burlington. I was just showing Cathy and Diane some photos of the holiday we had a few years ago. We went to Cape Cod for two weeks before the twins were born. Cathy is thinking of going there for her fiftieth birthday…"

"Surely not?" said Peter hurriedly.

"Don't you advise it Mr Burlington?" asked Cathy.

"No. I mean yes…yes I do advise it but I meant surely you're not fifty this year?"

"Oh I see, yes. Next summer is my big five-oh."

"Well, I wouldn't have thought that." Peter's repeated attempt at flattery was as clumsy as the first.

"How old do you think I am then Mr Burlington?" asked Cathy, looking a little worried.

Peter was not only in hot water now but drowning in it without a paddle or a rubber ring.

"Err…in your…forties." He had decided quickly not to go lower in case that sounded ridiculous. He had assumed that Cathy was well into her fifties already. She honestly looked it and to Peter she could have passed for a Saga Cruise frequent passenger.

"Well, she is still in her forties," chirped Diane.

"True," said Peter, wishing he had phoned Sobia instead of coming in person. He addressed himself specifically at Sobia so as to cause no further confusion. "Could I have a quick word, please?"

Sobia walked out into the corridor with him and Peter said "I just wanted to check you're coming to our house tomorrow...It's no problem if you can't. I'd quite understand."

"No. Yes I'm coming. Is it okay if I bring my family?"

"Of course," said Peter, without pause, hesitation, deviation or any risk of repetition. But his next utterance was a comprehensive failure "Yes...that would be...really, really great...It would be great to see your boys and your husband...I don't think I've seen him for...."

"They can be a bit of a handful but I'll bring some toys to keep them occupied."

Peter wasn't sure if she meant she'd bring toys for her husband too and if so what sort of toys he'd want to play with but he knew he couldn't ask that. He opted for his favourite word of the moment, "Great...see you all tomorrow about three. I'll let you get back to your holiday snaps."

He turned into first gear to walk back to the comfort and safety of his own office but Sobia's voice stopped him. "Sorry about the holiday photographs. I thought it might help to create a better..."

Peter stalled. "No need to explain or apologise. It's a good idea, you're doing a good job. See you tomorrow."

Peter walked away counting guests in his head. He was almost there. He had already asked Penny and she and her husband were coming. He just needed to chase Ann Brown. When he'd asked her at the end of a long and tedious governors' meeting, she'd mislaid her diary somewhere and couldn't say. If he phoned Ann, Rachel would have her definitive numbers for catering.

Unbelievably back at his office, Ann Brown was already there talking to Penny. He panicked. *Had he missed a meeting with his Chair of Governors? Surely not.*

"Hello Peter, I popped in because I wanted a word and Penny said you were free after your learning walk."

A *learning walk* was one way to describe the last twenty minutes of activity. The judgement however fell well outside the parameters of Ofsted's four point scale. The figure was over ten already, not including the twins.

"I wanted to show you something," said Ann.

"Of course. Come through."

Peter delayed consideration of whatever the problem might be by making coffees while Ann sorted through her bags for her glasses, her phone and other random items. As he sat down opposite her, she produced the latest edition of the Gazette and slid it across the table. Even upside down Peter could read the main headlines on the front page:

SCHOOL FAILS PUPILS A SECOND TIME
Inadequate teachers go on strike for more money

"I'm the bringer of bad news I'm afraid and it's not pretty reading. The feature links the Ofsted inspection to the teachers' strike next week and puts Whatmore in the *waste of time and space* category. Have a read yourself."

Peter slowly absorbed the two column article accompanied by a smiling photograph of himself outside the school gates by the school sign with its slogan; *Caring, Demanding, Achieving.*

The subtext was that a school already letting down its pupils was now going to close its gates for the day and deprive the poor children of even more of the bad education sadly offered. The article continued by portraying Whatmore's teachers as selfish, highly-paid failures trying to claim more money in their overstuffed pay packets while working one less day in a year already heavily punctuated by holidays as it was.

There was no accurate mention of the Ofsted judgement, only a blunt use of the word *inadequate*. Nor was it clarified that the strike was national and not just centred on Whatmore's catchment area.

Peter read the article again and flicked through the rest of the paper but the damage was all in the front page splash.

"It's really unfortunate that the teachers' strike and the inspection have come so close to each other," said Ann sympathetically.

"It's played right into The Gazette's hands. The paper has clearly kept the inspection's findings on file until it can find another damning story to wrap around it."

"So what's our response?" Ann asked.

"Well from a pragmatic point of view, we can't change the past. We can't change Ofsted's judgement and we can't change our minds on what we do next Wednesday. The strike will go ahead regardless and the article's out there in the public domain. If we try to respond in next week's Gazette they probably won't publish and it's too late by then."

"They could do us further damage next week on the day of the strike by interviewing and photographing our kids with their poor parents outside the locked school gates losing out on a whole day of education," Ann retorted, fearing the worst.

"The only way we can limit the damage to a small nuclear explosion is by sending another letter to parents which deals directly with the article and the strike next week. Although I don't feel inclined to apologise to the parents for something outside my control."

"Then don't. Don't apologise. Don't do anything!"

"How do you mean, Ann?"

"Perhaps this is one of those occasions where the best course of action is to do nothing. Everyone will have made up their minds by now…Some parents will kick up a fuss but most won't give a hoot. Our parents already think teachers are on too much money and are lazy part-timers who can't and shouldn't be respected by them or their kids…and that's just the supportive ones!"

"So what are you saying? Let it lie and see it through?"

"I'm just saying it's worth considering," Ann said raising her hands as if to stop traffic.

"I appreciate the suggestion, but my knee is still in jerking mode and I want to kick someone's bottom at the moment. I want to explain that this is a national strike and my staff are all hardworking people who deserve to be treated with some respect. The trouble is I can't say that having one day off won't harm the kids or I'll be leaving myself wide open when I tell parents about the importance of attendance. And then of course some of our working parents may lose a day's pay to look after little...Sanjita or William."

Ann started to move off the topic. "It's funny isn't it? We, as a nation, support the right to strike and are sympathetic to the plight of others who are being mistreated by their bosses but when it comes to being inconvenienced, then it's a different story. As soon as we can't use a train, or can't send our kids to school then sympathy goes out the window."

Peter was half-listening to Ann and trying to weigh up his options at the same time. Action versus inaction. This was not the first time Peter, man and boy, had met these two impostors and now he had to keep his headship when all about him were losing theirs and blaming it on him. He found he was coming round to Ann's approach. *What could he say in another letter to parents that would make matters any better? Was he throwing in the towel on the issue or on his career or was he not even getting his hands dirty so he'd have no use for a towel at all?*

His mood lightened. "Annie, my fair lady, I think you're right, I will be your Dr Doolittle. Hopefully by Monday morning most people will be using The Gazette as toilet paper."

"I thought everybody used cute Labrador puppies for that? I certainly do!"

"So we agree. Our action is inaction?"

"Agreed."

"Thanks for your insight on this Ann. If you hadn't made the time to come in today, I wouldn't have found out about this until later and then I'd have been bending your ear on the phone and contemplating shooting myself."

"That would have made a much more serious article for next week's Gazette. Anyway it's bad form for the party host to commit suicide the night before the guests arrive. It puts a real damper on the occasion."

"Okay. I'll leave the shotgun in the desk drawer. Does this mean you're coming tomorrow?"

"Indeed. Even if it's to check your pulse." Ann gathered up her things and left. But she left the newspaper on the table.

Peter knew the first casualty of the article would have to be the loss of an early Friday night departure from work.

"Get the team together for a short discussion at the end of the day, please," he told Penny. Then he rang Rachel, grovelled because he'd be later home than he'd hoped but by way of recompense offered up the final number of party guests expected on the morrow. He explained that Sobia's twins were coming and that it might be an idea to re-position some of the ornaments in their living room.

Unsurprisingly, Rachel agreed.

CHAPTER 21

Sobia and her family had been at Peter's house for almost an hour and she was trying her upmost to smile and stay calm whilst suppressing a range of fears gathering in a disorderly fashion in the back of her mind.

Over the last week Sobia had used all her powers of diplomacy and bribery to persuade her husband to accompany her to the party. He had not been keen on the idea but her gradual and subtle feminine charm and guile had won him round to the point at which he started to believe he actually wanted to go. Persuasion with her twin boys had been less subtle. It was a simple concoction of threat, bribery and more threat.

The first thirty minutes or so at Peter's house were spent as a tight family unit moving from one small group of people to another. The three men in her life smiled at appropriate moments, talked when required and behaved impeccably.

Just as the strain was getting too much for the boys, Charlie came to the rescue. The day was dry and warm and he suggested to Peter and Rachel that he took the boys out into the back garden for some games. Rachel smiled and agreed to the plan realising she valued the contents of her house even more than her plants, shrubs and lawn.

Sobia's husband jumped at the opportunity to stop pretending interest in teachers' talking about teaching and offered to help Charlie out. Julie's new friend also volunteered to join in the fun and games outside. Sobia wasn't quite sure who this Mark was and how long he had been *friends* with Julie but it was clear to her that he was a confident young man who had certainly thrown himself into the party.

This left three social sub-committees randomly spaced around the lounge talking about all things connected with education. Ann Brown, the Chair of Governors, Charlie's wife and Rachel were discussing the damning story in The Gazette; Julie, Neil, Penny and her husband were debating the merits of Ofsted inspections; and Peter was talking to Sobia about the school system and what was wrong with it.

Sobia tried to show interest while glancing regularly through the patio doors to check up on her boys. They all seemed to be enjoying themselves. She started to relax and gradually gained the confidence to mingle with the other guests and not keep looking out into the garden. She found it easy to talk to Peter and Charlie's wives because they were both happy to explain to Sobia how flawed and hopeless their husbands were but that they had their occasional moments. Sobia wondered if these admissions were coincidental or if they knew something about her own husband. They told each other amusing tales that illustrated their husbands' idiosyncrasies and more idiotic tendencies. Strangely, they all felt better for sharing and knowing they were not alone.

Later on Sobia spent a little time with Julie and innocently probed her about her friend, Mark. Julie, who appeared to have had a few glasses of wine, seemed quite happy to disclose various elements of her personal life that would normally be stamped private and confidential. Julie gave Sobia a fairly graphic account of the beginning of her relationship with Mark and the key actions and activities in their development plan. There was clearly no need for Sobia's probing to be innocent or otherwise; Julie had openly enjoyed a good deal of probing in the last couple of months.

Sobia talked to Ann Brown and to Penny and her husband for a while about holidays and foreign currency and realised being a mother, while joyous and rewarding at times, can also narrow your horizons.

The only person Sobia didn't manage to talk freely with was Neil. This was not out of choice. Sobia liked Neil, in a strange sort of way, but found it difficult to find a topic of small talk they could both engage in with confidence. She looked across at Neil standing by the patio doors looking out at the boys playing football and she could see a man torn between the comfort of the carpet and the turf of the football pitch. She was just about to go over to him when the Burlingtons started bringing food from the kitchen and placing it on the dining room table. Sobia helped. She was comfortably at home with food preparation and presentation.

Peter summoned the teams representing Brazil and England back in to attack the food. Rachel had included some child-friendly stuff for the twins and Peter had set up an area in the kitchen for the boys so they could eat messily and spill their drinks without fear and Peter supervised them while

Sobia and her husband and the other guests helped themselves to finger food.

Rachel went round topping up drinks and being the perfect hostess, pointing out which items were meat and which were vegetarian. The food and drink relaxed everyone even further. Neil and Mark got talking IT with Sobia and Penny's husbands; Charlie's wife was now engaged with Ann Brown on her perennial subject of holidays and foreign currency; and Charlie was playfully flirting with and teasing Julie and Penny.

Sobia realised that she was so absorbed in people watching that she was standing on her own so she grabbed a handful of crisps and headed for the kitchen. There she discovered Peter, Head teacher of Whatmore School, with two chicken nuggets poking out of his mouth like fangs, making her sons giggle uncontrollably. She joined the three daft children and became a fourth sitting at the kitchen table playing with their food.

In the next ten minutes of the mad hatter's tea party, Sobia realised why Peter was a successful Head teacher regardless of what Ofsted said. He was kind, considerate and a nice man. Although that doesn't win you awards for leadership or make Ofsted shower you with plaudits, in Sobia's book it made Peter *outstanding*.

While the boys tucked into some ice cream Sobia squeezed Peter's arm and mouthed very quietly, "Thank you." Peter blushed and whispered back, "You're welcome."

Once Peter had finished being a children's entertainer, Julie and Mark took over. They sat on the carpet at one end of the lounge with the boys and played *shops* and *wink murder*. More and more adults who could manage to sit on the floor, after eating and drinking so much, joined in. Mark took centre stage and the kids and the adults all seemed to love him. Sobia could tell that Julie adored this young man and had real plans for him as both a husband and a father.

It was almost eight o'clock by the time people started to make noises about leaving. It was at this point that Peter halted the conversation and laughter and said a few words. He thanked everyone for coming and he thanked his wife for all of her hard work in preparing the excellent food. Finally he said he hoped, no matter what inspectors and reporters threw at the school, that the outstanding team of people assembled in his home could keep smiling and carry on. It was a short speech but a moving one, prompting mutters of approval and a few watery eyes.

Just as the moment could have turned awkward, Charlie raised his glass and said "To Peter and Rachel." The leadership team and their partners repeated the words in unison and the party began the inevitable process of disintegration.

Charlie's wife had agreed to drive them home. It was usual for them, like most couples after a party, to spend the journey home criticising and analysing the hosts, the other guests, the house and the hospitality. They would normally also make sweeping statements about how they would have better managed the event themselves. In the case of Peter and Rachel's annual get together, neither driver nor passenger could fault the occasion. They had enjoyed all of it; the party, the company and the catering.

Charlie had particularly enjoyed meeting Julie's boyfriend and in his avuncular way he was pleased she had found someone to make her happy. She would definitely need some fun and balance in her life if she was going to be a Deputy Head soon. Charlie would be content and reassured in his decision to retire next year if Julie was securely in place supporting Peter with some strong Year Heads to lead the pastoral care of the school.

Charlie wasn't going to hang on at Whatmore out of loyalty. He was pretty sure that he was ready to go at the end of the year. Some people reach the end of their careers staring in fear at the blank piece of paper in front of them. Not Charlie. He already had a to-do list and an action plan in his head that was already more detailed than Whatmore's inspection report. He wanted to travel, he wanted to use his hands and he wanted to meet some real people who didn't live in schools. *And who would he do all this with*? That was Charlie's easiest decision. Why, the driver of the car of course. She was the one. He had messed about for far too long. He had screwed up other women's lives and now it was only fair to commit to this good wife.

No, on second thoughts, she was better than that, she was an outstanding woman and wife. Charlie took a sideways glance at his beautiful driver whom he knew to be street wise in all respects. She knew his faults and misdemeanours and yet she stayed with him and was seemingly happy to journey forward with him. He was a lucky man. There she was focused on the road ahead in her sexy short dress and long blonde hair looking half his age. He couldn't resist her and he needed to show his gratitude to her. Charlie was lost for words but he could communicate very effectively using touch. He slid his right hand across onto his wife's nylon clad knee and started to gently threaten her clutch control.

Sobia's journey home was less erotic but as loving. The boys in the back seat were chattering away about the fun they'd had with the mad adults playing silly games and making funny faces with food. It was lovely to hear the boys talking so enthusiastically about a happy occasion that could have been a special measures failure. No threats had been required at Peter's house; no punishment meted out. At Whatmore School her boys would have been sent to Mr Briggs to receive a merit award for good behaviour. But in the car both mum and dad were the praise givers and rewarders.

Sobia was also pleased to lavish praise and gratitude on her driver. Her husband had thrown himself in to the event and showed no signs of disengagement or apathy. He had been a model husband for the afternoon and she needed to reward him in some way. As the boys quietened down and started the process of drifting off to sleep, Sobia thanked him and promised him that the next weekend he could choose what they did as a family and if that meant entertaining his family, so be it.

Julie's drive home was a very quiet affair in comparison. Mark was driving as he'd consumed five times less alcohol than Julie. Julie had thrown herself into the party and from initial nervous apprehension in introducing her young boyfriend to her Chair of Governors and the senior leadership group, she had over-indulged herself with wine at the expense of food. Almost as soon as Mark started the engine, Julie had begun to nod off. Every so often Mark would look over to check on her or just to look at her. Even Julie's occasional snoring and snuffling were endearing and made him smile. After he had parked up outside their flat, he unclipped her seat belt and kissed her on the forehead to wake her up. Julie roused from her dream and verbalised her thoughts.

"You know I love you to bits, don't you?" she slurred.

"I do and I love you." And from that moment onwards they both secretly had marriage on their minds.

Neil drove home alone at a steady speed. He had drunk more than he should have but was confident he wasn't over the limit. He opened the front door to be met by Corinne. She was dressed in a white bath towel with a few drops of water dripping from her.

"Hi there. Did you have a good time?" she asked.

"It was good. Peter and his wife put on a fine spread. I could do with a cup of tea though. Do you fancy one?"

"I was hoping for something stiffer!" said Corinne, dropping the towel to the floor.

A good hour later Neil had the cup of tea he'd desired earlier before it had slipped down the Peckett order as other priorities arose. They lay in bed sipping tea, sharing a chocolate bar and watching a crime drama on Neil's IPad.

Neil pressed pause on the screen and said, "I'm sorry I couldn't take you to Peter's today. I felt it was a bit too early to throw you into the lion's den when we've only just started..."

"Started what...?" asked Corinne.

"Holding hands," said Neil, doing just that.

"Don't worry. It would have been awkward. I've only just started at the school and I'd be regarded as the lowest form of pond life at the Head's bash. It wouldn't have been wise turning up announcing I'm sleeping with one of the SLT."

"Corinne," replied Neil smiling at her from about eighteen inches or 45.72 centimetres or 457.2 millimetres away, "You do realise that sleeping with me won't enhance your career. If anything, it could be the worst career move you'll ever make."

"I'll be the judge of that. It works for me in the short term. The way I see it, if I have any IT issues at school in the future, all I have to do is drop my knickers to get preferential service." Corinne kissed Neil full on the lips. She amazed him with the difference in her demeanour and confidence inside and outside the classroom. Her teaching style was unsure and unsteady but on extra-curricular activities she was energetic and assured.

"Sounds a good arrangement to me. I'll just have to make sure your laptop continues to freeze up from time to time. How would you feel if I programed your hard drive to malfunction every other day?"

"I think I could cope with that but you'll have to remember to defrag your memory stick on alternate days!"

Tea, chocolate and crime drama were relished and finished and Neil was about to suggest that he was suitably defragged and ready for another upload when Corinne said out of the blue, "Oh, I almost forgot. A couple of hours ago I decided to have a quick shower. I got undressed and then would you believe it, there was a knock on your door and there was this woman standing there."

"It wasn't the woman from number sixteen was it? She often knocks the door and complains about the noise I'm making. I keep telling her it's not me…"

"No it definitely wasn't her. She just asked if this is where Neil lives and I said yes and told her I was your girlfriend. Then she started to cry and ran down the stairs."

"Didn't she say anything else?"

"No and to be honest I'm not quite sure I properly understood anything she said. Her English wasn't too good. She sounded Russian to me."

CHAPTER 22

Blank mind

Blank page

Peter stared at his laptop screen. *What was the problem?*

He could create a school policy for the governing body out of nothing or write a lengthy letter to parents that was convincing and heartfelt claptrap. But this was different. It was his first attempt at writing a novel and he couldn't get out of the starting blocks.

It was the day after the party. Rachel had rewarded herself by leaving Peter to do the final parts of the tidying up so she could spend time at her daughter's house. Peter had spent an hour or so emptying the dishwasher, re-loading it and binning all the empty cans and bottles that adorned any and every flat surface in the lounge. Then he ran the vacuum cleaner around for a second time. He had ticked off Rachel's list and now it was *Me Time* for Peter. He had made himself a coffee and sat down in his study to soak in the peace and quiet of a day alone in the house without family, friends or work colleagues. He deserved it surely? Yesterday's party had been successful. His considered judgement, after observing and analysing the outcomes, was that everyone was engaged, on task and had made progress.

Peter flicked through his diary and viewed the week ahead, which included the strike itself and the strife that would be caused before and after the school closure. Peter came to the conclusion that he also deserved to go on strike. So he closed his diary and opened his mind to the possibility of being a best-selling writer.

He could knock out a book in the next twelve months and retire this time next year before Ofsted re-visited the school. This plan sounded attractive. So what would he write about? It had to be about something he knew something about. The obvious options were; *Sixties and Seventies progressive rock, real ale, Disney, failing schools and failing Head teachers.*

Realistically it had to be about schools. He knew more about the first three on his list but he was not sure how to wrap a storyline around a boozy and ultimately tragic night out with Emerson, Lake and Pocahontas. But he could do a book about a school that was falling apart led by a Head teacher who was also falling apart. He could start the book from the moment the Ofsted inspectors were leaving the school and the Head and his team were left trying to put the school back together again. They would have eighteen months or so to improve or else the Head would lose his job. Great idea! Peter didn't know where or how he came up with this idea but it sounded a sure-fire winner. Lots of teachers would buy the book and he would be a millionaire in two years. Brilliant! He just had to write it now.

So Peter stared at his laptop waiting for the words to hit the screen.

He knew what he would call the first chapter so he typed it on the Word Document; *Chapter 1*.

He'd made a start but he was still in the blocks. And then in a blinding flash of genius he had a title for the book; *Waiting For Goodot*

Genius! He was pleased with that. It made him sound well-read and witty. The hardest part over, he just needed to fill in the blank pages with text.

He sat back smugly and enjoyed the moment. He was on his way. Perhaps it was time for some music or some more coffee or a bag of crisps. After all, an author needed to regularly feed his brain and fuel his mind.

Peter chose music from Greenslade, coffee from Douwe Egberts and a bag of crinkle cut from Walkers. Peter's appetite for writing was now ready salted and whetted.

He stared at the screen while eating and drinking and listening to music. The screen remained blank. So Peter decided to close his eyes and imagine a school and some characters that he could write about. His own school kept popping into his head. His team kept shouting at him *Pick me, pick me!* No he couldn't. He couldn't write about Whatmore. It was too close to home. Too personal. He didn't want to write a biography about a useless Head teacher. He wanted to write about what's wrong with the current education system. He wanted to get it off his chest before he lost his mind. And if lots of teachers bought the book, then that would be a bonus and he could retire early before he was sacked for being unprofessional or a mad man.

Yes, that's what to do. Write a book about the ideal school system and the ideal school called...Burlington Academy.

Maybe a little self-indulgent, thought Peter. Perhaps it would be better to set the book in a failing school but the Head is exceptional and leads the troops to glory. *That would work, wouldn't it? And that way I can keep the title I've already got!'*

So what is wrong with the system? Peter's fingers started to twitch and he began typing and ranting.

Peter stopped typing and flexed his fingers. He looked at the screen, in the corner it told him he had ranted and vented for 1376 words. He smiled to himself. This book writing is easy. The problem was that he couldn't publish this sort of stuff while he was still a practising Head teacher. Wouldn't it count as a form of whistle blowing or would it just be viewed as bad form to spill all the fifty-seven varieties of beans. When it came down to it Peter knew that his book would just be seen as the ravings of a lunatic who was whistling in the wind in the willows.

However, these were his darkest and deepest thoughts that he normally kept in a locked box somewhere between his fat neck and his bald pate. There would be a day, possibly fairly soon, when he could stop pretending to be a Head teacher and in his forced retirement he could pursue his dream of becoming a professional pensioner majoring in grumpiness.

He sat there practising being a grumpy old man, thinking what he would change if he was King Peter of Burlington. His hands started typing again...

Peter, Peter, stop it, snap out of it, you're ranting again," Peter, rebuked himself with a smile on his chubby cheeks.

A further pit stop for coffee was fast approaching and there was all that leftover food from yesterday's party crammed in the fridge. Peter had really enjoyed himself this morning. This was so much more fun than writing policies or action plans that no-one would ever really read. This was self-indulgent grumpy venting that need never leave his study or certainly not for a while. He didn't need an audience or a marker or examiner. This was true writing for a purpose and the purpose was to amuse himself in the land of never ever. Peter did feel guilty though. He thought about the rest of his leadership team. They were probably all working on school based stuff and here he was mucking about on his laptop, creating the beginnings of a manifesto so that all Earthlings could live on this mad, sad, bad planet with smiles on their faces.

Not all of his leadership team had their minds on Whatmore School, however.

Sobia was writing an email to members of her far-flung family. Often she would have to exaggerate and embroider the truth but today she could report positively on the Didially family without feeling guilty for spinning a yarn. She told them about the day she and her three boys had enjoyed at her boss's garden party and that today, while she was writing this, her husband and the twins were playing football in the back garden. She excitedly typed with freedom and hope about the present and the future and her movement was no longer restricted by fears or bruises.

Charlie's usual Sunday morning routine of a run followed by breakfast at the gym and a game of squash had been postponed. He had exercised when he and his wife had got home, during the evening and night and again this morning. If truth were told, he was now a spent force but a very satisfied and contented spent force that was happy to settle for breakfast in bed. While eating toast and swigging tea he had told his wife that he wanted to retire at the end of this academic year and that he wanted to begin a new chapter of his life which involved the two of them spending a lot more time together - perhaps travelling, perhaps buying a second home in a hot country near a golf course and a beach. *They could afford it, so why not?* You only live once.

His action plan was met with full support and a seal of approval. The only issue was when to tell Peter formally and finally. They came to the conclusion that if the decision had been made, there was no reason not to officially notify the governors now. So they got out of their supine state and sat side-by-side in their dressing gowns in their dining room and wrote a short letter of resignation to Ann Brown before commencing some essential research into affordable houses on the Algarve.

Julie was also in her dressing gown, with her laptop and school bags in front of her on the small table sandwiched between the kitchen and lounge areas of her open plan living space. She didn't feel very alive this morning. She had woken with a throbbing head from yesterday's excessive drinking and a post-it note stuck to her forehead saying. *At rugby practice, didn't want to wake you, I'll pop in to the shops on my way home, love you, Mark x.*

She would normally be touched by Mark's thoughtfulness but this morning she was too hung over to appreciate his sentiments. So she got up, made herself a large mug of coffee and decided to have a look at the application form for the Deputy Head position at Whatmore. That would definitely clear her head.

Without arrogance, Julie knew she would get an interview whether she wrote it sober or sloshed but personal pride meant she would try to do the best possible job to impress Ann Brown and the rest of the governors and particularly Peter. She knew he was her greatest supporter but with that advantage came the pressure of not disappointing him.

Over the last few weeks Julie had become a big fan of Peter's and she felt she could work well with him and learn from him. They were different people, very different but she needed to adopt some of the qualities he possessed if she wanted to lead her own school one day. After marriage and children, she hoped.

So through the fog of yesterday's wine, Julie tried to focus on the dancing text of the application form. Once completed faintly in pencil, Julie looked at what else she had to do. A letter of application including a paragraph on why you were the ideal candidate for the post, a paragraph on your philosophy of education and a paragraph on strengths and areas for development. This was the tough bit, all this in five hundred words. She could use up all of the words allowed just on her areas of development! She had to be concise, which meant a clear head. Perhaps another cup of coffee would help or perhaps the hair of the dog? No, definitely not. No more drinking. No more eating. Plenty of exercise. She may have to get in to a wedding dress one day and she wanted to look good and be the envy of some of her so-called friends.

Neil was in his flat on his own. Yesterday, it appeared that two women were wanting to share his pad and today he was left alone. Corinne had left early to visit her parents and would ring him later in the day but his other woman, who had travelled all the way from Russia, was nowhere to be seen. As far as Neil knew, he might never see her now but he was not leaving the flat today just in case she returned.

Corinne had driven off this morning without suspecting that this foreign cold caller was any more than a misguided traveller or visitor. Neil had decided last night not to tell Corinne about his lengthy relationship with a virtual woman thousands of miles from home and he was certainly not going to confess to her that he had sent this woman a considerable amount of money. What was he going to do? He wanted to speak to her, wanted to explain himself, wanted to make everything okay and he supposed that applied to both women in his life now!

His binary mind could not cope with blacks and whites today; everything was grey. So he sat down at one of the computers in his flat and stared aimlessly at the screen. The only way he could contact his Russian doll was by email and it had been weeks since she had used it. He supposed that she was still somewhere in the country but he had no idea where that could be. It sounded, from Corinne's description of the incident that his little Russki was very upset. Understandable, considering what she'd encountered in his flat doorway. A semi-naked woman. What was he going to do? Doing nothing seemed the best option. Doing anything just ended up with more complications and heartaches. But he had to do something. So Neil made a plan in his head. He would stay in the flat all day and wait for knocks on the door. Perhaps he would send an email and hope it would be read and responded to. Perhaps just something simple like: *Sorry I wasn't in, my sister is staying with me at the moment and may have surprised you. Can we meet up?* or *I've been missing you for weeks now and recently someone else has come in to my life. Someone who I can touch and speak to face-to-face* or *Why on Earth didn't you contact me in advance of your visit?"* or *I'm so sorry, I screwed up!*

Neil was just about to start the email when he was surprised by his phone ringing.

"Hi lover boy. Just thought I'd let you know I've arrived safely at my folks' house. I'm afraid I have a confession. My parents have just been asking me how I am and I happened to mention that I was seeing a really nice bloke. And…and they would like to invite you for lunch one Sunday…Only if you'd like to…No commitment you understand. What do you think? Is that okay or do you think it's too soon…I'm cool if you think it's too soon…Neil…are you there?"

"Yeah, I'm here, sorry I was a little distracted. Tell your folks I'd love to meet them. Whenever you like. What about next weekend? You'll have to warn them I'm a trained dinner supervisor and won't allow the throwing of food."

"Do you know something Mr Turner?"

"What's that Miss Peckett?"

"I think I may need to call on you later tonight to demonstrate in graphic terms why I fancy you!"

"My door is always open. You just have to press Enter!"

Corinne laughed out loud as she pressed the red button on her mobile and Neil chuckled inwardly at the thought of his door always being open.

CHAPTER 23

Some fifty loaves and the contents of twenty cereal boxes were consumed before Charlie left the canteen at the end of his breakfast supervision duty and made his way to Peter's office. Peter would be waiting for Charlie to give him the same briefing the Head had just given the staff. Charlie winked at Penny who was on the phone and walked straight in to the Head's office.

"Hi Charlie. Good weekend?"

"Not bad. Had to go to this dreadful party on Saturday afternoon but otherwise fine thanks."

"Yeah, funnily enough, we hosted a party on Saturday and all the guests turned out to be really awful. Still, we live and learn!" said Peter.

"Maybe we do; maybe we don't."

"That's profound for a Monday morning, Charlie!"

"Sorry, I slipped into serious just for a moment there. I won't let it happen again boss!"

They drank coffee and Peter reported back to Charlie on the staff briefing. Peter explained that most of it was about this week's strike and The Gazette's front page story. Peter had made it clear the school would be closed to all pupils but adults on the pay roll belonging to non-striking unions would be expected to be working inside the school for the whole school day planning lessons, marking pupils' books and holding subject meetings to prepare for the impending HMI visit. He had also made it clear that he didn't want anyone using social media during the day to suggest that this was an *easy* or *fun day* or commenting on the strike. Nor were staff to talk to the press about the strike.

"It sounds as if I had to lay down the law but actually everyone at the briefing was fine about the arrangements," said Peter.

"The staff will generally be alright. We perhaps need to say that we're taking a register on the day so we have proof who is here and who isn't. It may not stop the odd non-striker experiencing a sudden headache or stomach upset on the day but formalising with a register will help staff attendance."

"Good point, Charlie. We'll need to be out and about and also guard against any unwanted visitors rolling up on site." Peter took a mouthful of coffee and noticed Charlie was reaching into his inside jacket pocket. He was fairly sure that Charlie wasn't going to produce a gun and shoot him but Peter was almost as alarmed when he saw the long brown envelope being placed neatly on the table between them.

"I want you to give this to Ann Brown when you see her next. You can guess what it is. I've decided to take the plunge and retire next summer and I wanted you and the governors to know as soon as possible if it helps with future planning. I want to do this now so I can start my own planning for retirement. I don't want to be one of those old guys who hang on dilly-dallying about the right time to leave and then staying on longer than he should. I'll take my pension and lump sum next summer so my wife can look forward to spending it all."

"Oh, I wasn't expecting this today. I'm just pleased you're not jumping ship before next summer. It must be a good feeling to make a really important decision and be content about it."

"Yes it does. I actually feel I'm ready to grow up and be an adult fairly soon now. If truth be told, I haven't been the best husband in the world but I'm fairly certain it's third time lucky. I've found a keeper."

"So you won't be slipping the ball past her and scoring own goals from now on?"

"No, I'll be playing for the home team and not playing away," admitted Charlie.

"I'm glad....I mean, I'm really glad you've sorted out your future plans. It goes without saying that although I'll support your decision, part of me wants to selfishly tear up your letter and keep you here until the school crumbles to the ground. You're one of the few things in this place that doesn't require improvement."

"Hey, don't get sloppy on me. Save it for my leaving speech. Of course you know the other reason I'm giving you plenty of warning is it gives you and the rest of the staff more time to save up for my leaving presents!"

Leaving the Head's office, Charlie decided to head over to see Julie.

"Hey good lookin'," announced Charlie bouncing in, not at all concerned that she might be half way through an important telephone conversation or document.

"Hello Charlie, I was expecting a visit. So come on, I can take it. What do you want to start with; my underage boyfriend or the amount of alcohol I had at Peter's on Saturday?"

"That's a cheap shot Miss Osborne and a character assassination of a well-meaning colleague who just has your best interests at heart!"

"Yeah right. You may as well sit down if this is going to be an intense therapy session. What do you want to drink?" asked Julie

"Whatever you're having as long as it's not Alka Seltzer. Sorry...couldn't stop myself."

Julie smiled as she placed two coffees on her low round table. She couldn't be cross or offended by Charlie, no matter what. He might well be bad husband material and too old for her, but it didn't stop her having a deeply secreted crush as well as a growing respect for him as a work colleague.

"So where do you want to start?"

"I think it's only fair to begin by giving me as many intimate details about Mark and your relationship as you can without turning bright red," said Charlie sipping his coffee.

"Well, we bumped into each other in a pub and he remembered that I had taught him when I was at my first school. He was in the sixth form but I didn't really recognise him. It goes without saying that he's younger than me but we liked each other straight away and one thing led to another...I kept quiet about it because of the age difference and my past failures with men but we decided that we couldn't hide away forever..."

"Forever...so it's quite serious?" probed Charlie.

"It's serious and it's fun and it's great…"

"Julie, I'm really pleased for you. He seems a great guy. It doesn't matter what other people might think. You looked good together, really comfortable with each other…I bet you were nervous showing Mark off for the first time."

"God, tell me about it. That's why I had too much to drink. I didn't make a fool of myself did I? Tell me I wasn't embarrassing in front of Ann Brown?"

"I suppose it depends on what you regard as embarrassing. I have to admit, I quite liked your pole dancing routine in the back garden but I suspect it wasn't everybody's cup of tea!"

"Stop it Charlie. Seriously, was I okay?" Julie was almost pleading for the right response.

"You were fine. More than fine. You were great. Will you stop beating yourself up. You're going to make a brilliant Head teacher one day, if that's what you want. And more importantly you'll make a great wife and mother."

"Now I'm really starting to worry. Is that really you, Charlie, or has your body been taken over by a cloned robot with emotional intelligence?"

"A sort of AI with EI?"

"Exactly. So why are you being so nice to me? Don't tell me you want another private lap dance in your office like last Christmas. I still haven't recovered and I was definitely worth more than the 50p piece you shoved down my bra."

"No, I haven't got your stamina anymore and I don't have any loose change."

"That's a pity, I could have given you senior citizen rates and I do accept credit cards!"

Their flirty conversation was getting near the knuckle for a Monday morning and Charlie switched the play with some nifty footwork.

"I really popped in to tell you about a discussion I just had with Peter. I made the decision yesterday to take early retirement at the end of this year. I don't particularly want to announce it to the whole staff yet but I wanted you to know. If, or should I say, when you get the Deputy Head position here I'll still be around for the rest of the year to support you..."

"You're serious aren't you? You can't leave us...me...here...not yet." The magnitude of Charlie's news suddenly hit her. She was a grown woman who could stand on her own high heels but she needed people around her who cared. She knew Peter and Charlie cared about her and that Charlie, in particular, was both caring and fun. She needed men like this in her life, no matter what age they were.

"Look, you'll be fine. You'll be a Deputy Head soon and then maybe have a family of your own in the future. Peter really respects you. He'll be around for a few years. And with a bit of luck Mark will be around a lot longer."

Julie tried to laugh and smile while wiping a little tear from her mascara. "Sorry, Charlie, it was a bit of a shock and I'm being incredibly selfish thinking about me when this should be about you and your life. I should have said that I'm really happy for you to get out of this sinking shithole and don't look back."

"I understand. We all get used to people and things and sometimes it's hard to see what life will be like without them. But one thing's for certain, you and Whatmore will survive and succeed in the years to come. Hopefully you'll change your name and status and maybe the school will have a fancy new title as well but you'll both be the same underneath...Wow, that was quite a speech. Sorry! I've already apologised to Peter for being serious this morning!"

"I'm sorry too. I was expecting you to come in and just tease me this morning. I wasn't prepared for serious stuff."

"Well, that's the heady cocktail that makes a deputy...sweet and sour, serious and fun, with just a dash of sanity."

Charlie stood up to go but Julie couldn't stop herself moving quickly to give him a hug. "Are you sure you don't want a lap dance before you go?"

"Hey! We're both respectable teachers with partners...there again...perhaps we could schedule half an hour on strike day?" Their hug was broken but not the spell.

While Julie and Charlie had been verbally dancing around an awkward elephant in her office, Peter had been talking to Penny. After the post-party punditry, there was serious stuff to deal with although the first two items on Penny's list of incoming phone calls regarding strike day were Clive Howell and angry parents from a local planet where no-one is allowed any human rights.

Apparently, Clive wanted to know how Peter was intending to manage the fall-out following The Gazette's article on Friday. There was no mention of how the LEA were going to support one of their schools in this matter. Peter drew the conclusion that as usual, Whatmore would be on its own and therefore felt uninclined to speed dial Clive's number.

There were two different parents who needed to be spoken to. Both had been unreasonable and unpleasant to Penny when she explained that the strike was national and democratic. They were demanding that their children, two from one family, three from the other, should be catered for as it was the school's duty to look after them from 8am to 4pm each week day except at holiday time.

One mother took her argument further and criticised teachers for taking as much holiday as they did. Several years ago she remembered, when she had a job for a while, she wasn't allowed any holidays and it hadn't done her any harm. The other parent was threatening to go to the press about her children having to be left on their own in the house while she was out at work. Peter knew that when he returned the calls there would be no meeting of minds. In situations like this he found it was more effective to have the phone on speaker and less damaging to wear ear defenders.

Peter made a note to make all three calls under the mental sub-heading *Delay As Long As Possible*. Once Penny had completed Peter's morning by reminding him he had a meeting scheduled with *Call Me Rick* in about forty-five minutes, all thoughts of the party and his first novel had been filed under *Distant Happy Memories*.

Peter was tempted to break a confidence and give Penny the news that Charlie would be leaving. He knew that this would be hard for Penny to take in her stride and that it should be handled sensitively. So should Peter tell her or should he let Charlie tell her himself? Would Charlie think to single out Penny and break the news and a small portion of her heart in a quiet moment? The chances were Charlie would blurt it out in the staff room and within seconds the news would be viral and Penny would be hurt at being the last to know. But it wasn't Peter's news to tell.

"Are we finished?" Penny asked.

"Yes, I think so. Thanks Penny."

As she left his office, the phone rang and he picked up the phone. It was Charlie.

"I've just had a chat with Julie...I thought I'd tell her about my decision. It seemed only fair to tell her first."

Peter struck while the iron was hot. "May I suggest Penny should be second? Of course that's your decision..."

"You're right. Penny and I go back a long way."

"She'll also be upset; she thinks the world of you."

"Oh crickey. I've already had to cope with Julie tearful this morning. Are you saying that Penny might react the same way? I'm just an ex-PE teacher. I can only cope with tears when someone misses a penalty. Perhaps I shouldn't retire if all my adoring fans are going to get so upset."

"Don't kid yourself. Most staff will be cheering from the rafters when they hear the news. It's just that Penny's bound to find out soon because it'll be a governing board issue so she'll know from agendas and minutes."

"You're right, boss. Will you do me a favour? Send her down to my office on an errand and I'll tell her now."

"No problem."

"And Peter, thanks."

It didn't come easy to Peter to lie. Another reason he should never have been a Head teacher. But he called Penny straight away and sent her down to Charlie on a false pretext. Out of guilt, he then reached for the to-do list and braced himself. He would start with Mrs Angry and then speak to Ms Livid and finish off with Mr Perfect.

Some thirty minutes later Peter thought he could hear a knock on his door. He wasn't quite sure as his ears felt like they might be bleeding after the lively debate with Angry and Livid. When it came to Perfect, Peter felt that he needed a break or a breakdown before listening to any more verbal diarrhoea. So he was at his desk enjoying a moment of peace and quiet when the door opened to admit *Call Me Rick*.

"Are you ready? I knocked a couple of times because Penny's not at her desk."

"Come on in Richard...Rick...take a seat. I was just in the middle of something and I didn't hear you," said Peter, improving his skills as a bare-faced liar by the minute. "I just wanted to see how things are going. I'm hoping the HMI can see we've made real progress in all the areas that were under the spotlight. So it goes without saying that as well as SLT they will want to talk to key leaders in the school and you'll be one of them."

"Not just me surely?" asked Rick, fidgeting in his seat, paranoia beginning to course through his veins.

"Not just you of course. But I'm fairly sure that you will be seen, as will Jo, as leader of English. So I suggest we look at the areas in Maths that have been strengthened since Ofsted left us and where we, or should I say you, think we need to put greater emphasis in the next week or two. You need to be able to present as self-assured and confident about what the Maths team are doing and that you're moving forward and can prove it."

"Well yes, I see. Jo has been coaching me on how I should be assertive about the team's achievements. She also thinks I need a list of strengths and areas for improvement with evidence to back up what I say."

"So could you provide such a list in the next week?" asked Peter hopefully.

"I have it all here." Rick placed an A4 lever arch folder on the desk between them. Peter steadied himself lest he fall off his chair.

"Fantastic. This must have taken a lot of time to create?" Peter was seeking to ascertain if any of the content of the folder were Rick's own handiwork.

"Well Jo and Julie gave me a little help and guidance but I spent the whole weekend on it," he said proudly, as if he was handing in a lengthy piece of homework.

Peter was impressed and a little guilty that his weekend had consisted of very little school work - just drafting the start of a daft novel and partying with his higher ranking colleagues.

"So you're in a position to explain progress in Maths over the last few weeks and how you have taken the lead on it?" Peter expected a fudged response.

"Yes, I believe I am," replied the Head of Maths. Peter steadied himself again and wondered if they'd been transported into a parallel universe but grilling Rick produced only clear, cogent and concise answers. Peter couldn't think of any other words beginning with c that were apposite or he would have used them. Rick was impressive and at the end of the mock interview Peter told him so. Both men were hugely relieved.

When Rick left Peter's office having grown a few more inches and a new pair of testicles, he left behind him a man feeling good about being a Head teacher again. It was always uplifting and gratifying to see progress in teachers as well as pupils. He made a mental note to send emails congratulating Jo and Julie on the work they had clearly been doing in the background. Then he abandoned that idea, lifted his body out of his chair and set off to find them so he could praise them face-to-face.

Both took the sincerity of a personal thank you well and he left each of them the better for his efforts. Returning he found a sniffling Penny back at her desk.

"Are you alright Mrs Hinks?" he asked quietly.

"Yes, I'm okay as long as you don't leave me as well," replied the red-eyed secretary.

"I'll try not to. I tell you what - I'll retire only when you decide to retire."

"Deal," said Penny.

CHAPTER 24

"Talk about smelling a rat," said Neil to Charlie as they entered Peter's office at the end of the school day for the SLT meeting.

"It must have been a rat with learning difficulties if it decided to eat food off the floor in our dining hall," replied Charlie.

"What's this?" asked Peter who was re-arranging the furniture in his office for the meeting.

"Some kids reported that they saw a rat eating pizza at the end of lunch time," explained Neil.

"It must have really sharp teeth. It's normally rock hard!" said Charlie. "Are they sure it was a rat eating pizza or should I say a pizza eating rat? There are some Year 7 boys who could fit the description."

"They were fairly sure it was a rodent and fairly sure it was a piece of pizza. They caught me in the corridor and gave me a detailed description," said Neil.

"What do you think, Peter? Do we need to set up an identity parade?"

"Possibly. We might have success. No two pieces of pizza look the same when they come out of our canteen."

"You're both taking this too lightly. This could be a health and safety issue..." said Neil.

"For the rat maybe," laughed Charlie.

"Sorry Neil, we get sightings of rats every term. Our site staff see them from time to time and very occasionally pupils and staff see them scurrying about. Schools are great places for rats to breed in. Food aplenty and times in the day and night when they're left alone to scavenge. They do a better job than our cleaners," said Peter.

"Who does a better job than our cleaners?" asked Sobia, catching the last bit of the conversation as she walked in.

"Our family of rats."

"I suspect it's a very extended family. There are probably hundreds of them below the floor boards waiting for us all to leave." Sobia pointedly looked down at the floor.

"Who wants us all to leave?" said Julie, the next SLT arrival.

"Well, let me think," said Charlie. "How about the pupils, the teachers, the parents, the local authority and the DFE for starters."

"What have you heard Peter?" asked Julie looking worried.

"Well the word on the street is that we had a secret Healthy Eating inspection today and the free school meals passed with flying colours."

"Pardon…what?" Julie looked confused and then started to realise she was guilty of taking things too literally.

"It's only that a couple of kids saw a rat eating pizza in the dining hall today. Neil was just telling us about it. It's not the first time and it won't be the last. I'll report it to our site manager but I know what the reaction will be," said Peter.

"Perhaps we should get the site team to plug up any gaps in the skirting boards," suggested Neil.

"That would cost a great deal of money," said Sobia, "Half of the skirting boards around the school are rotten or damaged. It would be better if we could stop the pupils dropping litter and food."

"The trouble is it's very difficult to stop kids eating outside the dining hall. They all have chocolate bars and crisps stashed. I'm sure they think that their large blazer pockets were specifically designed for snacks. Kids like to eat on the move. Eating at tables with knives and forks is alien to most of them."

"Perhaps we're looking at this all wrong," said Charlie. "Let's tell our cook to start making food that's less appetising to rats. She's already successfully introduced a Healthy Eating policy by making the food inedible for children so we all don't eat as much. If we can just make the food revolting for rats as well as humans then we can solve the hygiene issue as well as the obesity problem."

"Right, I'll leave that one for you Charlie. Good luck. So let's get on with today's meeting and if we can all be careful not to drop biscuit crumbs on my carpet, I would appreciate it even if the rats don't. The main item is this week's strike and the action plan but a couple of other things first. Some good news; Clive Howell tells me he's leaving the local authority soon. Reading between the lines it appears that the local authority is getting rid of all of its advisers in the next year and he's decided to jump ship…"

"Perhaps he'd like to work here as a rat catcher," interrupted Charlie.

"I know you're all going to be devastated by this news and it's hard to imagine how Whatmore will be able to function without him but we'll just have to manage. I suppose we'll have to send him a good luck card nearer the time. I think that's enough don't you?"

Neil looked up from his IPad, "How about a minute's silence…from Clive…or is that too much to expect?" He had caught the mood and while the others were laughing he pulled up and played The Last Post on his device.

Equilibrium restored, Peter reported progress on Maths, making a point of praising the sterling work undertaken by Julie and Jo Slater in supporting Richard Perry. Julie played down her part in Rick's rise and re-directed the appreciation squarely at Jo. She spent a couple of minutes extolling the virtues of Jo as a teacher and staff mentor. As she talked passionately and enthusiastically, Peter and Charlie couldn't fail to notice Julie's own onwards and upwards progress as one of the new guard ready to take over the educational watch in the new game of thrones.

Peter moved on to the Ofsted action plan now it had been seen and approved by all relevant parties apart from the designated HMI. He wanted the HMI to come soon and see Whatmore while all the plates were spinning in the air.

The longer the wait, the more likely things were to change and Peter couldn't be certain the improvements would all be sustainable. The staff had been working so hard over the last five or six weeks and the pressure to improve was certainly telling. Senior team members had reported several incidents of teachers who for no rational reason were displaying over-emotional behaviour. It reminded Peter of a time many years ago when he was asked by an old Head teacher to front up an assembly to warn the pupils that a surprise visitor was going to be in school in the next week and they should all behave perfectly for five days. On day one the pupils all behaved perfectly. Day two most pupils behaved perfectly but by the fourth day the pupils were all behaving worse than ever because it had been too much of a strain to keep the act going. It was the same with Peter's staff now. They were trying so hard and the cracks were appearing.

Peter sat there thinking that a day's strike wouldn't be such a bad thing. It would give everyone a chance to re-charge their batteries. He kept these thoughts to himself while supposedly listening to his team discussing minor changes to the action plan; a plan that would always be a work in progress and would only ever be in its final draft on the day that it was no longer required or needed.

When Peter sensed that the discussions were going round in circles he moved on with "Thank you team, I think we've given this a good airing. It's getting late and I don't want to keep you, so let's just go round the table with any other business…Sobia?"

"It's not so much a school business issue, more a personal matter…" said Sobia. At this point all of the rest of the team woke up. "I know I should take my holidays outside term-time but I'd like to take next Monday off. My husband, without consulting me, has booked a long weekend break for the two of us in Paris. It's my birthday on Sunday and he wanted to treat me. His family are looking after the boys. I know I shouldn't have time off but I don't want to disappoint him and …I'll take Monday off as unpaid leave…"

"Nonsense," said Peter. "Go to Paris with our blessings. I am sure the school will benefit from your extra-curricular fact finding mission on the euro and the cost of living in France."

"Thank you…Peter," said Sobia, embarrassed and intensely pleased.

"Neil…any other business?"

"Well, I suppose I ought to tell you something before you find out anyway."

The others, including Sobia moved even closer to the edges of their chairs.

"I know you all think I'm a bit of a geeky nerd and my only friends are virtual but I want to let you know that…"

Each set of eyes started to look quickly at the other four sets of eyes and then move on. It was like a fast game of wink murder without the winking.

"I've started seeing someone…a girl…I mean…a woman. Corinne Peckett from the Maths Department."

"You sly old dog," said Charlie. "How long has this been going on? Don't tell me, she had problems with her equipment and you volunteered to give her a hand?"

"Well, something like that. A few weeks now."

"You should have brought her to the get together on Saturday," said Peter.

"Corinne would have felt awkward and to be honest, I would have done too. Not having warned you first."

"A pity you didn't. It would have taken some of the pressure off me and my new boyfriend," admitted Julie.

"No, we would still have stared at you most of the night," said Charlie, receiving the customary thump on the arm from Julie.

"Well, I'm really pleased for you Neil," said Sobia, "Corinne is a really lovely person."

"So are we all, Neil," Peter said. There were general noises of support from Julie and Charlie as Neil's head dropped to hide his embarrassment in his IPad.

"Julie, anything?"

"Well I suppose I ought to follow Neil with thanking you for the party and for all behaving perfectly in front of the guy I was trying to impress. I know it must have been hard, particularly for Charlie, but I just want to report that you all got away with it because Mark thinks you're all really nice people…..God knows why!"

"But we are all really nice people," said Neil.

"Apart from Charlie, of course," said Peter.

"He's alright in small doses, I find," Sobia said out loud without realising she had said it.

"I shall take that remark as a compliment after all the flack I usually get." Bullet-proof Charlie winked at Sobia and she glowed momentarily with pleasure.

"Anyway," continued Julie. "The other thing I wanted to mention officially is that I'm applying for the new position and apologise in advance if I go into meltdown before the interview. I'll be a bit nervous. It's difficult being an internal candidate."

"You'll be fine, Julie. Good luck to you."

"Thanks Neil."

"You have my full support, Julie. We need good women in charge. It's no use leaving it all to these men....nothing would get done," said Sobia who was not just coming out of her shell but had left it on the beach.

"We're coming in for some stick tonight Mr Briggs," observed Peter.

"It's a good job I'm retiring at the end of...the ...year..." The statement came from Charlie's lips before he realised what he was letting slip. Two people around the table knew it already but the others did not. Two uninformed jaws dropped. "Sorry to just blurt it out. I was planning to see you guys tomorrow before telling the rest of the staff."

"It's okay Charlie," said Neil. "I thought you'd retired already." The throw-away line eased the tension and paved the way for several more old codger jokes at Charlie's expense.

The consensus was that Whatmore would improve rapidly once he had gone. Charlie hoped they were all joking.

CHAPTER 25

Peter stared at his diary. It was the day before the strike and all was calm apart from the wet and wild weather outside. He had returned to his office from a particularly wet and wild break time duty checking on the wildlife situation in the dining hall.

Peter's staff briefing had pinpointed the need to clamp down on litter around the school and especially on food discarded on the floor rather than in the bins. He didn't mention the rat.

At least this morning there had been less food on the floor and there was no sign of a rat. It was a temporary victory of sorts.

Peter couldn't believe the diary. There were spaces without meetings. He could, in theory, do something useful like read a small percentage of the emails collected in his inbox. He could re-read the finalised Ofsted Action Plan, sitting proudly on his desk. He could attack his in-tray or tidy his top drawer. In the end he made a coffee, phoned Penny and told her to hold all non-emergency calls and stop any impromptu visits by staff as he had some pressing paper work to attend to. It sounded plausible and it was the closest he could get to physically padlocking his office door.

Peace and quiet and a cup of coffee. To Peter it was the Holy Grail. He knew it would be merely a small calm before another large storm but he would take it for now.

If the story of his career was a blockbuster movie, this would be the time when a passenger plane with a wing on fire was plummeting to Earth directly at the school's playground and Peter had twenty-six seconds to evacuate the school and save the Ofsted Action Plan. If this was a crime thriller, three police cars would be bursting through the school gates ready to take Peter into custody on some trumped-up charge. What Peter really wanted was a Disney film with a final shot of the Action Plan turning gold in his hands and a voiceover saying "What a wonderful career!"

Alas, no film director would consider making 'Whatmore – The Movie' unless some young good looking person was the Head teacher…

Peter drifted into a realm of fantasy in which each member of his SLT was a bizarre, quasi-cartoon character from a Disney film. The cast included an evil but vulnerable witch, a drunken sleeping beauty, a nerdy wally operating in a world wide web of his own and a little boy who told jokes and lies and when he did a certain part of his body grew and grew.

Peter sat on his throne, surveying his magical cartoon kingdom and wished for a happy ending to his reign as well as world peace. His world would have no weapons, no religion, no reality shows on TV and possibly no people. This was a sure fire way to create a peaceful world. He was in his fifties and he was tired of hearing the same news stories repeating on the television with only the names and places changing.

Peter could feel another book emerging. *The World of Education According to Peter Burlington*, if ever written, would be solely about teaching by modelling how to behave and treat one another. Of course, this wouldn't suit assessors and evaluators who need cold, hard data to analyse. What could they do with compassion and consideration? How would they be able to quantify it, tick an appropriate box or give it a grade?

Peter tried to imagine the world of education that Julie Osborne would be part of when she became a Head teacher in perhaps ten years' time. *Would she still be enjoying the job? Would she be reducing everything to meaningless grades? Would she be drinking heavily? Would she have left the profession because motherhood seemed more rewarding?* He sincerely hoped she could keep her humanity and sense of humour through her career.

Peter snapped awake and out of a long and complicated dream with a strong sense of impending doom. He stood and walked to his window to stretch his legs. He looked out over the staff car park to view cars of every colour and persuasion which would later be driven home by tired teachers with bags and boots full of planning and marking. Was it his imagination or had the rain stopped and was that the sun peeping through the clouds? He smiled and closed his eyes for what seemed an eternity and sang quietly to himself one of his favourite songs by The Beach Boys, *Disney Girls*.

There was a knock on the door and Penny entered his office. She closed the door behind her. Peter turned his head. "Yes?"

"Sorry to disturb you Mr Burlington." She looked concerned.

"What is it Penny?"

"I have a Mr Goode on the line for you. He's a Lead Inspector from Ofsted. Apparently we haven't been inspected for some years now and we're due a visit. They'll be here tomorrow morning."

ACKNOWLEDGEMENTS

I owe many thanks to many people for helping me knowingly or unknowingly write this book.

To begin with, the thousands of pupils I taught over the years – thank you and apologies! To the staff in schools that I worked with or against – thank you and apologies! The governing boards I served on and the schools I advised – I hope you can forgive me!

I would also like to thank some dear friends who have been very helpful and supportive in the drafting process of this book. Diane, Clive, Corinne, Mark, Cathy, Peter and Tony. I am forever grateful. Special thanks go to my wife Ann and son David for your love, patience, wisdom and encouragement. You both make me live and love.

Thanks to Caravan, Blodwyn Pig, Pink Floyd, Yes, Greenslade and many other prog rock bands from my past and present.

I would also like to acknowledge someone who I worked with some years ago who is sadly no longer with us, Peter Rickerby. In my opinion, the most caring and inspirational head teacher I have ever come across. You are greatly missed.

Thank you to APS Publications, particularly Andrew Sparke and his editorial assistant, Christine Ware.

And finally, my gratitude goes to the playwright J.B.Priestley. My storyline is created from the spirit of *An Inspector Calls* - a play for all ages and all times. My book rests at your feet.

IAN MEACHEAM

Ian Meacheam has spent most of his working life in education. Consequently he is well versed in the trials and tribulations of Ofsted inspections and found writing this, his first novel, a cathartic experience. He lives in Lichfield with his wife and they have one son. In his spare time Ian writes poetry and is a great fan and collector of Prog Rock.

MORE FICTION FROM APS PUBLICATIONS
(www.andrewsparke.com)

Abuse Cocaine & Soft Furnishings (Andrew Sparke)
Copper Trance & Motorways (Andrew Sparke)
Initiation (Pete Sears)
The Horned God (Pete Sears)
Nothing Left To Hide (HR Beasley)
Mister Penny Whistle (Michel Henri)
The Death of the Duchess of Grasmere (Michel Henri)
An Inspector Called (Ian Meacheam)
So You Want To Own An Art Gallery (Lee Benson)
Momentary Lapses In Concentration (Phil Thomson)

CLASSIC REPRINTS
Jeremy (Hugh Walpole)

Printed in Great Britain
by Amazon